CW00407483

the
Irish
Child

BOOKS BY DAISY O'SHEA

The Irish Key

DAISY O'SHEA

the
Irish
Child

bookouture

Published by Bookouture in 2024

An imprint of Storyfire Ltd.
Carmelite House
50 Victoria Embankment
London EC4Y 0DZ

www.bookouture.com

Copyright © Daisy O'Shea, 2024

Daisy O'Shea has asserted her right to be identified
as the author of this work.

All rights reserved. No part of this publication may be reproduced, stored in any
retrieval system, or transmitted, in any form or by any means, electronic,
mechanical, photocopying, recording or otherwise, without the prior written
permission of the publishers.

ISBN: 978-1-83525-080-8
eBook ISBN: 978-1-83525-079-2

This book is a work of fiction. Whilst some characters and circumstances
portrayed by the author are based on real people and historical fact, references
to real people, events, establishments, organizations or locales are intended only
to provide a sense of authenticity and are used fictitiously. All other characters
and all incidents and dialogue are drawn from the author's imagination and are
not to be construed as real.

PROLOGUE

ANNIE 1847

Annie remembered her dada going away on the big ship. She and her mother had gone up on the hill to wave as it sailed on, leaving them behind. After that, everything got muddled. She was angry with him for leaving: because he was so big and strong, he could have looked after them and fixed the problem Mam had with the praties. It hadn't been so bad, at first, but one day, when she went to the potato pit with her mammy, the praties had all gone black and smelly, and it was worse than anything she had ever smelled.

Soon there were only turnips, which she didn't like at all. But she was hungry, so she washed them down with water from the well. And all the while, baby Luke was getting to have Mam's milk, and it wasn't fair.

She vaguely recalled when her grandmam and grandada stopped being hungry, then one day they didn't get out of bed. After that, her mammy got tired all the time and cried sometimes, and Annie had to cuddle her better and remind her that dada would find his way home soon, but it didn't really get better because they were so hungry, not like before her dada left.

Then one day her mammy was laughing and crying at the same time because her dada had sent them a ticket to go on the big ship, so they could find him in the new country. She thought it must be further away even than Kerry, which was over the mountain. She was pleased he hadn't forgotten about them. She remembered riding on his shoulders, and holding on to his red hair, and she remembered falling asleep in his arms sometimes in the evening when he was singing his songs. He was so strong he could lift her and her mammy up together, but they couldn't lift him at all. She remembered him laughing until the tears ran down his face when they tried, but it was too hard to remember what he looked like.

It was horrid on the boat. Sometimes the boat went straight, but sometimes it went up and down and side to side at the same time, and people were being sick on the floor, making her sick, too. And it went on forever.

The lady in the bunk opposite them died one day, and the sailors came and took her away. Then there was a baby who went to sleep and didn't wake up, and the mother didn't stop crying until she just stopped one day and was taken away, too.

Sometimes people went up the ladder, to outside, but Annie wasn't allowed. She wanted to, because she could see a tiny patch of sky through the square hole, but her mammy thought she might fall into the sea and drown, and she was afraid if she went up on her own, she would come back and find her mammy and Luke had gone like the lady with the baby.

After a while she stopped being hungry and just wanted to go to sleep, but her mammy would shake her and get angry and make her eat the secret food. She didn't even know any more if Dada had been real.

.   .   .

One day the ship bumped into the new land and stopped moving. There was a lot of banging and shouting above them, and finally the hatch opened, and the sailors were calling for them to come out. Annie tried to climb up the ladder, but her legs were too tired to work. Someone pulled her up by her arms onto the deck then reached down to pull her mam up after her, with baby Luke clinging to her neck. She squeezed her eyes against the brightness of outside.

Mam was smiling weakly, and sort of laughing and crying at the same time. She hugged Annie close, her eyes roving the high banks of cloud and patches of blue above, as if she had never seen such a sight before. She whispered though her tears, 'Oh, praise be to God, we're saved. We're saved.' She squeezed Annie's hand. 'Now, we just need to get through immigration, then everything will be fine. Dada will be here to meet us, like he promised.'

'I don't remember what Dada looks like.'

Mam laughed. 'He's big, with a fine head of red hair, just like yours!'

It was frightening up on deck, with people pushing and shoving, trying to get to the little bridge to get off the boat, and just a few ropes to stop them tumbling into the churning water below. Annie could barely stand. She was weak from hunger, and so tired, and somehow everything moved strangely beneath her as she tried to walk straight, like the old man down the road who Dada had called a no-good drunk. She felt dizzy and sick, and then they were over the bridge, and her mam was pulling her along faster than her legs could manage. Mam said her new home was called Boston, but she didn't want to be here. It was big and dirty, and there were too many people. She hung on to her mammy's hand, and whimpered, 'Can't we please go back home?'

'Be brave, love. A little longer. Look out for Dada, eh?'

But the noise was overwhelming. Everyone was pushing

and shoving and talking too fast, too loud, and she couldn't
understand at all what they were saying. A man in a funny hat
asked her mam who they were and made a bad face, like the
angry priest did when shouting about their sins. They were
hustled through a building and out into another big, open place,
where people in strange clothes were waiting.

Mam found a place to sit, on some piles of wood, and Annie
leaned against her, too exhausted to even feel hungry. They
waited, and they waited. Where was her dada? Why wasn't he
here?

Then she saw him through the crowd, his red hair shining
like a beacon in the dusk. 'Dada, Dada!' she cried. She pulled
away from her mammy and ran towards him, her hands out.

She heard Mam cry out in alarm behind her. 'Annie! Stop!'

A group of men got in her way, grabbed at her, and there
was ribald laughter as she wriggled free, dodging, until the
coarse voices were lost in the darkness. Then she couldn't see
her dada any longer – and couldn't see her mam, either.

'Dada! Mammy!' she screamed, over and over, but she
couldn't see through the crowds.

Finding a platform stacked with barrels, she climbed up
some steps to look out over the dark docks, but the platform
jolted suddenly, and she fell, hitting her head. Feeling sick and
dizzy, she sank down, shut her eyes and put her hands over her
ears. Her mammy was gone and so was baby Luke. She said her
Hail Marys over and over and over, knowing that God would
bring her mammy to save her. She said them until she was so
tired she couldn't say them any longer. But her mammy still
didn't come.

1

ERIN

I fall asleep on the plane, which is what I do, and wake up as we're landing in Shannon.

The moment we took off, after the woman in the pill-box hat had done the arm-ballet explanations of what we should do if we crash, I felt myself begin to drift. Kenny, my husband, used to joke about it. *It's like a switch,* he'd say. *If I want you to stop talking, all I have to do is put you on a plane!* He was funny like that. I still miss him, and his betrayal invokes a strangely convoluted sentiment in my soul, like loving and hating him in the same beat. How could he leave me just as our life together was getting interesting? We were consolidating our future, giving our home the makeover required for our planned family.

Dad said from the start that it would never work, and in a strange way, he was right. Kenny was an artist, a dreamer, and that's kind of anathema to Dad's ambitious drive as a top lawyer in a competitive environment. But I guess I'm a dreamer, too, with all the requisite, fluffy lack of substance that comes with it. The only difference is that Kenny was struggling to keep his head above the rising tide of living, while I was living the dream.

The hard light of a new day hits me as the tyres hit tarmac, but there's no point in going over old news. One of the reasons I got on the plane in the first place was to put Kenny behind me, to get over him, so to speak. *You have to rely on yourself,* Dad said, *because people always let you down in the end.* Sure, he has an inflexible streak, or he wouldn't be so successful, but Mom is still with him after all these years, so they must have got something right.

Anyway, the last thing I remember thinking before drifting off is: *What's the point of all those safety explanations, when no one really listens?* If there's an in-flight emergency, people will naturally panic, so it's probably best to just sleep through it. I'm not so much a fatalist as a realist. If it's my turn, well, maybe God does have a plan.

I wheel my luggage out of the airport building and discover the car I've booked: a strange little thing, a Ford Escort, apparently, all angles. And the colour! More suited to a canary than a car. I wonder if the hire-car company bought vibrantly coloured cars to make them stand out against the backdrop of gloom that is overshadowing my first day in Ireland.

The sky is grey and bulging fatly as I climb into the car and turn on the motor. I attack the clutch and shift the stick into first gear with only minimal grating. I did get a couple of lessons in stick-shift driving before leaving Boston, thank goodness, but even so, it's kind of clunky. I wonder why the Irish don't go for automatics.

As I drive towards Roone Bay from Shannon, I understand why people left here in droves. One of my friends, a clarinet player in the Boston orchestra, who also claims a paternal line from this dismal little country, told me Ireland is *cosy.* He's been here several times, and raves about it, but he always comes home to Boston, to his neat condo with all its mod cons. Maybe being cosy wears off after a few weeks. I'll no doubt find out. But the overly sentimental images in travel brochures, with their trailing stone walls and super-green fields, is somewhat different now I'm seeing it for real in a light drizzle that shrouds the view.

I thought I'd be taking in the scenery on the way south from the airport, but actually, my eyes are glued in dismay to the amazingly tiny, pitted roads. As the cloud base is sitting about ten feet above me, the surrounding scenery is pretty much obliterated. It feels as though I'm driving through a tunnel of fog. I'm not comfortable driving at the best of times, but here my unease is multiplied by a thousand.

As occasional tractors and lorries loom out of the gloom and swoosh past on the wrong side of the narrow road, I find myself breathing in, as though that will squeeze the sides of my car in a little further. Somehow, each time we pass without a scrape. Then, when a little donkey pulling a cart clops dreamily the other way, its head bobbing to the music of its own hooves (the wizened woman slumped sideways on the seat surely asleep), I feel as though I've somehow slipped back into the 1930s, into the depths of the Depression.

I've thought about this trip for a while, but actually being here is weird. After the heartache, the planning, all the time wondering what I was doing and quite who I was doing it for, I'm still reeling. Maybe I'm also suffering a bit from the time difference as I feel distanced from reality, floating in a strange universe. I tell myself again, *I'm in Ireland*, to make it seem real, because I wonder if I'm really here at all. Maybe it's some kind of strangely discombobulated dream, and in a while I'll wake up in my parents' home, where I'd rebounded after my marriage came to a grinding halt and all my future aspirations had been blown out of the water.

Mom couldn't understand at all why I wanted to come to Ireland. What did it matter where our folks came from over 150 years ago? But she had my back in a discussion (argument) with Dad. She has a wickedly practical outlook on life, which is grounding, if sometimes daunting in its severity. Nothing in her home is ever out of place. Dirt simply isn't allowed. Broken things are instantly trashed, never sentimentally valued. She has no time for dithering over the past, which makes it all the more strange that she fought my corner, encouraging me to follow my inclination. Maybe she thought I should just get it out of my system.

She's all for me starting afresh, but I know she thinks I should do it in New York or Phoenix, even London or Paris or Prague, somewhere there's culture and, of course, music. I mean, what would I do with myself and my music in a little backwater like Roone Bay, where there isn't even a theatre?

There's probably a determined kind of crazy logic to her thinking, in that if she encouraged me, maybe I'd actually rebel, which is at the very core of my nature, as she well knows. It was my father's insistence that I should stop being silly and get on with my life that actually tipped the scales, of course. I hate being told what to do, and if I want to be silly, it's my choice. It would be easy to blame either of them for my present situation, but in truth, I'm not like the rest of my family and haven't a clue where I inherited it from. My somewhat bohemian disposition must have skipped a few generations before emerging in me. Maybe I'm some kind of ancestral throwback. Or maybe, as Mom thinks, I'll take one look at quaint little Ireland and go running back to civilisation.

Ireland isn't such a random choice, though.

My grandpa's ancestor, Luke O'Mahoney, came from Roone Bay as a babe in arms. His mother, Nellie, emigrated during the famine, seeking a new life in Boston, with her two children, only to lose her daughter on the docks the moment she arrived. That story had always bugged me. According to Grandpa, Nellie never found out what happened to the child. My heart bleeds for her, though she's long dead. How traumatic, to just never know. Even death would have provided a conclusion of sorts, as I know only too well, but that lack of knowledge must have been an open wound for the rest of her life. And yet she carried on living, working to provide for her son, Luke, who rose from nothing to become the forefather of my family's wealth. Without her determination, none of us would be around; not me, my father, my grandfather, and his...

I think, somewhere in the back of my mind, I have taken Nellie's grief to heart. It echoes my own in a strange way. My grandpa told me about Luke, but he didn't know what happened to Nellie. I've often wondered whether they left some trace of themselves here, in Ireland. Some distant relative, maybe, who can cast a light on the mystery. I might be clutching at straws. No, I know I am, but there's a strange sense of inevitability about me coming to Ireland, as though my own fate is somehow tied to Nellie's. Maybe I am a little mad, after all. Grief can do that to a person. But I feel, in some distant way, that if Nellie found peace, maybe I will, too.

Eventually, exhausted, I drive over a hill to see the faint curve of grey sea looming through the whiteout. I had debated coming by liner, which would have given me time to read and think, but ships aren't my thing, really. Being on a plane for a few hours meant I didn't have to be sociable to whoever was unlucky enough to be sitting next to me (Kenny said I snore). On a liner, I'd be trapped for a week with a bunch of people digging curiously into my life, wanting to know why I'm going to Ireland, or perhaps just eager to tell me their own stories. At the moment, my mind is too fogged with my own disillusionment to want to get involved with anyone else's problems.

I mash the car into first gear, and it whines reluctantly down a steep hill towards the curve of the bay until it reaches the first of a row of town houses marching down to the quay. They're painted in a surprising array of bright, discordant colours.

Kenny should be here, of course. He must have known how much I'd miss him. He would have been painting this scene in his mind, long before he photographed it and sketched the first lines onto canvas.

On the corner of a junction there's a large building, a bank, and further down the hill the road narrows and curves to the left, lined by tiny shops and bars. I stop by the side of the road, slip the car into neutral and remember to put the brake on. I sit for a moment, stunned with exhaustion, almost surprised to find I've made it to my destination in one piece.

After a while, I open my eyes and find a man standing by the car staring at me as though I've come from another planet. Or maybe he's just startled by the colour of the car, as I was.

I blink uncertainly. He looks kind of designer-scruffy, dark hair flapping in a fitful breeze, jeans worn thin as gauze at the knees. His hands are wedged deeply into the pockets of a checked lumberjacket, the collar of which is pulled up around his ears. He's strangely attractive, his ordinary features – the usual mouth, nose, eyes and beetled brows – coming together in some indefinable way to produce a charismatic whole. He could be a model, in a windblown, stubbly kind of way. Like me, he's probably hitting thirty or has maybe tipped over the other side. His unwavering gaze, though, has the almost-vacant look of someone who isn't quite in the present, but as he's the only person in sight, I wind down the window by two careful inches and ask for directions to the hotel. He stares some more then nods as if his initial supposition that I'm an alien has been proved right.

'Ah, American, so,' he says thoughtfully. 'You'll be wanting the new hotel, I'm after thinking.'

'Roone Bay Hotel,' I confirm. If there's an old hotel, I don't know about it, but I smile and nod.

Instead of speaking further, he points. I follow his line of sight through a hovering layer of mist, and there's the hotel on the other side of the valley, rising like a ghostly grey ship, its ornate gables disappearing into the heavy gloom.

'Thanks,' I say.

'Not a bother.'

He nods as though we've communicated. In the mirror, I see him standing there staring after me as I drive on down the road. *Weird.*

The road loops down towards the sea and up the other side. There's a sign for the hotel, and I turn up a steep drive to a substantial car park where there are just three cars nestled together as if for warmth. Not overly busy, then. I was told the holiday season in Ireland is short, due to the weather, but it's mid-September, the summer barely over. How can a hotel like this survive if the tourists are already non-existent?

After a moment of deep breathing, I adjust to the fact that I've reached my destination. It feels like a victory of sorts. A brisk wind tries to rip the door from my hand as I open it, but I grab it in time, climb out and stand with my back to the hotel. The chill wind seems to be scudding in from the heaving, white-capped Atlantic.

Roone Bay looks as if some giant monster from the deep has taken a bite out of the land, leaving the edges ragged from its teeth. I shiver and wrap my arms around myself. Even now I'm here, I'm not sure I made the right decision, but I'm not going to turn tail and run, giving everyone the opportunity to say *I told you so*. One of my strengths (as Mom sees it) or my failings (as Dad sees it) is to dig my heels in when I've made a decision and see things through to the end – bitter or triumphant or whatever.

I turn and survey the hotel. It's kind of cute, like the picture in the brochure, except for the lack of little fluffy white clouds floating serenely over it in a clear blue sky. The gables over the top windows are reminiscent of servants' quarters in Edwardian buildings, and it's painted the same steel-blue colour as the

Atlantic over which it stands sentry. It has the look and feel of something old, but I know it isn't. Some entrepreneur or other built it, my travel adviser told me. She thought the phoney historic aspect was deliberate, intended to attract us 'returned Yanks', as they call us, apparently, who are coming back to seek our Irish roots. But to me it seems a little out of sync with the surroundings. Ireland never had buildings like this, outside the city environs, anyway. It's strangely discordant, as though it's been uplifted from an English seaside town and dumped in the wrong country.

Being that I'm largely Irish by genes, despite being Bostonian by birth, I was always vaguely curious about Ireland but never expected to find myself here. I'm grateful times have changed. My own Irish ancestors, I gather, weren't the lofty kind; they were farmers, potato grubbers, poor as church mice. Poorer, even, as they didn't even have church candles to eat.

A blustery wind flaps sharp ends of hair into my eyes and whips the sea into foamy whitecaps. It's as uninviting as I imagined it would be, especially after the sun-filled holidays of my childhood, with their endless ribbons of yellow sand glinting under a hot – usually Mediterranean – sun. But that was then, and this is now. Anyway, it is what it is. I'm not here to build sandcastles. I'm in Ireland, the land my ancestors fled from over a hundred years ago, to tread somewhat warily in their footsteps.

If I can find any trace of them at all.

I have scant enough information. I know that William O'Mahoney left Roone Bay because of the famine, and Nellie followed him later, crossing the treacherous Atlantic with their two children on one of the coffin ships. I know a bit about their son, Luke, as he was my father's direct ancestor. I don't know what happened to their daughter, Annie, and maybe I'll never know. The lineage I have details her birth date but nothing else, her disappearance a mystery.

Really, I'm just curious to see where Nellie and William came from, and maybe then I'll be able to let it rest. It's better than being aimless, anyway. When my life fell apart, I was drifting through depression, and my eyes, for some reason, latched on to Nellie's O'Mahoney bible. The thread of births and deaths scratched inside the front cover called to me. For the first time I considered how I was linked by that thread to an Ireland long gone, and the strange thought came to me that if I knew where I'd come from, maybe I'd have a better idea of where the future might take me. Of course, I might be fooling myself, because looking into the past is slightly more doable than thinking about a future stretching ahead into empty silence.

When I go back to Boston, Dad will expect me to put all the bad stuff behind me and never to refer to it again, which is what he'd do. Mom will allow me to talk about it, get it off my chest, then she, too, will expect me to stiffen the upper lip and stop wimping out on life. Being here is probably me rebelling against their no-nonsense, practical outlook, which truly doesn't allow for nostalgia or wallowing in self-pity, all of which I'm presently enjoying, because it's all too raw to simply shunt aside. Maybe I am running away, as Dad thinks, but the desolation, the sense of abandonment I feel is real, and if I'm wallowing, maybe it's just my way of getting through it in one piece.

2

ERIN

I blink away my thoughts and turn back to the hotel, which has a kind of abandoned feel, like something out of a horror movie. I open the trunk, heave out the big suitcase and dump it on its wheels. I haul my vanity case from the back seat and loop my purse over my shoulder. Slamming the trunk loudly, I look around, hoping there's a porter handy, but the place seems deserted. I leave the big case standing and fight the buffeting wind to the front door with the smaller case. There I fumble and nearly drop the case, trying to work the latch. What kind of hick hotel is this? A rotary entrance would be a boon.

Somehow, I make it inside, and as the door closes behind me with a whoosh like an airlock, the whole place seems to expand with a sudden silence. I will say that everything looks neat and clean. Maybe because it's brand new, as the strangely charismatic man up the road suggested. There's a scrubbed pine counter, presently unattended, some comfortable chairs, a coffee machine, and atmospheric pictures on the walls: an advertisement for the *Titanic: The Queen of the Ocean, bound for New York via Queenstown*, and the iconic image from an English newspaper depicting the Irish as drooping matchstick figures during the famine. A third picture, much nicer, is – I peer closely – a charming monochrome photograph of Bantry market in the early 1900s, with girls in petticoats, women in beribboned hats, men in three-piece suits and flat caps, and an abundance of donkeys.

There's a framed photograph of Michael Collins – the Big Fella – on the counter. Of course there would be. The people's hero, who led the fight for independence from this part of the country, leading his determined army of Irishmen through the bogs and hills, in guerrilla warfare against the might of the English army. He looks so proud, in his uniform, and him only thirty-one years old when he was ambushed and shot. I study the image for a moment, wondering what drove him.

There's a massive disconnect between the conflicting scenes on the walls and today's comfortable mod cons, which I have no doubt is deliberate. It's probably not a bad idea to subtly – or not so subtly – remind us how lucky we are to be living in an age and location where there's social welfare, education and a modicum of personal freedom for women.

I pour myself a coffee from the glass carafe into a china mug and take a seat. There's a bell on the counter, but I wait, curious to see how long it will take before anyone notices that I've arrived. I smile to myself. Kenny always said my sense of humour verged on mischievous, but right here and now, coffee is just what I need. As long as it doesn't rain, obliging me to run out and rescue my big case, I'm not in any hurry.

But nor are the hotel staff, if there are any. Perhaps they would have been better served to have put a picture of the *Mary Celeste* on the wall, the ship infamously found abandoned by its crew for no perceivable reason.

I'm tipping on the edge of dozing when the main door opens, releasing a flurry of Atlantic weather into the foyer. Darn. It's raining, after all. An ancient man comes in, battling my big case through the door. He's wearing brown corduroy pants, a waistcoat, a collarless shirt and a flat cap, epitomising my mental picture of an Irish farmer. It seems the fashions haven't changed for men, here, in the last seventy years! I jump up, instantly embarrassed to have left my case to be rescued by someone old enough to be my great-grandfather.

'Oh, hey, you shouldn't have! I was just waiting for someone to come and give me a hand, but really, I could have brought it in myself. Now I feel really bad!'

'Sure, it's no problem,' the old man says, stretching, favouring the centre of his back with both hands. 'The heavens are about to open, and we couldn't afford a lawsuit over a wrecked case, now, could we?'

It takes me a second to realise he's joking, and I echo his grin. 'My father's a hotshot lawyer, too,' I respond in kind. 'You really don't want to go up against him!'

'So I gathered,' he says.

So, he works here. Mom had no doubt booked the hotel in the firm's name, to get better service. She probably stressed Dad's importance, him being the managing partner and major shareholder, but I doubt anyone here would have heard of him. 'I found coffee, and the drive from Shannon was a bit scary. I was just chilling for a moment before going out to rescue my stuff.'

He looks amused. 'Scary?'

'Narrow roads, hairpin bends, potholes and a tiny car with a manual shift.'

'Ah,' he says. 'Welcome to Ireland. Shall I show you to your room?'

'You can do that?'

'I can,' he says. 'I'll leave a note for Grace to say you've arrived. I haven't a clue how this booking-in system works. I take it you're Erin Ryan?'

'That's me.' *Am I the only guest due to arrive today?*

'I'm Noel.' He scans the back wall and unhooks a key

attached to a piece of wood that could double as a tray. 'Room thirty-six,' he says. 'You can leave the key here, at the desk, if you go out. Grace has given you the best view in the house, up in the gods. It's not the biggest room, but if you don't like it, you can change. Are you staying long?'

'I don't know. I haven't really made any plans, other than getting here. My great-great-great – I forget how many greats – grandparents emigrated from Roone Bay during the famine.'

'Ah, a quest into the past?'

'Not really. Just a vague itch that needed to be scratched.'

'What were their names, your great-great-great-something grandparents?'

'Nellie and William O'Mahoney. She was a Crowley before she married William.'

'Both good local names, for sure.'

'I know they came from Roone Bay, but that's all I know. I'm kind of curious to see where they lived. Is there a land registry or something?'

'Not from then, no. You might find some birth records up in the church, but those were bad times. After the famine, whole families had disappeared, and there were few enough left who could name them. And so many houses empty, and farms left vacant...' He shakes head. 'Bad times, all right.'

'Surely there was a record of people in the parish?'

He shakes his head again. 'Not then. The only people who had records were the land agents, and that was for the sole purpose of collecting rents for the landowners. Largely, land agents were men who feathered their own nests. They would have had to be ruthless, not the nicest of people, to do that job. But when the famine took hold and the landlords scurried from the sinking ship, the land agents were hot on their heels, saving their own lives. The big houses went to ruin, and many were then burned out in the fight for independence, so what records there might have been are all gone.'

'But Roone Manor, behind the hotel, won't that have records? That was owned by the local landlord, wasn't it? Some baronet or other.'

'My dear, the manor was abandoned and wrecked, 150 years ago. There are plenty of these magnificent old piles abandoned around Ireland. This one was a sad sight, nothing left except the walls. It was rebuilt recently.'

'Oh. It looks as if it's been there forever.'

'That was the intention.'

I sigh. I kind of knew these things but had hoped I'd find more when I got here. 'Well, I guess I'll just get a feel for the place, anyway.'

'Young Finn Sheehan might be able to help,' the old guy adds. 'He's interested in local history. I understand he's documenting the graves in the area – those that weren't mass famine graves, of course. For those, no records will ever be found.'

'And where will I find this Finn Sheehan?'

He purses his lips and pauses, as if wondering whether he should have mentioned the guy at all. 'Well, he isn't the easiest person... I'll see what I can find out for you. Now, if you'll follow me. You're on the top floor, but we do have a lift!'

The room certainly has a view. Well, it would have, if the fog would only lift. It's nice, too – its subtle apple-green decor quite calming.

When the old guy leaves, I push open the double window and lean out over a Juliet balcony. I shut my eyes and lift my face to the wind. I could be on a ship sailing into the past. I can almost hear the singing sails snapping tautly behind me. I have the strangest sensation of standing on the edge of Irish legend, the fitful blast whipping my hair into needles that flay my cheeks. I'm floating in a void, and somehow the pain feels good. It makes me feel alive for the first time since Kenny abandoned me, and for a moment I imagine his arms sneaking around me from behind, his lips on the back of my neck. He would have revelled in this moment, finding words to describe things that would later materialise in his art. He was pure poetry, and I'm lost without him.

The chill spatter is like tears on my face, and eventually I find myself curled up on the floor under the window, crying, the driving rain puddling around me. I'd come here to leave him behind, but it seems I've brought him with me. Will he ever let me go? I pull the windows shut, grab a towel from the bathroom and mop up the floor angrily, telling myself to grow up, pull myself together. I wonder whether Dad was right, after all, that this was a really bad idea.

Eventually, I wend my way back through the deserted hotel, and a tall, thin, unsmiling lady brings me a dinner I didn't order. She apologises that there isn't a choice, but she's done the best she can in the circumstances. How very peculiar. Despite myself, I enjoy the dinner and ask for a bottle of wine that I can take back up to my room. I'd feel daunted, sitting drinking in solitary contemplation of the vast dining room or the well-appointed foyer area. In all honesty, I'd expected to find Ireland a little unsophisticated, but I suspect this journey to Hicksville is going to provide me with some amusing anecdotes to regale the family with when I return.

3

ERIN

The restaurant is all but deserted when I emerge from my room after a long but troubled sleep. Aside from a salesman (presumably) wearing a dated pinstripe suit, who is deeply engrossed in a copy of the *Irish Examiner*, I'm pretty much alone. Breakfast, it seems, is self-service, nothing cooked, but at least here, as in reception, coffee is steaming on the heater. I take some available slices of bread and pop them in the toaster, then carry everything to a table by the window, which is mostly obscured by a river of water. It's like being back in the dorm at school. I've been in quite a few hotels with my parents over the years, but I've never served myself with toast before.

The weather is abysmal, and I wonder how persistent the rain is going to be. It could be midwinter not autumn. I'm beginning to understand why the holiday season has come to such a quick end. I mean, Roone Bay isn't exactly your average holiday venue. There's no sunshine, no sandy beaches, no nightlife. I suspect that the only travellers here at this time will be salesmen or people like me, searching for roots that have long vanished. I suspect my quest is likely to end before it gets going. Well, I can at least get an idea of where Nellie came from, even if I can't find the exact location.

I miss out on lunch and eat a chocolate bar in my room while reading a novel I bought at the airport. It doesn't grab me, but I plough through it, simply to waste the day, between times sinking into a troubled doze. The drive wasn't just scary, as I told Noel; it was traumatic. I'd known it would be, but it was a fear I needed to conquer. Mom had advised me not to drive but to use public transport. I know she was worried for me, but if I'd done that, I'd still be travelling now. Besides which, I have a feeling if I didn't have a car, I'd be stuck totally in Roone Bay. There's probably a bus to Bantry once a fortnight.

In the evening, I sit waiting to be served by a silent girl who can't be more than fifteen years old, and when she finally brings me a thick chunk of soda bread and soup, the bread is steaming hot, the soup lukewarm. Weird. I choose ham and cabbage from the menu as my main meal, and kind of expected it to be made into a pie, or a dish, rather than exactly what it said: boiled ham and boiled cabbage. It's accompanied by a huge dish of potatoes well cooked, in their skins, liberally lathered with butter. I'm stunned. Am I supposed to eat all of them?

When the girl comes to clear, I ask, 'What do people do around here in the evening?'

She looks confused for a moment then says, 'We light a fire to get warm and watch TV.'

'Just like back home,' I say, trying not to laugh.

'You're from America, aren't you?' she asks, a little shyly.

'Sure am. My folks were from here, though. Back in the 1800s. They were O'Mahoneys.'

She nods sagely. 'There are plenty of O'Mahoneys around here, all right.'

She takes my dishes and leaves, and I don't see her again. Probably just as well as the dessert menu seems to revolve around ice cream, and it's not exactly ice cream weather. I hear clattering in the kitchen so assume someone must be working, but I eventually head up to my room with a wry shake of the head.

This morning, two other guests roll down in the morning, a smart couple who must be husband and wife, as they snip and grumble through breakfast. I watch them drive away and think how sad it is that so many love stories end in disillusionment, each partner blaming the other because life hasn't turned out to be a fairy tale. I haven't left the hotel yet, thinking I'd wait until there's a break in the rain, but as it's obviously not going to stop any time soon, around lunchtime I slip on my windcheater and run to the car. Surprisingly, it's not as cold as I expected, just very, very wet. At this rate I'll be needing an ark not a hotel. I don't fancy my chances going for a walk in the countryside.

I drive around the town and discover that the shops and houses are built in a loop descending from the hotel, towards a small quay, and back up the other side. There's a small area of more modern housing on the hill behind them, but I'm guessing that this is still largely a fishing village surrounded by a farming community, the population scattered in the countryside around. Some fishing boats are moored by the quay, and I find another quay along the coast road, past a ruined church and an ancient graveyard. When the weather turns, I decide that's going to be my first port of call. See if I can locate any O'Mahoneys or Crowleys there.

I drive to Bantry to the west, and that seems to be altogether bigger and more cosmopolitan, if it's possible to use that word in southern Ireland. I don't stop, though, but head back the other way, towards Skibbereen, just to get my bearings. I'm moved to find that in such a small area I've already passed two signposts leading to famine grave sites where, as I understand, unnamed bodies lie in rows.

Skibbereen has the dynamics of a thriving little market town with a plethora of bars. I wonder just how many bars one town can support, and kind of understand why the Irish who ended up in America were all labelled drunkards and thieves. Of course, the poor everywhere drink to drown their circumstances, and I'd probably steal to feed my children, as Nellie might have done after arriving in Boston. In fact, it's amazing that she did survive. Like many others, she must have gone through hard enough times before taking the desperate voyage to America. She must have been one strong, determined woman.

It's late in the afternoon when I drive back to the hotel. Two days lost, nothing achieved. I'm not in any hurry – my time is my own – but it's frustrating all the same. I'm not looking forward to phoning Mom later, because she'll be on at me to come home, and she can be pretty insistent. I'll lie and tell her I'm having a wonderful time.

When I head back into the hotel foyer, this time there's a woman behind the counter. She's pretty, immaculate in a way that suggests she's not from around here, with the hassled appearance of someone who's trying to fit too much into her day. She smiles a welcome and has the key to my room in her hand before I can even ask.

As I take it, I ask, 'Am I the only guest now? The place is kind of, ah, deserted?'

'I'm afraid so,' she says, and I realise instantly that she's English. 'What with the Troubles, people are staying away from hotels.'

'I didn't think the problem extended down here, to West Cork?'

'Not so much, but people are scared all the same. There have been a few hotels targeted out of the cities.'

The Troubles.

I know about this, but being American, I felt distanced,

immune, somehow. It's Irish Americans who are funding the rebellion, after all. I don't agree with how they're going about it, though. Innocent people get caught up in random violence, and people fighting a cause can be blinded by the needs of their own crusade. 'I'm surprised the hotel hasn't just closed, then,' I comment.

'Mr O'Donovan, the owner, won't hear of it. The old hotel is up for sale, and if people need a place to stay, he said, he's not going to be dictated to by people who haven't learned to fight with words not guns.'

'Good for him.'

'But we haven't had any problems here,' she adds hastily, probably wondering if she's put me off staying in Ireland at all.

'There was a guy, Noel, who booked me in when I arrived. He was going to introduce me to a guy called Finn Sheehan, to help with tracing my ancestors. Might he be around?'

'Who, Finn or Noel? Noel is Mr O'Donovan, of course. The owner.'

'That old guy in the flat cap, he owns all this?' I wave my hand around loosely.

She nods. 'Sure, and Roone House, up the back. He went to America to earn his fortune and came back with one, which isn't the usual story,' she adds with a faint grin.

'Slightly unusual, to say the least,' I agree, amused. 'But why on earth was he here, showing me to my room?'

'The chef walked out on us, and the lady who was going to manage the hotel didn't arrive at all. I'm having to do everything except make the beds! I'm sorry if you aren't getting the service you expected. I hope the dinner was all right last night? Noel's housekeeper is helping out. She's doing her best, but like the rest of us, she's not really employed to do that.'

'It was fine,' I say.

She looks relieved. 'I'm sure he'll find someone soon. He's advertised, up in the city.'

'Just as well I'm the only visitor at the moment, then.'

Her hassled look returns. 'Sure, but we have quite a few bookings in a month, and a party arriving next week. I don't know how we're going to cope. I'm Grace, by the way, and this isn't really my job. He took me on as his secretary, sort of. Mostly to write his memoir, but that's taken a back seat at the moment.'

I reassess, looking around the place with new eyes. A staffing shortage explains everything. 'But what about this Finn person. Can you tell me where I can find him?'

'Finny Sheehan? Yes. He has a property down towards Colla Quay. But the thing is...' She pauses for a moment, and I wonder what the thing is. Noel had hinted at something; now Grace is doing the same. 'Finn isn't the most sociable of people,' she says carefully. 'He's kind of a loner, if you know what I mean?'

'Well, maybe I can talk him around if you'd let me know how to find him?'

'Well, I guess it's up to him...' A strange look flashes across her face, but she describes a tiny cottage, not far from the quay down at the far end of the town, past the graveyard. 'Will you be wanting dinner tonight?'

I take pity on her. 'No, I've eaten already.'

Her eyes light up. 'If you take the key with you, you can let yourself in. It opens the main door, too.'

'Thank you. I'll do that.'

'And good luck with Finn.'

The rain seems to have run out of impetus for a moment, though the gloom hasn't lifted, so I decide to walk. I wonder whether I'm going to regret that decision as the occasional large splat finds its way loudly onto my windcheater. I march determinedly past the quay, up the hill, taking the road to Colla

Quay. I pull the hood tightly around my face. Truly, I'm happier not driving, and the walk will do me good.

It takes me longer than I anticipated, though. Two minutes in the car but nearly half an hour on foot.

The cottage is easy to find, exactly as described, with its blue door and three windows. It's tiny, like half a house – a shack, even. There are no lights inside, and it has an air of desolation. Surely no one can be living here?

I knock on the door and step back. Silence. I step back further and see a thin wisp of smoke trailing from the chimney. So, he is around. Or was until very recently – this Finn Sheehan who is not the most sociable of people. I knock again, repeatedly, and finally hear the latch ping open.

It's the guy who directed me to the hotel two days ago. He's standing in his socks on a mat decorated with two doggy footprints. He's bigger than I thought. Not tall but stocky, muscular. Not someone you'd want to tangle with on a dark night.

He stares blankly at me for a moment then says, with recognition, 'Oh, it's you. What do you want?' His tone is soft, but there's no hint at all that he cares about what I want. I can see it in his face, that he wants me to go away and leave him alone.

'Noel O'Donovan, up at the hotel,' I say, slightly nervously, 'he said you might help me. I'm looking for information about my ancestors. Nellie and William O'Mahoney. They came from Roone Bay back in the famine. They...'

'Sorry, I can't help you,' he says.

He backs away, and I'm left facing the blue door that he's closed in my face.

Oh. Well, that's that.

I walk on down to the quay and gaze over the dark expanse of water. I must be standing not so far from where Nellie must have stood, watching her husband sail off to America to seek a new life for them both. She must have wondered whether she would ever see him again. But she must have hoped and dreamed. That's all we have in this life, really. Hope that the bad things we're so afraid of don't actually happen, and dreams that something good will eventually come our way. Of course, one can be disappointed.

At that thought, my loss, my loneliness, comes rushing in on me like a wave. Everything I ever believed in, my future, my love, simply gone. The sobs well up, unstoppable, and tear out of my throat in a harsh cry. I sink to my knees and double over, retching. I haven't eaten anything, so bile burns my throat. Then the heavens open, and cleansing rain lashes down on me where I kneel. I lift my face to it and push back my hood, letting the rain wash over me. I came here to get away from my grief, and here I am, on a foreign shore, on my knees, howling it into the heavens like a banshee.

I told Mom I didn't need the anti-depressants any longer. I didn't like taking them in the first place but had allowed myself to be persuaded. The fog of calm that settled over me when I was taking them had distanced my grief, all right, but it also stole my personality, and I wanted it back. I didn't tell Mom I'd stopped taking them, and I didn't bring them with me, sure that I was in control. But I'm not. I want to be the person I had been, before: dynamic, fun, busy with life. In love.

That's what I came here for, I realise.

Not to find Nellie but to find myself.

And I've failed, just as Dad said I would. *There's nothing left to find over there*, he said with a moue of distaste, and he was right. I should go back now and let my parents take me back under their protective wing, keep me safe, as they've always done.

But right now, I'm too tired.

It's easier to just let go. I slip to the wet stones and curl, hugging my knees. I have no inclination to rise. I don't want to face my thoughts any longer. I just want them to go away.

As that thought trickles into my mind, I hear music cutting

through the sheeting rain. I don't know if I'm dreaming, but perhaps I'm not. This is Ireland, the land of myths and fairy mounds. Bright and cheerful, yet haunting, the tune cuts through the gloom, its tripping melody made for dancing. It reminds me of the Pied Piper story, a river of rats then a stream of children following the magic pipes to another world, where there's always warmth and light and music, and they will never have to cry again from hunger.

I'm not cold any longer and feel myself drifting. The music lifts my soul as it glides seamlessly from one tune to another, the wild reels morphing into happy jigs then sliding to slow airs, the notes hanging on the breeze until I don't know if I'm dreaming or still hearing them.

I hear stones shifting, clattering, followed by the happy panting of a dog. There's the strange sensation of a harsh tongue licking my wet cheek. I weakly bat it away. I don't want to wake.

'Whiskey, what have you found? Whiskey, leave!'

It's a man's voice. Then I hear him swear, and feel arms reaching under my back and knees, lifting me as if I'm a child. I want to say 'go away, I'm happy, leave me alone'. But I'm carried, jolted, over the rattling pebbles, and finally laid on a soft surface, and consciousness fades.

4

ERIN

People say when you wake after trauma, or a coma, there's a moment of confusion. *Where am I? What am I doing here? How did I get here?* But strangely, I know exactly where I am, even though I've never been here before. I'm in Finn Sheehan's cottage. He picked me up off the beach and carried me here. I recall the strength of his arms as he lifted me. I recall turning my face into his jacket, feeling safe there.

There's a fire burning in a cast-iron wood burner with a glass door, with a huge German shepherd – Whiskey, I seem to recall – stretched on a rag rug before it, cooking her toes. And I'm on a small sofa, covered in blankets, dressed only in my underwear. My clothes are on a rack to one side, steaming, as is a threadbare yellow towel.

My eyes focus on a chair set ninety degrees from the sofa, and he's there, hunched over, staring at me from under lowered brows. Or glaring, I'm not sure. He's as good-looking as I recall but tougher than I remember, his mouth set in a hard line. Close up, his workworn clothes seem less seedy and more of a statement: this is who I am. Take me as you find me.

'I'm sorry,' I say, hauling myself up, hugging my knees under the blanket. 'I can go back to the hotel. I'm okay now.'

His face relaxes slightly. 'What the hell were you doing?' he asks bluntly.

I smile faintly. 'Giving up, I think. But I'm over it now.'

There's another long silence as he digests that information, and I add, 'I heard music. I thought it was the fairies. Was that you?'

He crooks his finger towards the windowsill where a black-and-silver concertina sits.

'You're a musician.'

'I play a few tunes. Have you eaten? It'll warm you. You look way too thin.'

I'm too thin because I couldn't eat for nearly a year without throwing up, so I lost a bundle of weight, but I don't mention that. 'I'm hungry,' I admit. 'I felt sorry for the woman in reception. She would have had to cook for me because the chef walked out, and I think she had a family to go home to.'

He snorts, and his expression softens. 'I can make a cheese sandwich. And tea.'

'Please. That would be great. Thank you.'

He hammers up the stairs, and comes back with a pair of sweatpants and a hoodie. 'Here, put these on. They're clean.'

I dress while he's out in another room. I hear the clatter of cutlery and crockery, then he's back, with plates and mugs on a small tray. 'Sorry, it's not the Ritz. I don't have a table. Are you warm enough?'

I nod and make inroads on the sandwich. Eventually I ask, 'Did you call an ambulance?'

'Do you want me to?'

'No, I really don't. I just wondered.'

'I would have if I'd thought it necessary. It would have taken the ambulance at least half an hour to get here, though, even if it wasn't already out on call. My first thought was to get you warm and dry. Then I could see you weren't in danger. Apart from a danger to yourself, of course. You want to tell me why you want to kill yourself?'

'I don't want to. At least, I don't think I do. I came to Ireland to' – I shrug – 'I don't know, see where my ancestors came from or something. They came from Roone Bay, but I don't know which house. Noel said you were the man, so I came to ask for your help and you shut me out. So I walked down to the seashore, and, ah, everything just hit me, out of the blue.'

'You still haven't told me why.'

He's persistent. I contemplate telling him to mind his own business, but I guess I've just made myself his business. Maybe he saved my life. Maybe I do owe him an explanation. I purse my lips and stare at the coffee mug now clutched between my hands. 'I was in a car wreck,' I say softly. 'My husband, Kenny, was killed. He was an artist. A gentle, kind soul. I miss him so much.'

I blink hard, pushing back the threatening storm of emotion. There's another long silence. This Finn guy doesn't believe in filling the spaces. He knows I haven't told him everything, but he doesn't fish for more. Maybe he realises that to say more, now, would break me.

'I'd best take you back up to the hotel,' he says eventually. 'When you're feeling up to it. This place is a rumour mill. If you're seen coming out of my house in the morning, they'll have us married by lunchtime.'

I grin despite myself and find it echoed on his face. He's not such a grump, then, and has a sense of humour. I wonder why he hides himself under that dour facade. I push the boundaries a little. 'So, will you help me find out about my ancestors?'

'Maybe there's nothing we can find.'

Well, that's more positive than a door shut in my face.

I feel quite drowsy but strangely content, sitting in a stranger's house, warm from the food and tea, basking in the flickering firelight. I notice that there's a storm lamp behind me but no lights turned on. I glance up at the ceiling in surprise. 'Don't you have electricity?'

'No. No running water, either.'

'Goodness.' So that's why I hadn't seen any lights on as I waited outside. There weren't any. 'I didn't think people still lived like this.'

'It's just me and Whiskey, and we manage just fine.'

I flush slightly. 'Sorry. I wasn't being judgemental.'

His shrug and lopsided smile offer an apology. 'I was prevaricating. I bought this place as an investment. One day I'll expand it, put in the facilities. But it came up for sale, and it made sense to buy the place outright rather than get a new place with a hefty mortgage on top. I don't like being in debt, and I've got no family to worry about. But most of all, it's right by the sea. The sound, the smell, her moods. The fierce danger when the storms are down. The treacherous calms when the sun is on the water.'

I stare at Finn, thinking I'd never have expected such poetry from someone who looks like a down-at-heel builder. Of course, the lilt in his Irish accent helps.

He does with words what Kenny did with paint.

I wonder what he'd make of my parents' home, where I have a private bathroom and dressing room attached to a spacious bedroom. Or the tall, prestigious brownstone where Kenny and I shared those two brief years and which has now been empty for another two.

Our very different worlds have gently collided, and I wonder if fate had something to do with it. Perhaps Finn is meant to help me in my quest, and the fates aren't allowing him to say no. I smile at my own fanciful thought. I'd speculated with Kenny about whether something was meant to be, and he'd laughed. *No such thing as fate*, he'd argue. *You get out of this world what you put in.* But if that was the case, what had he done to deserve to die in a car wreck?

I'm curious about Finn. I wonder if he works and, if so, what he does. I've decided he's not the uneducated bum I'd supposed him to be when I asked for directions when I arrived. I'd like to know why he's hiding behind a gruff smokescreen and why he's making it so hard for people to communicate with him.

'Do you want to tell me what happened?'

I realise he's seen the scars on my body. I don't think he's prying so much as trying to understand. I'm tired but have no reason to hurry back to an empty hotel room; I can't think of a good reason to disagree.

'I don't want to bore you,' I say, shrugging.

He says quietly, 'Whatever it was, it was traumatic. Perhaps it will help to talk?'

I nod, and it spills out.

5

ERIN, TWO YEARS EARLIER

Kenny has just finished his first major art show. By the time we finally leave the exhibition hall, we're exhausted but thrilled. Kenny's exhibition was the best yet. Our throats are sore from talking, and my face has a permanent ache from the plastered-on smile I retained while discussing his work with various art aficionados. We're looking forward to reaching the hotel and chilling out before making the drive home. The staff will do the donkey work tomorrow: pack the pieces in crates and deliver the sold paintings to their new owners. The rest, which isn't so many, will be transported back to Kenny's studio, in the eaves of my brownstone. It has been a long haul to this triumphant moment, from the get-go to the final hour. I'd done a massive amount of administration: the PR work, the advertising, the auctioneers, the art dealers, the fine-art magazines, the catering, the invitations... Everything was coordinated to the best effect, and our success was reflected in the number of paintings sold.

I'm so happy it's almost indescribable.

Kenny called his exhibition *The Passionate Sky*; his paintings are about nature in all its raw glory: storms roiling with thunderclouds and sheet lightning, orange and purple sunsets, the serenity of endless blue vistas over white sand, and stark nights magically dusted with stars and an overshadowing moon. The foregrounds are almost foil to the skies. Kenny can reach into the soul of nature and daub it into being, turning the dazzling white canvas into something surreal, yet so deep I can almost reach out and touch his envisaged universe. Kenny is down to earth, practical and generous, yet views the world from a subtly different platform than us mere mortals.

He'd experimented with watercolour and charcoal and oil paints before I met him, but had discovered his forte using thick acrylic paint dabbed on in rich layers with a palette knife. When one peers closely at his work it just looks like splodges of colour, but the further back one stands, the more the scene evolves and draws into focus. I don't get how he can do that, working close to the canvas, while seeing, in his mind's eye, what the viewer will eventually see from a distance.

We're both thrilled at the result but glad it's over. It will be another year before we have to do it all again, and in the meantime, Kenny can lose himself to another theme; maybe still water, he's mused. He envisages deep reflections in marshes, lakes and quiet seashores, so I am anticipating a few jaunts to places of interest so that he can commit the scenes to memory and capture the light and depth of each moment on film. I love him so much; he's such a beautiful change from my family's inherently pragmatic take on life.

I'm driving us back to the hotel I'd booked on the outskirts of New York, well away from the noise and the lights. I glance at him, taking my eyes from the road for a split second. 'You're wonderful,' I say.

'You're prejudiced,' he responds with a lazy smile.

'Sure am. I'm the luckiest wife alive, to have snagged the best up-and-coming artist, who's going to become a household name and keep me in the style to which I want to become accustomed.'

'Living in a garret on dry bread and water?'

'With you, that would make me happy.'

'But a little luxury wouldn't do us any harm.'

He sneaks a grin, and I know exactly what he means. I like being able to live comfortably, and helping Kenny achieve his dreams is an added bonus, one that he didn't see coming, either. It was a while before he accepted that I wanted to share everything with him: my home, my life, my wealth. When he met me, sweeping me off my feet, he fell on his at the same time but had a hard job accepting it, knowing what people would think.

And he was right. People thought the worst.

My grandfather had given me a little nest egg when I turned twenty-one, and I invested part of it, with Dad's help, in a three-storey brownstone terraced house. At first, I rented it out and stayed with my parents, but when I met Kenny, then a penniless artist, everything changed. He had nothing but his skill when we moved into the house and set up home together. Dad said I'd regret it, that Kenny was a parasite who wanted a rich wife to springboard his career. Mom tried to tell me that he wasn't good husband material, but Kenny has proved them both wrong.

My affluent background, of course, has already attracted some propositions that were clearly two-faced or even downright fraudulent, but I like to think I'm a good judge of character. Kenny loves me, absolutely. I know this. He's a brilliant artist with vision, but he's also a good husband, stable and undemanding. He hadn't been prepared to compromise his dream, but neither would he have seduced a wealthy woman to further his dream. And yes, I fund his career, but I believe in him. The success of his first major exhibition validates my faith.

I'm smiling with self-satisfaction as we speed down the freeway. It's great to prove my parents wrong in matters of the heart. I'm proud that I didn't put my bank balance before a gut feeling that Kenny wasn't some kind of monster on the make but was the man I believed him to be: sensitive, artistic and loving, true to himself in a commercial world.

I'm sure my parents entered into marriage like a contract. Like-minded people making a decision for a future that wasn't so much about love as protecting their interests, walking in the right circles and feeling secure in their future.

I kind of like the excitement of taking a chance, of going with my inner feelings rather than common sense. But, with the brutal realism I inherited from my father, I also knew that Kenny was unlikely to have succeeded without my input. He would have sold a few paintings, sure, but he wouldn't have been able to put them out there in prestigious exhibition halls where they could be seen by people who would recognise his talent. Success isn't always a matter of being good; it's about being recognised. I'm able to open doors that had previously been slammed in his face, and, despite Dad's dislike of the bohemian mindset, in the end, he, too, helped kick Kenny through the door to success, albeit a little reluctantly.

I'm mulling over our triumphant entry into the world of art when Kenny cries out, a wordless scream of horror that sends a panicked shockwave through my body. A huge semi-truck driving towards us on the other lane has lost control. The wavering cab veers left then right, before hurtling across the grassy median into the oncoming traffic, and jack-knifes in front of us.

The traffic is dense. In the instant before we're consumed by the desperate mayhem of panicking drivers, my mind shoots through many scenarios, seeking a way out before discovering there isn't one. There's an orchestra of brakes and squealing tyres and metallic thumps as cars bounce off each other. I experience a moment of sheer terror as the vehicles surrounding us make rash evasive manoeuvres that add to the devastation.

Then the trailer flips like a fish out of water, bringing the cab crashing down with it. The impetus drives the wall of iron inexorably towards us, sending a firework display of sparks from the tarmac.

Then: nothing.

6

ERIN

So, now Finn knows. In the morning, I find that the heavy weight bowing down my soul has released its hold just fractionally, as if Finn has saved me from more than a near-death experience on the beach. I feel guilty for unloading on him, but he did ask. I'm working through depression, but I don't think I'm suicidal, as he supposed. Maybe my strange behaviour was something to do with stopping the anti-depressant pills too suddenly.

As I stretch, it takes me a moment to realise that the overwhelming silence is because it's finally stopped raining. I clamber out of bed, pull on a robe and stare out of the window in astonishment. The sky is a dome of blue. The Atlantic is sparkling. The horizon is a gently curved line splitting the two. There are a few clouds brush-stroked high above; mare's tails, Kenny called them.

After the last two days of gloom and torrential rain, it's hard to reconcile the sight with my recollection of nearly dying on a windswept beach last night. Perhaps I dreamed it, after all. Perhaps I hadn't been gathered up by a rugged stranger and saved from my own stupidity. That, without a doubt, is something I'm not going to share with Mom. She'd be over here like a shot, pills in hand, persuading me back into the twilight zone I'd been trapped in for the last two years. I think, now, that I'd been something of a zombie, just doing what I was told, going where I was steered. I almost laugh. I must have been acting like a model daughter; quite out of character, in fact.

I feel surprisingly strong this morning, as though I've clambered over another obstacle in a course designed to keep me down. Since Kenny died, until I made my somewhat bizarre decision to come to Ireland, I hadn't even tried to climb out of the pit of my apathy. I wasn't even sure I wanted to. I allowed my parents to take control over my free will, as I was not capable of doing so, and couldn't even find the willpower to try. And Mom is a force to be reckoned with when she's on a roll. I'm her only daughter, so her possessiveness knows no bounds. She didn't ever think Kenny was good enough for me, but in her eyes, maybe no man is, unless he's like Scott Freel, my father's carbon-copy trainee.

Maybe she was right that I needed the tranquillisers at the time, but my decision to come to Ireland flew in the face of her wishes. I love my mother, but if I'm here, and she's there, distance diminishes her well-intentioned, controlling influence. Maybe that's subconsciously why I was determined to come, knowing that the only way I'm going to move on is to do it myself, rather than be steered in a direction I might later regret. And that direction is directly towards Scott Freel. He's personable enough and destined to become a partner in Dad's law firm, if I'm reading it right. He has that clean-cut chin and confident stance of a man determined to go places. I suspect his somewhat relentless pursuit of me – with my parents' benevolent approval, of course – has just a little to do with ambition.

It's too soon after Kenny, I said, but that was a lie.

With Kenny, I knew right away that he was *the one*, whereas with Scott I seem to be expected to make a sensible and educated decision for my future, which isn't in the same ball park at all. He'd make a good husband, Dad said. Stable, reliable and well able to support a family. He's probably right, but maybe he didn't think that comment through before he uttered it, because it's quite clear that having children isn't on my agenda. Maybe that's why I wanted to run, to drag myself out from under the blanket of care that was smothering me. And here I am.

So, what now? I need to stop mulling over things and act.

I've been told there's a library in Roone Bay, so I make that my first port of call. I walk up the long road through the town, away from the hotel, minding the uneven and broken sidewalk, dodging the tufts of grass pushing through the gaps. I find the library, a modern building, all brick and glass, hiding behind a small grocery store.

At five foot three, I'm shorter than most of my peers, but at the information desk, I find myself peering down at the librarian, a petite, neat woman around my mother's age. She's wearing horn-rimmed glasses that sweep up into points, a statement from a few years back. At first glance she seems dauntingly severe.

'Can I help you?'

'Hopefully,' I say with a smile. 'I'm seeking information about someone who lived here before the famine.'

'We call it the Great Hunger now,' she corrects.

I'd heard that term, but I'm curious about it. 'Why?'

'Famine suggests that there was no food, but Ireland was a major producer of crops. The people here starved while food was being exported. It was a crime, so it was.'

'I see.' I don't want to get into the rights and wrongs of it so move on quickly. 'Well, I'm actually trying to find out about some ancestors who left from Roone Bay back in the 1840s and landed in Boston.'

'What was the name?' she asks in a somewhat softer tone.

'Nellie and William O'Mahoney. William left in 1846, when he was about twenty-two. He made it to Boston, I know, and got a job on the railroad. He sent her the money to follow after. Their son, Luke, was my great-something grandfather.'

'Well now,' she says, 'you're nearly local, so you are!'

The change in her expression from dour to beaming was as sudden as the flash of a light bulb. I laugh. 'Not quite. But is there any way I can find out where she lived? Just to get a feel for her, if you know what I mean.'

She shakes her head. 'Sorry, girrul. There are O'Mahoneys around, sure enough. The bar in town is owned by an O'Mahoney, but if any of them are your relatives, well' – she shakes her head – 'it might be impossible to discover the connection, so.'

'Are there remnants of local lore – newspapers, birth certificates, rent agreements, whatever?'

She shakes her head. 'Not local news, no. Not then. You'd be best talking to someone in the historical society, but, sure, there won't be much from back in the day. They have a few letters and suchlike.' She grimaces, adding, 'With so many dead, and not even their names remembered, it would be a wonder if they had anything specific to the people you're asking after.'

That was pretty much what I expected, but I persevere. 'So, where is this historical society? Can you put me in touch with them?'

'Well, they meet occasionally at the library, but it's fairly informal. The best person to talk to is Finn Sheehan, but—' She stops herself abruptly, and there it is again. What is it about Finn that has people clamming up? Is he an axe murderer or something?

'But what?' I ask.

'Well, maybe I should have suggested Joseph Keery. He's a retired school teacher and is very knowledgeable on Irish history.'

'Well, really, I'm looking for someone with specific local knowledge. Maybe Finn is the person I should be talking to, after all.' I don't mention that I've already met him, and certainly have no intention of exposing the somewhat embarrassing circumstances.

She grimaces. 'I shouldn't say anything, but Finn's taking a break from work at the moment. Trying to sort himself out, decide what to do with his life.'

Sounds a bit like me, I think. 'What does he do?'

'His father's a fisherman. Runs a boat out of the harbour, below. Finn started out with him, but fishing wasn't for him. He went up to Cork, got an education and eventually joined the coastguards.'

'I guess that's a hard life, too,' I hint, wondering what Finn's problem really is, what there is to sort out. It sounds as if he already made his life choices, and with some determination. Another man might have stayed fishing with his father then later blamed the father for ruining his chances.

She makes a decision and gives me directions to Finn's cottage, justifying herself by muttering, 'Well, sure, you can only ask. But in the meantime, why don't you write a note for our noticeboard? It might be that someone will see it and be able to provide some more information. You could put a piece in the local newspaper, too. The office is over in Bantry. But, sure, you could write and post it to them.'

She fishes a fat yellow telephone directory out from under the counter, flicks through the pages, then jots down the telephone number and address of the local newspaper. 'Martin Kelly is the man who deals with letters – maybe address it to him.' She jots his name down, too, and pushes it across the counter.

'I'll do that, thank you.'

As I grab the scrap of paper, I sense she's sorry she ever

mentioned Finn's name. It's the small community spirit at work, closing ranks when a stranger hoves into view.

She tries to be helpful, though, and skilfully redirects the conversation. She soon has me assessing a pile of history books. Some are weighty tomes, some glossy publications, but all cover the broader aspects of the famine: political overviews, acts of parliament and quotes from persons of importance at the time. Some are books I've already read, and they aren't what I'm seeking, but out of respect I choose a couple of books to take to the counter. 'Is it possible to take these back to the hotel? I'll be staying for a few weeks, so can I get a temporary library ticket?'

'Sure you can,' she says, pleased, and efficiently busies herself with taking my details before issuing me a cardboard library pass. In the time I've been here, half an hour or so, no one else has come in, so I suspect the library isn't inundated with clients.

I take the books back to the hotel and begin to read, but they really don't hold my interest. I doze for a while and think about what I know of Nellie O'Mahoney, which is very little.

When, as a child, I first heard Nellie's story from my grandpa – Gabriel – it had sounded like a fairy tale, so far back in history it was impossible to gauge. As I grew older, though, I realised it wasn't so long ago, five or six generations, because *his* grandfather, Luke O'Mahoney, had been speaking of his own mother not some far-distant ancestor. Nellie's story trickled down through family lore, word of mouth, so I'm not sure how much truth is in any of it, but Grandpa Gabriel had the Irishman's gift for telling a story, and to me it sounded real enough. I always loved a good romance, and to a child with imagination, Nellie's story was more intimate and emotional than a traditional fairy tale.

7

NELLIE 1842

Nellie was fifteen, nearly old enough to be a wife. Several times she'd seen William at a distance leading the master's donkey cart along the boreen. She wondered about William in a way she hadn't wondered about any of the other lads who cast eyes in her direction. She knew who he was, of course. In the townland, everyone knew everyone, and knew all their business, too. She knew William had been orphaned some years before and had no home to call his own. He slept in a rough lean-to made with stones and branches, roofed with turf, which leaned against the side of the master's stables.

Autumn had come around. Nellie had just collected a bundle of straw from the threshing and was carrying the bulky load on her back when she saw him walking towards her. His strong arms were brown from the sun, and he had a jaunty neckerchief knotted above the collarless shirt that looked as though it had passed down through many siblings. His feet were bare, like hers, and muscular calves stretched from the raggedy ends of his pants as if he had shot up too fast in the growing. His pants were knotted at the waist with twine. She stepped aside

with lowered eyes, to let him pass, but he didn't move the weary
donkey on.

'Young Nellie Crowley,' he said softly in the native tongue.

She raised her eyes, shyly, and met his. She had never seen
him so close. It was as if time stopped, he was so handsome.
Beneath the ragged clothes, he was lean as the master's grey-
hounds, fit and able as any young man she had seen, with hair
like fire. His face beamed with the pleasure of meeting, and that
was surely because he had a fancy for her?

'William O'Mahoney,' he said, hand to his chest in intro-
duction. His smile was like a flash of sunshine on a dark day.
'I've been watching ye this long year. Ye have grown into a fine
woman, young Nellie. Will ye maybe have a fancy for me?'

She blushed and said nothing, absolutely tongue-tied, but
gave a faint nod. She'd known instantly that she was in love. He
told her, later, that he'd known it, too. He said she was like a
fairy child, slim, barefoot and beautiful. Dwarfed by the
massive bundle on her back, he had also seen that she was not
work-shy so would make an honest man a good wife. *That's the
girl I'm going to marry*, he had told his friends, *and there's not a
body will stop me.*

Nellie went back to the tiny cottage that was her home and
did her chores with new vigour, sweeping the stone floor,
remaking the straw mattresses for the winter, and told her
parents that William O'Mahoney was going to come a-courting.
Her mother carried on spinning, shaking her head, and her
father grunted. She was the youngest and last of their children,
and maybe they were wondering how they would cope if she
left, as had her older siblings.

His courtship was constant and careful for nearly a year,
bringing little gifts for Nellie and her parents, who couldn't
blame their youngest daughter for falling under his spell, as,
indeed, they also did. He was polite and kind, ready enough to
help Thomas with the tilling or Mary with bringing in the turf

for the fire. He would help Nellie turn the sods over the praties in the lazy beds to increase the yield, and fetch water from the well on the hill. Despite the ragged clothes, he carried himself with dignity, and him always with a ready laugh and a song on his tongue.

Nellie was the youngest of her many siblings, save for the two little ones after her who had passed too soon from sickness. Each year as she was growing, her older brothers and sisters had walked out of their lives, to England, to Canada or Australia, seeking to better themselves, they said. They had no interest in scratching a living from barren land as their parents had done before them, not even able to buy shoes after the tithes and rents were paid.

Nellie's parents were relieved to invite the banns at church and welcomed young William gratefully into their family home, the one-roomed cottage made of stones that had been Thomas's father's before him and made by *his* own father's hands. It was a sound building with a good patch of land for growing their praties. The thatched roof, replaced many times in its life, held down with ropes and field stones, kept the weather at bay. The unglazed windows were on the west, away from the blast of weather from the sea, and the half-door, the same side, was closed only when the chickens and suckling pig were brought in to save them from an occasional spark of frost. What more could a man ask for, save young blood to provide comfort when the blindness of age came?

William had no wish to leave Ireland. He loved his country: its hazy green hills alive with yellow gorse and its bogs of iron-black water rimmed with rushes. He loved the music of the sweet streams bubbling down from the wild mountain, the mystical fairy mounds, and most of all he loved the music of the people, which was in his blood. He would stay with Nellie, he promised, be a son to them and farm the little patch of land that sustained them. And so he did, for two happy years, while

Nellie, after a couple of mishaps, brought little Annie into their lives.

Then news travelled along the boreens about a mysterious dark fog that rolled in from the sea and settled on the lazy beds, so the potatoes blackened and turned to slime. It seemed like a strange-enough tale until they experienced it themselves. When the blight settled its deathly vapour on the land, as had the locusts that once destroyed the crops in Egypt, it was as if the earth itself had betrayed them. They had grown the praties, harvested them and dug them into clamps for the winter as their people had been doing for a hundred years or more, but one of the clamps was fine one day and black as the devil's soul the next. Their other three clamps survived and were rationed throughout the long winter. Some were kept for seed, no matter how hungry they were, because without them there would be no planting in the spring.

There were those who said God was punishing them, but for what, Nellie's mother had no idea. They were God-fearing people sure enough, and didn't they go to mass and confess? And wasn't God after forgiving them for their sins?

William had heard tell that turnips and carrots didn't get the blight, and had planted a few to try out. They weren't as nutritious or filling as potatoes, but as more potatoes blackened, and the hunger bit, they were grateful to be eating them.

It would be fine the next year, they were assured.

But the ground was sick, and the next year they lost more than half of their planting, and the following year even the seed potatoes blackened and died, and there were no praties to eat, and none for the planting.

In desperation, Nellie made the three-day pilgrimage up the wild track on Hungry Hill to the Holy Well. It was autumn, turning towards winter, and hunger was biting at the gut. The long, yellowing grass whispered in a faint breeze, and shards of cold rock cut her bare feet. She pulled her shawl tight around herself, and on bleeding feet she walked nine times around the well clockwise, before kneeling to pray to the Lady for her bounty. *Take me if you will, but please don't let my family starve*, she whispered. Then she cupped her hands and drank the holy water.

But the Lady, it seemed, had turned her face from Éire. The people grew thinner and weaker and more wretched. Where Nellie used to see ruddy faces and smiles, now she saw gaunt desperation. Where there had never been theft or violence, she heard tales of people harmed, or worse, for the smallest hint of food.

That year, the master of Roone Hall sent his agents out to offer men the fare to leave Ireland, to go to America or Australia, to start new lives. It wasn't for charity, Nellie's father said grimly; it was because sheep were fetching a good price, and he wanted the land.

He was proved right. After the neighbour's menfolk had left on the ship for Canada, and their wives couldn't pay the rent, he had the roofs pulled from the cottages and evicted the women and children. They begged on their knees – *For the Love of God, what about our children?* – but the land agents didn't listen. The women begged from neighbours who were already starving, and dug shelters into the ditches or traipsed up the hill to the rock shelters where it was said the ancient gods used to reside, where the magic circles they had carved into the rocks could sometimes be seen in the early morning sun on a clear day. But when winter came, they died where they lay, of cold and starvation, their children in their arms.

It was said there was charity and food, miles to the north, by the city, but the inhabitants of the Tírbeg townland were already too weak to walk so far, and those who left never came back to say whether it was true or not.

A black cloud of depression blanketed Nellie's family. What had they done to deserve this? Did they not work hard enough, and obey the priests, through whom God was speaking? But the priests, too, were hungry, and holding on to the notion that God had a plan.

William, in dismay, finally told Nellie that he must take the master's bounty. He would go to America, where gold was there for the taking, and send money back for his wife and child, so they could follow in his footsteps.

8

ERIN

Two weeks pass almost unseen, while I wonder quite what I'm doing here. But the hotel is a calm place to be despite its lack of facilities, and I began to realise I had done the right thing. My friends and relatives were trying to be kind, but sometimes I just wished they would all stop trying. The alternative was to go away and give myself space to think. I lost myself in a few fairly forgettable novels and took silent walks down to the quay and the beach. Several times I thought about knocking on Finn Sheehan's blue door, but found myself reluctant to do so, for reasons I can't explain. But this morning my dozy reveries made me jolt with a sudden realisation. What an idiot! I was seeking Nellie O'Mahoney, but in fact I should be seeking her parents, whose name was Crowley. William himself had no kin alive when he married Nellie, and moved in with her and her parents. How could I have missed that little detail when I had so often perused the lineage scribed in such tiny scratched pen marks in the front of Nellie's bible?

I remember the exact time I became more than just vaguely interested in Nellie's story. It can be nailed down to the day Grandma Ethel died and Grandpa Gabriel passed Nellie's bible to Dad, who had no interest in it at all, so gave it to me. I was delighted and enthralled. The small book, with a brown, mottled cover embossed with a gold design, its thin-as-gossamer pages printed in two columns of minuscule print, had once been in Nellie's hand! It made her real, somehow. I wonder if Nellie was ever able to read it.

A hand-me-down bible is a bit of a cliché, but I treasured it, grateful that Dad hadn't consigned it instantly to a thrift store. Imagining Nellie's desperate struggle to survive after she left Ireland, to actually hold something in my hand that she had once held in hers, forged an unexpected link to the past. It brought us closer, made her a real person, no longer a fireside story repeated by an old man.

According to the inscription in the front, it had been a gift from Adelaide Becker, Nellie's employer in Boston, when she started to work for them as a maid, which indicates that they were God-fearing Christians. Adelaide and Kurt Becker once owned a cotton manufactory, which, I discovered, had gone into liquidation many years ago. I found no trace of the family; though, even if I had, it's doubtful they'd have any knowledge of a maid from several generations back.

I didn't become consumed with finding out more about Nellie until after the accident, when I was floating in a kind of half-life with no sense of direction. But as I was recovering, Nellie's bible somehow found its way to my bedside, and I found my eyes gravitating towards it. I experienced a strange sense of empathy with the long-dead woman, as if I had followed in her footsteps, our individual griefs bringing us closer together.

When I made the decision to come to Ireland, I thought there would be archives to trawl through. I hadn't expected there to be a vacuum into which whole families simply vanished during the famine. It had been rational, I thought, to assume that the priests would have made a list of all the poor souls they buried, but that had been naïve. I had no idea of the sheer scope of the problem they had been coping with.

Once I started to read up on the subject, I learned that on the back of the famine, epidemics of cholera, smallpox and typhus had raged across Ireland, ravaging a population already weak from starvation. The priests who bravely tended to their diminishing congregations would have been inundated simply by the sheer task of laying the dead to rest in the vast burial pits that served as graves. The priests who died are listed in church annals, as are the deeds they did and the manner of their deaths, but no list exists of the Irish population who feature in history as statistics, their anonymous deaths immortalised by the weight of their numbers. I'm not sure what to do next, though, if this Finn guy isn't going to help.

I go down to breakfast in the morning with no real plans. As I pass the foyer, though, I'm stopped in my tracks. There's a little girl sitting on a seat by the window. A tiny violin rests on the seat beside her, and at her feet is a school bag which has fallen over, ejecting some books onto the carpet. As it's Saturday, I assume her mother is working here, and she's been told to sit quietly and entertain herself.

'Hello,' I say. 'And who are you?'

'Hello,' she replies politely, without a trace of shyness. 'I'm Olivia, but I like to be called Livvy.'

I'm not sure if I detect an English accent; if so, it's been overlaid by Irish nuances. 'Then Livvy it is. My name's Erin, which actually means Ireland, in Irish.'

'That's funny,' she says, grinning. 'Being called Ireland, I mean.'

'It is,' I agree. I indicate the violin. 'Do you play?'

She sighs. 'I'm learning, but it's too hard.'

'It sure is, but that's the point, you see. When things are hard and you manage to get it, it's so much more exciting than if it was just easy. Do you want to show me what you can do?'

She grimaces and reaches for the instrument. 'I'm learning the D scale.'

'Oh. Aren't you learning any tunes?'

'My teacher says I have to know the scale first. And the archippelas.'

Goodness. Why would a teacher start with scales and arpeggios? 'How old are you?'

'I was eight last week.'

'That's a perfect age to play tunes. Do you know "Twinkle, Twinkle, Little Star"?'

'It's a baby song,' she says dismissively.

I wonder, very briefly, if I should be overriding her teacher, but it astounds me how easily some people put children off playing an instrument. 'I agree, it is a baby song, but the tune is nice. Shall I show you?'

She shrugs, and I pick up the violin and play the tune through, softly. I can see she's impressed. 'Do you want to learn it? It's easy, I promise.'

She nods, uncertainly, and I explain while illustrating slowly, the violin strangely tiny under my fingers. 'You play that string for the first two notes – that's G and G. The next string for the next two notes – that's D and D, then the first finger for the next two notes – that's E and E – then take the finger off for a longer D. That's the whole first line of the song. The last part's a bit harder, and you need three fingers for C, C, B, B, A, A and a long G to finish. Do you want to try? We can do the first part a few times before going on to the middle part of the song.'

'Okay.' She scrapes the bow up and down, and, after three tries, beams as the first lines resonate harshly through the empty room.

'What do you think?' I ask.

'It's okay. But it doesn't sound nice, like when you do it.'

'That's just practice. Try being gentle with the bow. Hold it like this.' I show her how. 'Now try again, as soft as you can and still make a noise.'

She does, and we share a delighted grin, because she knows she's already improved. I surprise myself by still being there after half an hour, by which time Livvy has learned the four lines. 'So, you get on and practise that, and next time you come in you can play it to me.'

'Will you play me a tune?' she asks. 'A real tune, I mean?'

My mind goes cold at the thought. 'Maybe next time. Besides, the thing is, this violin is too little for me. My fingers don't go in the right places.'

'Have you got a big violin of your own?'

'Yes, but it's back in America. I didn't bring it.'

'Oh.'

As she's mulling that over, I get the feeling I'm being watched and turn to see Grace, the reluctant hotel manager, watching from the door. I wonder how long she's been there.

As I turn, she walks over, smiling. 'Hi, Erin. I hope Livvy hasn't been bothering you? I don't have anyone to look after her today because Sean's working, and Grandma and Mum are off shopping in Cork city.'

'Absolutely not. I'm the one who's been bothering her. She was sitting quietly when I came over and asked her to play me a tune. She's doing really well.'

'She plays the violin, Mummy,' Livvy says. 'She's really good.'

'I got that,' Grace says, smiling.

'But I didn't get good too quickly,' I tell Livvy hastily. 'Do you know what my father used to call my violin when I started?'

She shakes her head.

'He called it my vile din.'

Grace laughs then has to explain to Livvy why it's funny.

Livvy looks sad. 'Didn't your father want you to play?'

'Not really. He wanted me to become good at working in an

office, so that I could go and work in his firm. Only it wasn't what I wanted to do.'

'Well, I think you should do what you want, and not what your father tells you to do.'

'Thank you,' I say then give her a sly smile. 'Actually, that's exactly what I did do, but don't tell!'

'Well, I need to get on,' Grace says. 'We have some bookings over the next few days, and I need to make sure the rooms are ready.'

'Can I help at all?' I offer.

She looks horrified. 'Goodness, no! You're on holiday!'

I lean towards her fractionally and whisper, 'I'm a little bored, actually. I could do with a task.'

'Well, we'll see.'

I suspect that asking to help out was a mistake, so I add, 'But when Livvy needs more help with the violin, I really don't mind.'

She nods. Perhaps that's acceptable, at least.

I was going to walk around the town, though I pretty much have it sorted. But when I look out of the window, I see the rain has started to lash down once more. *Doesn't it ever stop?*

I wander up to my room and try to get interested in one of the books I picked up at the library, but Livvy and the violin have unsettled me. I feel the darkness descending, and a headache building, so I take an aspirin and lie down, my hand reaching for the comfort of the old bible. I try to imagine what it must have been like for Nellie, brought up in this tiny back-water of a place, where religion was the glue that held the community together and being poor meant surviving each day, producing an endless string of children and trying to feed them. I wonder if she'd been happy with her lot, or whether she had secretly wished for something better, perhaps even just something a little *more*.

9

NELLIE 1846

Nellie didn't believe that the streets of Boston could possibly be paved with gold, as they had been told, but there was housing and food aplenty for anyone who wanted to emigrate. And with a child starving at her knee, William said he had little choice.

'I have to go,' he reiterated as the day of his leaving grew ever closer. Maybe he was assuring himself, as Nellie hadn't actually disagreed. He tightened his arm around her back. 'Trust in me, my sweet Nellie. I'll find a place to live, over the sea, in America. I'll find work, and when I have the money saved, I'll send for you. It won't be so long – you'll see. Then we can be a family again, and our Annie will grow up in a new land and never know hunger again.'

With his strength beside her, it would have been easy to believe him, but she'd seen too much grief. She had also seen other men disappear over the sea, never to be heard of again, and their womenfolk left in dire need. But as he said, there was at least hope over the water. Here, hope had died, from one cold shore to the other, right across the land, as friends and family and strangers fell victim to starvation, and were praying to God that the next year would bring better times.

There was nothing to stay for, though. Her parents, their frail bodies whittled away to ghosts, had drifted away quietly on the back of the flu epidemic last winter, and she was trying to be brave. The house already seemed empty without their solid presence, and she was scared of coping without William, even for a little while. She was afraid for her Annie, but also afraid for William on that unforgiving, deadly sea, if the rumours that filtered back home were true.

But he was right – he had to go.

In just two years, what had started out as the rumour of a strange black fog had turned into a national disaster. There were no potatoes, no grain and little enough Indian corn on the market, even if she had the money to buy it. It was bad now, with so many dead or evicted she was afraid to ask after her one-time neighbours or friends. They kept quietly hidden in their cottages, emerging only to go to mass with the dwindling congregation.

If William had not been married, and had no child to protect, maybe he would have stayed in the land he loved. Maybe he would have taken to the road and headed north, seeking the soup kitchens, as so many already had, but he took his vows to protect his family seriously. He had decided that emigration was no choice but a necessity if they were to survive. They'd heard there were not enough jobs in England, and the English were turning the starving Irish away with fists and worse. Australia sounded too alien, too frightening, but America was a big country, with land still for the taking.

He put his hands on Nellie's shoulders, holding her at arm's length, staring deep into her eyes. She put her hands up, rested them on his and met his gaze with equal intensity, drinking deep of the sight, committing him to memory. He was a shadow of the man he had been, but behind the sallow skin, his eyes still burned with love. He must be fearful of the unknown, as she was, but they both had to be strong. They had discussed it over the flickering light of the turf fire throughout a long and hungry winter, through a spring that promised food and another summer when the land had belched poison, the black rot settling over the diminished crop like a blanket from hell.

She thanked the Lord for William's insistence on planting a few precious flowers and different vegetables, despite the derision of their neighbours. Turnips didn't satisfy a working man's belly the way potatoes did, but they didn't turn to foul black slime overnight, and would see her and Annie through another hard winter. It might be a year before William could send the money for the fare, he said, but he would send money for the rent so they wouldn't be evicted from their home. She must eke out the secret store of turnips for herself and Annie, and survive as best she could until he sent for her.

It went against nature to withhold food from the skeletal figures who passed by, begging, but she would have to be strong, or she and Annie would join the multitudes who died where they lay, in ditches and along the roads, until the whole land stank of death. She would do as William said and hide away in their cottage, keeping herself away from people, even the priests and those she had grown up with, because disease now raged on the back of the famine, picking off the weak and the starving.

She thought it would be harder for William, who felt guilty for leaving his family behind as he faced the unknown: a new land, a new life.

But it was a big leap from understanding that he had to leave to accepting it with equanimity. She would miss him desperately, not least for the way he put his back into the land to provide for them. Their marriage was still young, but it was hard, in this second desperate year of blight, to recall how bright the future had seemed, laid out before them in yet unborn generations. How quickly it had vanished, she thought. All that hope, that excitement for the future, trampled underfoot by the black rot.

.   .   .

'Walk with me, Nellie,' William said softly.

He hoisted the quiet and withdrawn four-year-old Annie
into the nest of one strong arm, took Nellie's hand with the
other and led the way up the hill. She would miss him more
than he knew. He was still her sweetheart lover, with his riot of
red hair, clear blue eyes and deceptively slim build. Though he
now looked as if a breath of wind might shake him like a reed,
he could dig ditches and pull carts with the best of the men.
She had known he was a good man from the moment his wide
smile had caught her, and she hadn't been wrong. He was a
strange mixture of male strength, combined with the inner
sensitivity more befitting of a woman. What other man in
Tirbeg had planted a rose bush for his young bride as a wedding
gift? He had courted her with primroses from the hedges, eggs
from wild birds' nests and the rare gift of a shawl, spun and
woven by his mother many years past. It was a treasured gift,
her only legacy to her son, save for the gentle beauty of his
lilting voice, which could turn out a ballad that would make the
fairies weep.

He led her up past the well, holding her steady as her bare
feet slid on the moss-covered stones, past the stunted grove of
oaks, onto the weathered grey shale with its overhanging rock.
The faded autumn grass folded under the onslaught of a chill
wind blowing in from the ocean, its dying plumes battered back
into the land. It would spring forth next year, Nellie thought,
uncaring of the pitiful tragedy unfolding across the land, and
hide the graves beneath a fresh green mantle.

While Nellie had her gaze on William, he kept looking back
at the town snuggled in the curve of the bay, ingesting the sight
with the desperation of a man who might never see his homeland again. They wedged themselves beneath the jagged weight
of the pulpit rock, sheltered from the wind, and scanned the

southern coastline where Ireland dipped its toes into the unforgiving chill of the Atlantic.

In the distance, sea and sky melded, seamed by a dark shadow. Somewhere over the bottomless sea, America waited.

They clung to each other, and as they watched, a ship in full sail drifted slowly across the horizon. A ship like the one he would soon be on.

'When your ship sails down from Ireland,' she said softly, 'look for me, here. I'll be watching, sending my heart with you to America, my love.'

'And I'll take it, sweet Nellie, and keep it with me always, until either I can come home or you join me there,' he answered and began to sing, so softly it was like a breath of wind, an emigrant song that had somehow echoed back over the vast expanse of water:

> Oh, Érin grá mo chroí, *you're the only land*
> *   for me.*
> *You're the fairest that my eyes did ever behold.*
> *You're the bright star of the west,*
> *You're the land Saint Patrick blessed.*
> *You're the dear little isle so far away.*

His soft, sweet singing seemed distant, as if he were already on his journey, his homeland a hazy dream in the back of his mind. Annie hummed along tunelessly, sucking her thumb and stroking her father's hair, and Nellie fought back tears, so as not to alarm the child further. She was, Nellie knew, already aware that something strange was happening, that they were all tired from hunger, wasting to shadows of the people they had been two years ago.

When the day came for William to leave, his words were almost harsh as he lectured. It had all been said before, but it was perhaps his way of coping with the knowledge that the time was upon them for him to depart; for only God knew if they would meet again in this life.

'No matter what happens, keep the seeds safe. If the harvest turns sour, you must harden your heart, my sweet Nellie, and stay alive, for me and our Annie. Keep your stores hidden, and don't tell anyone you have food. You must put yourself and our child first. Annie must live, or what has this all been for?'

She saw newly creased lines on his face as he struggled to contain his inner turmoil. She knew he was torn in two by the decision to leave his family behind in a land weighed down by the dead. He should not be leaving her behind, and yet he could do little else. They did not have the money for another two passages.

That night they lay in bed silently, holding each other, waiting for the dawn. There was nothing left to say, but words rattled in hollow repetition around the chasm of grief that was Nellie's mind.

It was barely sunrise when they heard the donkey come trotting down the road, pulling the tiny cart with its weary load of passengers. William kissed the still-sleeping Annie then hugged Nellie tightly before pushing her clutching fingers gently aside. He climbed onto the seat with his meagre belongings tied into a strip of sacking. He waved with false cheer, saying, 'I'll send a letter, Nellie. I promise, I'll see you again, *a stór mo chroí.*'

Her smile wavered through unashamed tears as he called her the treasure of his heart, because she truly didn't know whether she would ever see him again.

10

ERIN

I must have fallen asleep reading. It's dark outside, and I'm lying on top of the green candlewick bedspread, fully clothed, shivering. Thinking and dreaming had mutated into a deep sleep, the best I've had in months, but the fading remnant of my ever-present nightmare of the accident is hovering, waiting to re-emerge the moment I close my eyes. I lie there for a while knowing that further sleep is going to evade me. Whatever possessed me to go to sleep during the afternoon and evening? I'm still dressed, so grab my windcheater and slip silently down the empty stairwell. I make sure I have the key with me, its enormous fob just about fitting into my purse. At the door, I slip on the waterproof, mostly to cut out the night chill.

The roiling black thunderclouds of a few hours ago have blown away, and the sky is littered with stars and a full hunter's moon glowing with a faintly red aura. The light has a sensational, almost mystic quality that permeates my soul with the faint shiver of... not apprehension but a portent of something cataclysmic on the horizon.

Outside the hotel, I pause, entranced by the blanket of peace, overwhelmed with memories. Kenny would have been quietly thrilled to be here. In Boston we rarely saw stars, too much light being generated by the city. When we felt the need for peace, we would drive out to Harold Parker State Forest and camp for a weekend. It was always a serene time, lying together in the darkness listening to the pines creaking and the rustling of night creatures, while whispering our future plans. Kenny got a lot of artistic inspiration from those forays into the wild, taking photographs to remind himself of special moments. Dad said he was cheating, painting from photographs, but Kenny never painted from a photograph he hadn't taken himself, so there was always a deeper side to the end result as the memories filtered subtly into his work. He would have loved this visit to Ireland and been mentally storing the rugged scenes: the rocky shores, the lighthouse blinking away in the distance, a black sea pitted with whitecaps reflecting in the moonlight.

I miss him so much it's a physical ache. I wonder when grieving stops, when I can pick up the pieces of my life and get back to living. Will it ever happen, or will I forever be a ghost in the system, haunting life from a distance?

I drift slowly down through the deserted town, just the hint of lights peeping through cracks in curtains to remind me that other people are still awake. Before the accident I was always a little afraid of people, of being mugged or murdered, but afterwards I went out of my way to walk the streets, as if subconsciously encouraging harm: here I am, mug me, put me out of my misery; why am I still alive, wondering what to do with my future? But here and now in the cold light of the moon, in a different country, I could be the only person in the world, walking in the overwhelming silence.

I pass the little road that leads down to the quay and start to march back up the other side of the town, intending to circle back to the hotel along the lane that passes behind the bank. Halfway up the hill, I stop short, startled by the faintest sound of music and for a moment wonder if I'm imagining things.

Perhaps I've succumbed again to the legends of moonstruck fairy mounds, where the little people play tunes to steal humans away into their magical empire.

Though what they would want humans for beats me.

But no, I really do hear music. As I pass Nancy's bar, which looks dark and closed from a distance, I realise the music is coming from within. It's barely discernible, but as I stand outside, listening curiously, I realise there's a live music gig going on inside. The distant murmur of dialogue penetrates the silence then a muffled shout of laughter. Then I hear it again, the hint of a fiddle rasping away at a tune, only the shrill higher notes penetrating the thick walls. There's also the rhythmic beating of a drum and the hint of a reed instrument – a concertina or maybe a button box. I had heard of lock-ins where the doors are barred, and those inside carry on drinking and dancing and singing, and am amused to have unexpectedly discovered one.

I perch on a windowsill, and although I can't exactly make out the tunes, I feel included in a strange way, simply by being here, experiencing this nocturnal, secret event. But maybe it's not so secret that the local guards don't know about it. Maybe they turn a blind eye to what is surely the national pastime – if they aren't in there having a pint themselves!

I pull my windcheater tighter around me and listen hard, to see if I can make out the tunes, but the old walls, nearly a metre thick at the base, are doing a good job of muffling the sound.

I don't know how long I'm there, in a strangely contented, dreamy state, despite the cold, when a voice I recognise says, 'What are you doing, standing outside? Are you trying for hypothermia again?'

Like the fairy folk I was thinking about, Finn seems to have materialised out of the gloom. He's holding a concertina case, so I assume he'd been playing, and wonder if the music session is grinding to a halt. 'I was trying to listen,' I say, almost guiltily, as if he'd caught me doing something illicit. 'But I couldn't hear much from outside.'

'Why didn't you just come in?'

'The door's locked.'

'Ah. I guess you didn't know. After eleven, the back door is open. Down there.'

His hand, ghostly white in the moonlight, points to a little alley I hadn't noticed previously. I nod, embarrassed, and push myself to my feet. 'I'll know next time. I'll be on my way, then.'

'Are you going back to the hotel?'

I nod again.

'I'll walk you back.'

'You don't have to. It's the wrong way for you.'

'It's not raining, and I'm too wired to sleep.'

He starts down the hill, and I hop and skip to catch up, feeling obliged to keep step. 'That was you playing?'

He casts a sidelong look with the hint of a smile. 'Not just me. There were a few others. Are you interested in our traditional music?'

I shrug. 'I'm curious.'

'Well, maybe you should come in and listen next time. How long are you intending to stay in Roone Bay?'

'I haven't set a return date. I have this peculiar need to find Nellie O'Mahoney's house before I go back. Everyone tells me you're the man to go to. But, of course, I get it if you aren't interested.'

I see him mulling that one over.

We're at the foot of the hill, where the road turns to go back up the other side, when he stops and says, 'Come. I want to show you something.'

Coming from a man I barely know, this should set alarm bells ringing, but there's something deeply meaningful in his tone. I don't speak, but we turn together, down towards the quay. We walk along the small stone-built harbour wall, past the double rank of fishing boats bumping gently against a row of old tractor tyres that hang into the water. In daylight, the boats are worn, the paint dulled and peeling, but in the stark moonlight, they take on a cold, pristine cleanliness.

Finn stops at the end of the quay and leans on the rail, peering out over the dark sheen of water. For a moment I stand slightly back, studying him. His body language is intense, somehow, and his shoulders are hunched against the fitful breeze which is blowing straight onto the shore.

'I come here sometimes,' he says finally. 'At night, after the music. I love the quiet, the way the sea is different at night. It's the only time I get a real sense of the past, maybe a glimmer of the emotions the emigrants must have felt as they contemplated leaving Ireland for good. They must have been heartsick at the thought.'

I look out to sea with him. Maybe it's his presence, or the sensitivity of the words, but I have an epiphany. I came here to find the physical presence of Nellie's home, and what she had left behind, but what I need to do is discover the more emotive side of Ireland: what it means to be Irish, what it meant, back then, to live poor but maybe with a measure of contentment, then to have it all ripped away, suffer the hardships and losses brought by the Great Hunger, and then have to sail away to an unknown future. When people told me Finn was the man to go to, I don't think they meant this, but I feel chastened, educated, just by standing here beside him.

He turns to me, and, with insight, he says, 'You get it, don't you?' I nod silently, and he carries on. 'The sea's been here since the beginning of time. She's seen everything, since before famine, before humans, before the dinosaurs. We're nothing to her, just flames that flicker briefly and are gone. The Atlantic is one of the ancient gods, all-powerful and self-interested. When you see her like this, she's a cheeky child testing her boundaries. See the white spume? The moonlight touching the tips, like fairy dust? But she can turn to anger in a moment and rip boats to pieces as if they were made of paper.'

She, he says. To Finn, the Atlantic is a woman. Does he think we're like the Atlantic, us women? Temperamental, uncaring? Is that what his problem is? That a woman has hurt him so much that we're all lumped into the same boat?

'The lady in the library told me you work as a coastguard?'

'I do. I'm taking some time out, though. Sometimes the work gets to me.' He halts suddenly, as if he was on the verge of telling me why then changed his mind. He turns abruptly and begins to walk. 'Let's get you safe home.'

'You don't have to...'

He frowns. 'What kind of man lets a woman walk alone at night?'

I hide a smile. How very old-fashioned and chivalrous, I think. And here, where the road is empty, with no revellers, drunks, potential muggers or rapists lurking in the shadows.

'So, have you found out anything at all about your ancestors?' he asks. 'Who were they? Did you tell me? I've forgotten.'

'Nellie and William O'Mahoney, but her name was Crowley before she married.'

'There are many families with those names here. You understand that you might not be able to trace back to your Nellie?'

'I know. But they came from Roone Bay, so here I am. I know William went first, taking the money provided by the landlord. He worked, saved enough money for Nellie to follow. She had a daughter, Annie, and by the time she left another child, Luke – whose line I come from.'

'They survived the trip, then – made a life there.'

'They survived the trip,' I say, nodding. But knowing what she experienced on the other side of the water is a story I can't feel comfortable talking about, not here, now, when my own grief is so raw.

We've arrived at the hotel, and I take my leave. 'Thank you. For walking me back,' I add, in case he didn't know what I was thanking him for.

'No problem,' he says and turns, walking away fast as though annoyed for exposing some part of his inner self to me down by the water's edge. I watch his back until he's lost in the harsh shadows. He's a sensitive but troubled man. I don't know why – and very much want to find out.

But as I lie on my bed, still unable to sleep, I recall another snippet of a story my grandfather told me, and I find myself lost once more in the past.

11

NELLIE 1847

Nellie slowly turned the handle that drew the bucket up from the well, each pull a mammoth effort. When it was within reach, she slipped the block under the handle as a brake and leaned over the well to draw the bucket towards her, before tipping the water carefully into the carrying pail. She paused for a moment to catch her breath, so tired it was hard to think. As a child she had loved coming up here with her mother to get the water. Standing on the knoll above with William, the day he left, was an image carved into her memory. The bleached backbones of the peninsulas in the distance descended into a purple haze, and beyond the black, rocky shores, far away, the curve of the sea twinkled innocently in the distance.

And somewhere beyond that was America – and her William. She had to believe he had arrived, that he was still alive. But deep inside a betraying little voice asked, if he was, why hadn't he written?

It was hard to recall those early days, when a filled stomach and hard work had made her sturdy, ruddy with health. They had been happy days, with herself, her parents and siblings crammed in their cottage as tight as turf in a basket. They were all gone now. Some for soldiers, some into service, some to marriage, some in foreign climes for work she couldn't imagine. She didn't know if any of them were still alive. And her parents, gone, too. They had, she knew, starved themselves so that she and little Annie could live, before wasting to nothing and taking themselves off to the God they trusted in, within two days of each other. Wherever they were, it was in each other's arms.

The priest, himself as skinny as a scarecrow, had collected them on the donkey cart, to lay them in the mass grave without even a headstone to mark their passing. One day, she thought, when times were better, she would remedy that. She would have a stone carved with their names and placed at the edge of the burial ground: *Thomas and Mary Crowley*, she would write, *who sacrificed themselves that their daughter might live.*

Crowley had been her name, too, before she became Nellie O'Mahoney and made her vows to stay with William until death did them part. It was death that separated them now; not their death but the unimaginable deaths of others.

She turned to the strip of dark sea visible between the hills. The Atlantic was so huge and deep they said monsters lived there, waiting to pull the unwary ships down to their gloomy lairs. It was temperamental, like a wayward child. Blue and serene as it sometimes seemed, when the sky was lit with sunshine, it could change in an instant to slate-grey menace as dark clouds bustled in, shunting the sailing vessels on irritated whitecaps towards the land. On the fringes of Ireland, the lintels of many windows and fireplaces had been created from thick planking from broken ships. Wood was scarce and that foraged from the shore an unexpected bounty despite the manner of its arrival.

And over the water was her William, in America, the land of plenty. She wondered, just briefly, whether he had found another wife and was living quite happily with her. She shook

her head, dismissing the deceptively upsetting image. Her
William would not have done that.

She had just turned twenty-three when he left, a little over
a year ago, though it seemed like ten she was so lonely. She
remembered the day as if it were yesterday. He had gone to
Roone Manor and queued up with the other lads from Roone
Bay, to take the bounty offered by Lord Roone: the fare to
America. It was best the men went, they had been advised, for
they could find work, and send money home to pay rent and
feed their families, or bring them over to America. William,
who had been so tall and strong and handsome when she had
first seen him walking the master's donkey, had looked as old as
her father on the day he left. He had been a skeleton wrapped
in skin, his face gaunt and grey, as hers was now. He'd held her
tight and whispered into her dark hair, 'Hold on, Nellie, my
sweet Nellie. Keep our darling safe. I'll send for you both.
That's a promise.'

Another year of hunger and suffering, and she had heard
nothing, and the longer she heard nothing, the surer she was
that he had died; maybe in that strange land so far away, or
maybe on the ship taking him there. But she knew she would
not survive another year as even the turnips were refusing to
swell in the damp peat.

The only good thing was that the master's land agents had
disappeared overnight, so there was no one to demand rent or
throw her out of the cottage when she couldn't pay. A while
back, it had been rumoured that the land agents had stockpiled
grain sent in as relief, so the starving had gathered at Roone
Manor, beating at the gates and demanding their share, only to
be turned harshly away with whips, some dying where they fell,
unable to find the strength to walk home. At this threat to his
safety, the master had abandoned his manor, fleeing like a thief
in the night, taking his promises with him, driving his carriage
between hedgerows scented with the stench of death.

William couldn't write, of course, any more than she could read, but there were those who would write a letter for a fee, and the priest would read them out on Sundays after mass, bringing hope to the families who were desperately clinging to life. Every week she waited for news, and every day grew a little darker around the edges, as the pall of death smothered the land, sinking lower over the mountains and coming to rest in the valley where her cottage nestled.

She sighed and heaved up the bucket, reaching for Annie's hand. Luke was snuggled, asleep, against her body, inside her shawl. He had yet to learn hunger, but his need for solid food was growing. William had left before Luke was even suspected, and she desperately wanted to tell him that he had a son. He would be so proud. Though, she thought, Annie would always be special. Maybe because she was the first and had arrived as the promise of a large family stretching into the future, as generations had done before them. Annie was a wide-eyed, contemplative child, looking younger than her almost-six years, as she took in the death surrounding her with resignation, as though it were normal. But it wasn't normal! It wasn't how life was supposed to be!

'Please God, send me a letter,' she whispered.

Annie's sidelong glance, her pale blue eyes just like William's, was a blow that sprang tears to Nellie's eyes. The child understood more than she should and accepted her hunger stoically, perhaps believing the priest when he told them death wasn't to be feared, because it would take them to a better place. There, maybe her grandparents would be waiting, the turf glowing in the hearth and tables laden with bread and potatoes.

It was hard to remember what potatoes tasted like, but even thinking about it sent a sharp pain through Nellie's gut, stopping her breath on a cry. She couldn't cry. Not when her children needed her. It was hard to recall a time when she wasn't

terrified for her children, terrified of the death that surrounded
her, knowing that one day it would come marching up the hill
and steal them from her. It wasn't just the hunger she feared. It
was the swathes of sickness that were striking the young and the
weak: cholera, consumption, fevers and measles.

She didn't travel any longer; she didn't dare – not to neighbours, not to the farm for milk as she had done once, for there
was none, and not even to mass, where the diseased dragged
themselves in a last appeal for succour. She wondered if she,
too, would heave herself there in a last plea to a God who wasn't
listening. It surely wouldn't be long.

She had nursed the last hens, bringing them inside the
house every night to keep them safe, guarding the eggs like the
precious gems they were. But despite William's admonitions,
they had died, one by one, their laying days over, with no grain
to keep them fat, and the rooster long gone to the foxes, who
were fatter than they had ever been. She shuddered, knowing
what the wild creatures were gorging on. The foxes were
growing ever bolder, brazenly walking the streets as if
reclaiming the land for themselves. If William were here, maybe
he would trap one, provide them with meat for a few days, but
she had no knowledge of these things.

She had dried strips of chicken above the fire, and they had
taken minuscule portions at a time, to suck and chew, relishing
the unaccustomed treat. But even they were gone now, and it
was just the turnips left. The turnips that her neighbours must
never know about, for they were all that stood between her children and certain death. She was not still alive by the grace of
God, as the priests would have her believe, but by William's
foresight. She was faint from exhaustion and the overwhelming
weight of defeat.

There was nothing Nellie could do except hope – and wait.
She had no money for the fare to America and no way of
earning it. All she could do was keep toiling, keep surviving, not

just because she had promised William she would, but because her children needed her to. If she had not had that incentive, she might have simply walked up the hill to watch the last sunset fall behind the sea, turning it the colour of blood.

Spring was the harshest time. The few apples she had harvested were rotting as quickly as she could sort them, and the turnips were as weathered and wrinkled as old men, but would be rationed for a while yet. She had sown thick rows of turnip seed, but the roots were thin as blades of grass and would take a long while to thicken.

She could barely recall what William looked like and wondered if her faded dreams bore any relation to the reality. Even memories of her mother were disappearing, and there were times she envied her for being at peace, not having to struggle on any longer. Her mother had been a whirlwind of health, just a few years back, working as hard as her father on their biteen patch of land, perhaps more so, because after the day was done, she would be sewing by the light of a candle, making clothes or mending, while her father was snoring by the fire's glow.

She couldn't recall her father at all, though he had made nearly everything she now used. As a child she'd been enthralled as he had treadled the pole lathe, turning knots of wood into bowls, legs for the chairs and knobs for the doors. He had even created the clever wooden lid on the water bucket, which hinged when it was poured.

Though he was no more than a distant memory, she was grateful for the barrel he'd bought from the wheelwright, which caught rainwater from the slated roof that was used for washing. This meant that the clean and sparkling well-water that cost so much in energy to collect was only needed for drinking and cooking. She and Annie drank a lot of water to briefly still the griping pains of an empty stomach.

Her childhood, and the first year of her marriage, with the

singing, the dancing and the bountiful potato harvests were a
dream that surely couldn't have been real. Now, it was a
struggle just to survive each day.

When a letter finally arrived, brought up by a new young priest,
still plump from the seminary, she put her hand to her mouth,
almost too afraid to ask, *Was it from William?* then found her
tongue and her manners. 'Will ye please to come in, Father?'

'I will,' he said softly.

At the table her father had made, the priest's soft hands that
had never seen manual labour carefully sliced open the thick
brown envelope. He read quietly for a moment, while she
waited, her breath caught on hope.

'This is this good news, Nellie O'Mahoney,' he said finally.
He was obviously pleased for her. 'There's a letter, a ticket for
the passage to Boston and a little money for you in addition. You
can join your husband in America, praise be to God!' He
imparted the news with relish, as though he had personally
instigated it, but Nellie was fast losing faith. This blight must
surely be the work of evil, and why had God not intervened?

'Money?' she asked, seeing none.

'The brown and yellow paper is the ticket for the passage to
Boston from Cork; the one with green is a bank draft,' he
explained, touching each in turn. She knew her colours, even if
she couldn't decipher the words that were written. 'The bank in
Cork will change it into money before you leave. You will need
provisions for the boat. They're supposed to provide food and
passage, but I've heard rumours that it's not always so. Best to be
prepared.'

As he separated the sheets of paper on the rough table,
Nellie reeled with shock. She hadn't yet considered the fear of
leaving her home to travel to America with her two children,
and it hit her hard. It was an unknown journey almost too big to

contemplate. If it had been just her, maybe she would stay, try to survive another year... But the thought of seeing her children laid in the ground from hunger or sickness stiffened her resolve. She would put her trust in William.

In the aftermath of her shock, the priest gave her a watery, tired smile, asking, 'Will I read the letter now?'

'If you please, Father,' she said.

He cleared his throat and read. *'To my dearest wife and sweetheart, Nellie O'Mahoney. I hope this letter finds you and little Annie well. The voyage was a trial, and I thanked God several times for getting me safe to America. It seems I am not a good sailor.'* The priest held the letter away a little, squinted and asked, 'Does your husband speak the English?'

'Badly,' Nellie said, remembering, with a little laugh that was almost a sob. 'He was brought up with the Irish, as I was.'

'But he doesn't write?'

She shook her head.

'Oh, then I suspect the scribe helped make the sentences. You speak it well enough, which is useful, as you would not gain employment in America otherwise.'

He went on: *'It was hard to start with, so many men looking for work, and the hunger biting, but I met with Danny O'Brien from Roone Bay, would you believe? He put me by way of some employment, building the new railroads for Boston. It is hard, dirty work and badly paid but, praise be, I am well. I am sharing a house with other men from Cork, but when you get here, we will be able to get a room of our own. I trust you received the money I sent you for the rent.'*

He raised his eyebrows in question. Nellie grimaced and shook her head. The failure to receive any letter at all was the reason she had supposed William had died. She wondered where William's hard-earned money had gone. Stolen, no doubt. There had been a time nothing was ever stolen in the townland, and not just because people had nothing worth stealing. Their innate honesty had been as cruelly blackened by the blight as had the potatoes. Desperate times made criminals of everyone.

The priest continued. '*I have been saving my wages, every penny, so that I can bring you here to me, my dearest Nellie. Enclosed with this letter is a ticket for the passage, which you must present when you embark on the ship from Cork to Boston, which departs 25 October, weather permitting. I am finding it hard to contain my joy at the thought of my family being with me again. I miss you so much, mo stór, and our precious little angel, Annie. The boat journey will be bad, I cannot deny it. Bring as much food as you can carry, keep it hidden, and keep yourself safe. God willing, I will be waiting for you on the quay in Boston.*'

'Oh my sweet William,' Nelly said, tears falling freely.

The priest was helpful in a lot of ways, having travelled, himself, from Cork city. He explained to Nellie that she should hold on tightly to her belongings and sew what coins she might save into her petticoats for fear of having them stolen. He added that she should maybe take something warm to wear for the journey. She raised her brows a little, and he coloured, realising, perhaps, that she only had what she was wearing. 'And the child? Has she a shawl? Never mind. I'll find one. And maybe some shoes for yourself.'

Unable to find words for his generosity, Nellie sank down on her knees and asked Father Patrick for his blessing.

She didn't ask where the well-worn shoes and thick woollen shawl he brought up later came from, but she washed the latter thoroughly and set it to dry before the fire, knowing with grim realisation that someone else's misfortune was her luck.

Then, for the first time in months, she and Annie ate a full bowl of mashed turnips as she explained that they were going on a ship, and that Dada would be waiting for them in America. By this time, the quiet and withdrawn little girl could not recall her father. Snuggling together for warmth that night, Nellie dredged up memories of happier times, painting a picture of them as a family once again. As Annie sank into slumber, Nellie buried all thoughts of failure. It would be a hard journey, but she had survived over a year of famine without William and would survive the journey to get to him.

12

ERIN

The days seem to drift away without direction, and grow into weeks, and I begin to wonder whether I should be booking my flight home. I do feel lighter and less burdened than I did when I arrived. My little night-time jaunt and that strange communication with Finn Sheehan fractionally eased the heavy burden I carry in my heart, but I remain curious to know why he's also burdened and with what. The hint of something traumatic had been communicated by the librarian, and his own cryptic comments added to my belief that he's a troubled soul.

I want to find out more about him, but I don't want word filtering back to him that I'm delving into his private business, so I decide to bury my curiosity for the moment. Maybe he'll tell me, in his own time, in his own words. Maybe he will come around to the idea of helping me in my quest. Our brief moment of communication might have paved the way, I don't know. But it had certainly helped me, and I wonder, now, if that had been his intention.

After the accident, I had moved back in with my parents, and their kindness and support somehow made everything worse, because they were just waiting for me to, I don't know, get over it. I can almost hear my father saying, *Give her time...* And meanwhile, they would both be making plans for my future, assuming I didn't have the strength to make my own plans. My decision to come to Ireland in search of my roots had been quite a shock to both my parents, who aren't at all interested in the past. Back then, I thought their concerted efforts to dissuade me quietly amusing, but here and now I feel lonely. It would be too easy to skitter back to Boston and sink back into the half-life of social rounds my parents enjoy, and not have to think any longer.

But, no, I won't be that person. It's not me.

I run downstairs with the intention of being proactive, doing my first trawl around the graveyards, seeking gravestones with names and dates on them, but Livvy is in the foyer, her little violin beside her. I had almost forgotten about her. I remember that it's Sunday, so no school. She beams at me, and I know that if I simply run through the door and away, she'll be hurt.

I walk over, a smile on my face. 'How're you doing, Livvy?'

'I got it,' she states. 'Do you want to hear?'

'Sure,' I agree.

I sit in one of the comfy chairs opposite her. She unclips the case, pulls out the violin and tightens the bow. There's heavy concentration on her face as she gets her fingers in the right position and proceeds to play the stanzas I taught her.

'Well done!' I exclaim when she's finished. 'So, I guess you want to go on to something new?'

'Yes, please,' she says happily. 'Then I'm going to show my teacher.'

Oh dear, I think. Teacher is going to hate me for interfering. I spend half an hour teaching her the second part of 'Twinkle, Twinkle, Little Star'. She's a quick study, all right. Then I tell her I have to go out.

'Will you still be here next weekend? Can I do some more?' she asks.

I can't think of a good-enough reason to dampen her enthusiasm. 'Sure,' I say as I head out the door, suddenly realising that I have committed myself to staying for another week.

There's that large graveyard on the way out towards Finn's house, along the small road that circles the bay. I'd decided it would be a good starting point, and now seems as good a time as any. From what Noel told me, I wonder whether Finn's already done that and has a list, but he's holding me – and everyone else, from what I understand – at arm's length.

I wander down through the silent town. The bar, the small baker's with its café, a small grocery store, a post office and a dinky food store, all closed. At the top of the rise the other side of the quay, I pass a dilapidated hotel on the right, closed for years, I guess, as it has grass growing on the gutters and what looks like a tree sprouting from a chimney. Further up, the prestigious bank building, which displays no sign of decay at all, is also shuttered, its windows solidly barred. Further up there's another hotel – I hadn't noticed that before. It looks closed, so perhaps that's why Finn directed me to the *new* hotel when I first arrived. I wonder if the inhabitants of Roone Bay resent the imposing hotel on the hill, as it sucks all the business away from the old order.

It takes me a good twenty minutes of striding to get there, past a row of tiny cottages that look inhabited, and out onto a country road. I pass a derelict cottage where a few glass panes hang precariously in rotting frames. The roof has completely fallen in, and the shrubs from the yard have crept indoors to inhabit the living space. The ivy dressing the walls lends an air of desperation, as if it's trying to make the bare house respectable. I wonder if the ruined cottage had been Nellie's home, but it seems there's no way I'll ever know.

Inland, the hills rise steeply above the town. Discoloured

grass and patches of gorse fringe lines of exposed rock. Scoured smooth by the weather, they glint in the cold light, and beyond that more hills rise in tiers, disappearing into the misty distance. Presumably a stiff walk up the hillside would provide a good view of the bay, but I'm not tempted to find out.

At the graveyard, I pass through a small wrought-iron gate and discover a network of well-trodden paths between the tightly packed graves. Long strands of lichen hang like sparkling Christmas decorations on a few stunted, wind-sheered trees. I read somewhere that the presence of lichen indicates clean and unpolluted air. Not something I was familiar with in Boston, I think wryly.

Thankfully, the clear air of last night has remained, and a cold, cloudless sky allows a weak sun to cast a hint of charm over the roofless church. The modern polished granite headstones shine like coal, but the older stones are mottled white, painted with splashes of yellow and black lichen.

From an initial scan, I see that that the older graves are nearest to the road, and the field slopes steeply down towards the bay, before which a newer field has been incorporated into the graveyard. Many graves, even the old ones, have been decorated with plastic ornaments, strands of rosary beads, bunches of dying flowers and a plaster-cast Mary, whose peeling blue gown bears the signs of yearly coats of paint. I start at the top and systematically begin to trawl through the stones, finding those dating from pre-famine and post-famine years, but I find nothing from the 1840s. On the older stones, the inscriptions are often so weathered and covered in lichen as to be unreadable. However, I persevere and find several generations of O'Mahoneys, but just two Crowleys. I make a note of those names and dates, but don't hold out much hope of tying them in to Nellie's family. From the note in Nellie's bible, I understand that her parents died during the famine, before she left for Boston, and even if this couple were related to Nellie, I can't see how I'd be able to work that out without researching an extended family history, and I'm not sure I have the headspace for that. As the Crowleys I'm looking for will have been poor crofters, I wonder whether they could even have afforded grave markers at all, and whether they had family left to place them.

After a couple of hours, I'm only quarter way through the graveyard. I sigh in frustration. I haven't the first clue about tracing ancestors. I'm guessing there's some kind of skill to it. I wonder if there's a book about that kind of thing and decide to pay another visit to the library. I've written a note for the librarian to pin on her noticeboard, as she suggested, and also a piece to put in the paper. If they will print it, of course.

I sit on a stone and stare out to sea, strangely enjoying the fact that I'm on a quest, even if it is *on a hiding to nowhere*, as Mom would say. The sun is as high as it's going to get today, being October, but it's still chilly. My stomach rumbles, so it must be lunchtime; I decide to head back to the town and get something to eat.

As I'm walking back along the road, a blue Mini pulls up beside me. Finn winds down the window. 'You're still here, then? Have you got a minute?' he asks. 'There's something you might like to see.'

Have I got a minute? 'All I have is time,' I admit, amused.

He pushes open the passenger door, and I slide in. His handsome face is bland, expressionless. He's wearing different jeans, still tired in a scrubbed-clean sort of way, and his brightly checked shirt is open at the neck, exposing a T-shirt and a sprinkling of chest hair.

I'm curious to know if he's going to help me, or if this is a temporary glitch in his decision to remain aloof. 'Where are we going?'

'You'll see.'

He doesn't waste words, but I soon work it out. As we drive up the winding road towards Bantry, we turn at the somewhat unimpressive signpost pointing to a mass famine grave, which I'd noticed when I arrived. We wind up a narrow lane and stop in the entrance of a grassy field bounded by ancient gorse and shrubby trees. The ruin of a tiny church squats sadly in the centre of the wide green space. It has a small graveyard to one side, enclosed by an eroded, low stone wall glued in place by the ubiquitous ivy.

In silence we walk across the bumpy field, side by side, but distanced as the strangers we are. Physically, Finn dwarfs me, though his stature is stocky rather than tall. He's a mass of muscle, his thighs straining against the worn fabric of his jeans at every step. I wonder if that's the legacy of starting out in life as a fisherman with his father; hard physical work and long hours. I can't see him sitting in an office. He's wearing Doc Marten boots, and in the sunshine, strands of grey hair shine like silver at his temples, lending a cultured elegance to his worn persona.

On the grey concrete gatepost where a broken wrought-iron gate hangs open, a blackbird is singing, his yellow beak wide. He flaps away, calling in alarm as we approach.

Finn indicates for me to walk through first, and we head towards the ruins of a church, within which there are yet more gravestones – a couple created from old, white stone; a few, surprisingly, of more recent black marble, incongruous in this ancient environment. He kneels by an old, weathered stone and caresses his hand respectfully over the overlapping circular splashes of lichen.

'I found this a while back, but it didn't mean anything,' he says. 'Not until you told me who you were looking for.'

I crouch down close and struggle to make out the words, already dimmed by a hundred years of weather, but Finn reads them out loud, as if knowing them by heart. '*Thomas and Mary Crowley, d. 1846, who sacrificed themselves that my children could live. Your loving daughter, Nellie, 1885.*'

I try to take this in, frowning. 'That's incredibly moving, and tragic, but it can't be my Nellie. She emigrated in 1847 and never came back to Ireland.'

'Perhaps she did, and you weren't aware of it,' Finn suggests.

'She would have been over fifty by then,' I muse, doing the mental calculation. 'It's a shame whoever carved this stone didn't put her surname.'

'That would have been the clincher,' Finn agrees, standing, and dusting his knees absently. 'This stone always interested me as it was put in here years after the famine. I suspect the parents are here, somewhere, and this Nellie, whoever she was, came back to place a stone when she was able. Maybe when she could afford it.'

I nod. He provides a speculated scenario, and although logic suggests this stone was not placed by my Nellie, the names of the parents are the same as those written in Nellie's bible. They were names common to the era, of course, but is that too much of a coincidence to ignore? Might she have come back to Ireland? It's not something that had ever occurred to me. But if she had, might there somewhere be a trace of her journey, her arrival and her address?

This small graveyard, most of its stones dedicated to people no longer known to anyone alive, is kept manicured and tidy. The Irish respect their dead, even those vanished so long ago that not even their names are legible.

'There don't seem to be many graves,' I say doubtfully.

Finn's expression morphs into one of shocked surprise, presumably at my ignorance. 'Not many?' he echoes in disbelief then waves his hand, encompassing the whole field surrounding the small church. 'That's the famine burial ground. All of it. There are estimated to be around seven thousand people lying under the turf. You were walking over them to get to the church.'

'Seven thousand?'

Finn's cynical expression softens. 'A lot of people don't get quite how many people died. There's another famine grave, just a few miles away, in Skibbereen, with over nine thousand souls, and another' – he indicates with his head, towards Bantry – 'with an estimated five thousand. Nearly a quarter of the Irish population died, and thousands more emigrated, many of those dying in the attempt. We'll never know the true figures. Cork and Kerry and Connemara were badly hit, being so rural and inaccessible at the time.'

We're outside the church wall now, and I view this green field with new eyes. I feel slightly nauseated at the thought of all the bodies underfoot, packed head to toe, or even on top of each other, as though I'm in some kind of horror story and bodies are going to start rising out of the field.

I want to run, escape.

As if realising my distress, Finn takes my hand and pulls me to sit on the ivy-blanketed wall. He lectures quietly. 'Before the potato came to Ireland, the people used to grow oats, like the Scots, and other vegetables, too. But the potato could be grown in such numbers, with such ease, poor people became healthy, lived longer and bred more, but they were totally reliant on the one food source. Never a good plan, eh? It was a disaster waiting to happen. It's easy to get bogged down in the whole tragic issue of large numbers of people dying in a horrific way, but they were so prolific, they outgrew the land's ability to sustain them. And the greed of the landlords and all their flunkeys kept the mediaeval system going. And there was the Roman Catholic Church, promoting big families, saying it was God's will...'

'All those poor children who starved to death,' I agree softly.

He nods. 'But history is what it is. Dwelling on the sentiment doesn't help them now, but we have to learn from it, stand back and see the larger picture. The enormity of the tragedy meant that Ireland could progress, move away from its serf-and-landlord culture. Those who survived were able to own the land. They learned to grow different food again. The population stabilised. The economy became Ireland's own, not a meal ticket for the gentry.'

We're sitting over thousands of dead bodies, I think, discussing them in the cold light of economy. Emotion wells and trickles out of me. I feel guilty that I'm not just crying for all those people I didn't know but for my own small tragedy. Wordlessly, Finn puts an arm around and pulls me close. I don't push him away. I'm starved for that physical comfort.

'I didn't mean to upset you,' he says softly. 'I thought you'd be interested in the Crowley stone and everything it stands for.'

'I am. Very,' I admit, slashing at my tears with the back of my hand. 'I didn't mean to let it get to me.'

'Kenny's death must still hurt. It doesn't take much to trigger grief, when it's that raw.'

He recalls Kenny's name. That surprises me.

'So, what do you know of this Nellie?' he asks. 'Do you want to tell me?'

I take a breath; push my grief back into its box.

'She was sixteen when she married William O'Mahoney. He emigrated to Boston in 1846, when the famine was hitting its third year. He found work in Boston and sent Nellie the fare. She followed him in 1847. Those dates are in the diary, so that's fact.'

I drift into the past, remembering the story Grandpa told me. I try to put myself in Nellie's shoes and imagine the hardship, but fail dramatically. I tell Finn what I know, though I don't know whether it's even the truth.

13

NELLIE 1847

Father Patrick drove Nellie and five other women from Roone Bay to Cork city on his cart, which was to bring aid back, such as it was: too little, spread too thinly to save anyone. Nellie was sure she heard him mutter that, unlike the bread and fishes, the good Lord didn't see fit to provide enough for his Irish children in their hour of need. It was almost enough to make one lose faith, so it was. He helped his pitifully thin passengers to change their bank drafts into coins, as none of them had any comprehension of how such things worked, but even with coins, Nellie found there was little enough food to be bought, and it was priced extortionately.

Nellie tucked her coins into the pocket she had sewn into her petticoats, which were already cumbersome, secreted with the last of her shrivelled turnips. Awed by the sheer size of the buildings in Cork, she clutched Annie's hand tightly as they walked the final long miles from there to Queenstown Quay. For two days they waited under what shelter they could find, huddled tightly with other passengers, in a chill breeze spattered with rain, praying for the wind to turn and bring the ship safely to berth. Then, finally, a bleak sun pushed aside the dark clouds, and on the horizon, white sails were spotted.

It would take six to eight weeks to reach America, Father Patrick said, depending if the weather was kind, but he said he would pray they didn't hit any storms. She was aware, from the serious tone of his voice, that she should be prepared for the worst, but until she was on board, she had no idea what that might mean.

They waited, packed like cattle in pens, as water and food were carried on board, for crew and passengers, they were told. Finally, they began to embark.

The men on the dock were hard, scrutinising tickets, and brutally pushing away those who were trying to scramble on board with none, wielding sticks where necessary. It was a ragged horde of humanity that was herded onto the ship, down steep ladders into a hold. Many berths were already filled by the time Nellie clambered down, so she elbowed her way into a berth with more ruthlessness than she even knew she owned, for her children more than herself.

The bunks, no more than wooden shelves, were tiered three high, and she would have preferred to be on the bottom, for the children, but the moment she saw a middle bunk with a space, she lifted Annie in first and thrust Luke into her daughter's arms, before heaving herself up with some difficulty, hoping that everyone was too busy to notice her heavily laden skirts. It was a free-for-all, men and boys scrambling up to the top tier, while many, by the time the passengers had stopped flooding in, had no bunk at all but packed themselves into spaces on the floor. There was a foul smell rising up through the floor planks, and there were mutterings that rats had been seen.

Finally, the hatches, which would be opened for an hour every day so that they could maybe take a turn around the deck, were slammed shut and battened tightly, sealing them in. They'd been informed this would happen, as the sailors needed the decks clear so that they could manage the ship, but she instantly felt claustrophobic, and had to clench her teeth and fist her hands to stop herself from crying out and running to the ladder. Nellie wasn't the only one afraid of being locked in this enclosed, stinking hole. Knowing they were below the water line, for people who had never even learned to swim, it was a horrific experience. Around her, people were praying, crying or sitting in petrified silence.

Nellie prayed out loud, too, in a low whisper; cuddled Annie and Luke tightly to her breast. She had learned that prayers were no more than the sound of the wind but hoped that her voice would provide a little comfort to her children.

The buzz of noise gradually died as the frightened passengers listened to the shouted commands above deck. She guessed most were terrified, as she was. Eventually, there was a strange rocking movement as the ship eased away from the dock. It was the point of no return, and anticipation was tempered by a collectively held breath as the ship groaned and heaved its way out of the harbour, its planks sighing with exhaustion. Few of those starving souls, packed like rats in a sewer, had even been on a boat before, and this experience would have daunted the hardiest of bodies.

In the darkness, Nellie realised there were tears on Annie's face and reached for her hand. The poor child must be even more frightened than she was. Thank goodness Luke was too small to know anything but the comfort of a mother's love. She began to sing, softly, a lullaby, in her native tongue.

> *Hush,* mavourneen, *hushabye,*
> *Your dada's out a roving,*
> *Across the fairy hills and bogs,*
> *To catch a hare for you and me*
> *So hush and cease your crying.*

Hush, mavourneen, *hushabye,*
The smiling moon is shining.
The path is clear, the heart is true,
He'll catch a hare for me and you,
So hush and sleep, mavourneen.

It took her a moment to realise that the low murmur around and above was that of a hundred voices joining in. A soft sound, a sad sound, drifting around the cramped environment, as if every person there had once heard that song in the cradle and knew that the verdant green fields of Ireland, where hares danced in play, were lost to them forever.

She almost wept, herself, at the all-pervading pathos.

The motion of the ship made many people ill, but there was nowhere to be ill or do one's business except through the floor slats, into the scuppers below. Nellie thought she would never get used to the smell, but after a while, she ceased to notice it, except when the ship listed, and the filth from below sloshed up through the boards, soaking the emigrants' rags with the stench of human waste.

She was grateful to be on the bunks, and also that neither she nor her children succumbed to the seasickness that added to the overpowering smell, and which William had undoubtedly experienced.

The voyage seemed to go on forever, and it was all Nellie could do to live one day at a time and keep her children alive. Fever raged through the emigrants, and Luke became ill, but thankfully recovered after an anxious couple of days when Nellie was nearly going mad with the thought that she was going to lose him. Neither Nellie nor Annie took sick, maybe due to

William's foresight, and the fact that they had not been so emaciated as others when they came on board.

She welcomed the brief glimpses of daylight now and then as the hatches were opened to let in a breath of salt-scoured air, but each time she caught sight of Annie, she wanted to cry. The little girl, who had been lost in the beauty of her childish world just a few short years ago, seemed to grow ever more wraithlike and distant, her eyes seeing something beyond the reality that bound them. Nellie was terrified she was seeing death written in Annie's listless eyes. She prayed out loud every day, injecting as much energy into the words as she could discover in herself. If Annie could still believe, it might help to sustain her through this seemingly never-ending trial.

Despite feeling desperate for sunlight, she rarely ventured on deck, because she could not carry the baby and keep Annie safe at the same time. For the same reason, she kept to herself and did not try to befriend anyone, for fear of her secret stash of food being stolen. At first, the food from the galley included dried biscuits and strips of salted meat, but after a while, it was just boiled oats or rice, lowered down in buckets to be fought over and scooped out by hand. It tasted mouldy, when she could fight her way through the grasping and fighting to even get some. All the while, Nellie was supplementing herself and Annie in the darkness, with tiny scrapings of turnip, until there was little left, and from then on, she gave her portion to Annie and hid the griping pain of her own hunger. The water became increasingly brackish, and there were times that Nellie wondered if it wouldn't have been better to have died quietly in her own cottage rather than face this ordeal.

Nellie lost track of the days, early on. She tried to keep a scratch on the wall beside her, but there were other scratches from previous passengers. She was exhausted, and the days and nights could sometimes only be counted by the times buckets of food were sent below. She was surviving now, not for a new life

for herself and William, but for her children. If it were not for
Annie and Luke, maybe she would have just lain in her bunk
and faded away, as so many others, already wasted with hunger,
did on a daily basis. Those who died were taken away by the
sailors in the morning and slipped into the cold water that
surrounded them, with a few quick words from the captain to
ease their passing. Eventually, as the numbers dwindled, and
bunks became free, there were no emigrants sitting on the filthy
floor boards at all.

Nellie instinctively knew that survival was not just down to
the food and water, but the sheer will to live, sustained by the
shared spirit of her brethren. Sometimes she would lilt a song in
the Irish tradition, without music, and bring to mind the fairies,
the legends, the rolling landscape and loves long gone. Others
would join in softly with the well-tried airs. Sometimes another
would diddle a tune by mouth, or another scratch out a tune on
a fiddle, and someone might find the energy and a tiny space in
the gloomy hold to step out the rhythm, as their fathers had
done before them.

Wherever the Irish go, Nellie realised, they take their
heritage with them. She wondered if William was singing
hopeful songs as he waited for them to arrive in Boston. He had
already endured this voyage, so he must know what they were
going through. It would be good to hear his voice again, feel his
arms wrapped around her, his chin resting on the top of her
head as it had so many evenings when the setting sun had
brought a halt to labour. She remembered his voice, his songs,
his touch, but it was hard to remember what he looked like. She
wondered if she would even recognise him as she searched the
faces in Boston.

Sometimes the ship ploughed straight, but other times, it rose on
mountainous waves and slipped down into seemingly endless

chasms. Each time she would hold her breath, as it seemed the ship was descending straight into hell. Then there would be a crash, the long groan of complaining timber and it would rise again. In those hours, Nellie held on tightly to her children and prayed.

There was one storm when everyone clung to stanchions or bunks, sometime being flung like rag dolls if they released their hold by accident. For several hours, they listened to the screaming wind, felt the sea battering the wooden sides of the ship and leaking through until the floor was awash, expecting every moment for the ship to turn over. When the storm abated, passengers and sailors worked together to bale, hauling buckets to the hatch and throwing the salt water back out into the Atlantic. For a brief time after, the ship smelled cleaner, the air below less foul.

She had expected to feel excited, empowered by their imminent arrival in a new land, but when there was a yell that land had been sighted, she was almost too exhausted to care. Some cried with relief, but she waited stoically, not tempting fate by rejoicing too soon. Overall, they had been lucky with the weather, she understood from a few comments shouted by the sailors in English, and had arrived within sight of America after only seven weeks. She translated for those many souls who only had the Irish. God willing, they would make harbour soon. Nellie was finally buoyed by the knowledge that there was an end in sight. She had endured the voyage because her children needed her to but would surely be pleased to feel land under her feet once more, even if it was somewhere alien and new. And at least in the new land they would be provided with food and shelter.

14

ERIN

When Finn drives me back down the hill from the famine burial ground, we're both silently lost in the past, but as we reach the outskirts of Roone Bay, he asks, 'Have you eaten?'

'No, I was just going to grab something in town when you hijacked me.'

'There won't be anything open,' he reminds me with a smile. 'I can drop you back at the hotel, or I've got the makings of a sandwich if you want to come back to my place.'

'Oh, I forgot it was Sunday. Thank you. I'd love the company, if you don't mind.'

I'm not daunted by his lack of conversation. In a way, I'm comfortable with it, companionable silence being better than an endless need to talk of nothing of consequence. I recall my parents' social gatherings with a shudder, the sweeping tides of dialogue that flowed over and around me, when I pasted a smile on my face and made inane responses to comments I hadn't even heard.

Finn's home, in daylight, is more interesting even than I recall. Downstairs is simply a single room, with an open-slatted wooden staircase rising at the back wall like a ladder. The back door leads to a lean-to kitchen tagged onto the back of the house, which was fitted with a basic counter, a few shelves and a Calor gas camping stove. The sash window at the back of the room isn't blocked by curtains, and through it a large proportion of Roone Bay is visible. I suspect at night the lighthouse will pulse its warning into the room.

He fills a kettle from a gallon container of water and puts it on the solid fuel burner in the living room. He pushes open a lever, letting the air flow, and within minutes it's belting out heat. His actions are neat, practised and unselfconscious.

The plastering in the main room is rough, basic. A rag rug is all that lies on a concrete floor, but the place is swept clean and tidy. There's a bookcase containing books on the sea and Irish history, which I suspect are not there for show and that he has read cover to cover. The contents the room are deeply personal. Aside from the basic living necessities, he has an eclectic selection of possessions – not ornaments but artefacts mostly to do with the sea. Some sea shells, three dark green glass fishing floats hanging in the window in a net. A boat's steering wheel on the wall.

On the windowsill there's a compass in a brass housing. I pick it up and turn it this way and that, stunned by the simplicity of two pivots providing a total ability for the compass to remain level. 'Clever,' I say as he returns with a tray of sliced, buttered bread, chunks of cheese and various pickles.

He places it on the floor, giving a half-smile. 'Most things to do with the sea are clever. Innovation is often created in the harshest environment of all. Like the sextant.' He gently picks up a contraption from the top of the bookcase and hands it to me. 'Careful, it's a couple of hundred years old. Obsoleted by new technology but amazingly accurate to someone who knew how to use it.'

'The workmanship is exquisite,' I say, examining it. 'But I'm not actually sure what it is.'

'It's for celestial navigation. It measures distance and the horizon in conjunction with the stars at any given time.'

'Can one person have that kind of knowledge?'

'Now? I'm not sure. But then? It's how Captain Bligh was able to navigate his way to safety after the mutineers cast him adrift in a small open boat, and how Shackleton navigated to South Georgia in the Atlantic, after his sailing ship had been crushed by ice.'

He pats the seat beside him, and I sit down. Our thighs briefly touch, and the heat of his presence warms something inside me. I move away slightly and clear my throat, realising my sudden hoarseness is from attraction not embarrassment.

'What is it about the sea that fascinates you?'

'I don't know. Born to it, I guess. My father's a fisherman. I started out with him at a very young age.'

'You didn't want to be a fisherman, though? I guess it would be a hard life.'

'I'm not afraid of the hard work.'

From his physique I believe him but say nothing.

He compresses his lips, deliberating, and finally admits, 'It got to me, the flapping and dying of the fish we caught. I decided I'd rather save life than kill it.'

'So, that's why you became a coastguard?'

He glances at me, one brow raised in query, then nods.

'Grace mentioned it in passing,' I say, though I can't recall if it was her or, perhaps, the librarian.

'Grab some food.'

I perch on the edge of the sofa and lean down to reach for a large slab of bread and some cheese. We balance the plates on our laps and eat in quiet companionship. I got the impression he was distant and stand-offish, to start with, but find he's a fairly easy person to be with. Quiet, thoughtful and non-judgemental.

Beyond the window, now we're quiet, the faint shift of the

tide against pebbles is shushing a lullaby, but I'm not sure I'd like it here so much if the weather was bad.

'The sea doesn't come up this far,' he says as if reading my mind. 'Though when it's stormy, salt water is blown onto the windows.'

'I heard that the sea level is rising.'

He casts an amused glance. 'So it is, but if the sea ever rises this high, I'm sure we won't be around to experience it.'

'What did your father think, when you said you didn't want to follow him into the fishing trade?'

'He understands. Fishing is a hard life, and what with new boats getting bigger all the time, the small fishermen are losing the trade. It costs a lot to keep the boat on the water, and the income barely covers it. He's put the boat up for sale, and if he can't sell it within a couple of years, he'll decommission it. It will become just another rusty hulk gradually turning back to nature.'

'The end of an era? That's sad.'

'Maybe. But it's no fun working those hours in those conditions.'

'No, I guess not.'

'So, what do you do?'

'I, ah, I don't have to work,' I say, embarrassed. 'I inherited a legacy from my grandpa a couple of years back. I was supporting Kenny. He was an artist, and I'm sure he would have made it big one day, if...' I pause. 'So, what will your father do, when he retires?'

He stares for a moment, his sympathy palpable. 'I don't know. But I do know he'll drive Mum frantic.' A little gleam of amusement pops onto his face then fades. He adds, 'I really don't know, and that's the truth.'

'I'm sure he'll find something,' I say.

He shrugs. 'It doesn't always work like that. I've seen a couple of men Dad's age retire and then die of a heart attack or a stroke a few years later, when life simply had no structure any longer.'

'Well, we'll have to find him something to do,' I state.

'We?'

I flush. 'Well, you, I mean.'

'So, have you got any plans? Do you know how long you're going to stay in Ireland?'

I shake my head. 'I kind of came on a whim, to get away. Dad's a lawyer. He's been pushing for me to join the firm in some capacity or another, and there's a guy working for him who... but I'm not sure.'

'If you're not sure, then it's a no.'

'Is it that simple? I'm not so young.'

'The biological clock is ticking and you want to have a family?'

'No!' I say, a bit too quickly, a bit too harshly.

His eyes widen slightly. 'Sorry. I didn't mean to offend.'

'It's all right.'

I can't tell him why, but after the accident, children simply aren't on my agenda. Not any more. I feel suddenly oppressed by the questions, by the thought of a mindless future stretching ahead of me. Kenny had become my everything. Without him, I'm directionless. It's not only the retired who lose their *raison d'être.*

I guess my distress has transmitted itself to him, because he puts his plate on the floor and squeezes a hand on my shoulder as he rises. 'If you're finished, I'll walk you back up the hill.'

'No. Really. Thank you,' I say hastily. 'I need some time on my own.'

He nods and leads the way to the door. There, he surprises me by taking one of my hands in both of his. 'Time doesn't heal wounds, Erin, but it does help us to cope with them. Take it easy, okay?'

I nod. 'Okay. And thanks for the lunch. I enjoyed it.'

'Not a bother.'

He shuts the door quietly behind me, and I wonder why I said 'okay'. It's not okay at all. But somehow, him telling me it would be okay makes it seem as if it could be. One day.

I walk slowly back past the derelict house, past the grave-yard, through the town and up to the hotel, wondering if that's the end of our brief communication. On my right, the sea is grey and choppy, and I can faintly hear it murmuring in the spooky Sunday silence. The small row of shops, their inner blinds drawn, look like blank, eyeless faces. There are no people anywhere, which is weird. I wonder if they're all at church, or whether they've been abducted by aliens.

I was interested to see the Crowleys' gravestone, and despite an unsubstantiated wish for it to be part of my story decide it can't be. Nellie never came back to Ireland. She survived a fairly horrific journey to get to Boston, had a dreadful start to her life in America but lived there, as far as Grandpa knew, for the rest of her life. After those first horrible years, her fortunes changed for the better. The date of her death, 1894, at the age of seventy, is noted in the bible, which was handed down through Luke's family, so she must have stayed in Boston. The Crowley gravestone must surely be just a coincidence of names common in this part of Ireland. But the stone niggles at me, making me question everything I thought I knew.

15

NELLIE 1847

When the ship finally docked, the tears Nellie had been holding back finally ripped from her, as if the floodgate had broken. She cried as if she would never stop. She cried for the hunger, for the dead, for the loss of her home, and for the fact that she and her children had survived.

There was a short delay before the steerage passengers were allowed to climb wearily from the bowels of the ship, to blink in the afternoon sun of a foreign land.

We're a straggling bunch. What must they think of us? Stinking from the hold, unwashed save for an occasional dash of salt water, barely clothed, thin as rakes, without a decent piece of baggage between us.

As she stepped from the plank onto dry land, it moved beneath her feet and she nearly fell. Beside her, another woman had wavered and was on her knees. There was laughter from the sailors behind and a few taunts.

'Take yez a while before ye finds yer land legs,' a man said, in a kindlier tone. 'Jest move along now, best you can.'

The cabin-class passengers had disembarked first, and although they looked deathly pale, they had luggage and had managed to clean themselves. They were directed towards a building first, where they queued, waiting to go through immigration gates, and the steerage passengers like herself clustered behind them in a huddle.

Through an iron fence, she saw a crowd of people milling, presumably seeking family or maybe seeking newly arrived passengers to rob. She had been warned by a sailor as they disembarked that people here could be cruel. Strangely, she hadn't expected that. She still had a few coins sewn into her petticoat, but aside from that, she had little worth stealing. Unlike so many of her fellow passengers, at least she had shoes, and she gave thanks for Father Patrick's kindness. The priest had warned her Boston could be cold in the winter. Maybe William could find a way to get shoes for Annie, too.

The docks were confusing and terrifying, bristling with action and noise: men shouting, the clanging of metal trolleys, the clop of horses and thumping of goods being thrown from the decks of ships. There were carts pulled by enormous dray horses, the like of which Nellie had never seen before, pulling huge wagons with wheels bound in iron. Everything here was bigger than back at home. The horses, the carts, the buildings, even the people. Her eyes were everywhere, wide with astonishment, fearfully drinking in the strangeness.

A voice yelled, 'Out of my way!' and she jumped back, pulling Annie aside as a man in a wide-brimmed hat drove a cart through the throng of scarecrow-thin emigrants, seemingly without any care for their lives.

Behind, at the ship they had just left, a bustle of activity was taking place. Barrels were being unloaded and shunted to one side, and more barrels, presumably water and victuals, were stacked by the wharf, ready for loading. The ship, she realised, was being readied to head back to England and Ireland within the week, to collect more emigrants. She wondered quite how many people this new land could hold. But it was a vast land, she had been told, where they could find a patch of land to farm and grow clean, white, wholesome potatoes.

Nellie stood in line with the other emigrants at the gate, waiting for her turn. Before her, men in suits and hats like pudding basins with rims were checking their passage details, taking names and allowing some people through the gate that presumably led out into Boston. Other people were sent to one side, to sit disconsolately hunched against the wall, looking too tired and exhausted to even care.

When Nellie's turn came, the man looked her up and down as if she were a horse. 'Name,' he said brusquely.

'Nellie O'Mahoney,' she said in a small voice.

'Have you family here?'

'My husband, William, is working on the railway. He will be here to meet us.'

He wrote something down in his book then glanced up again. 'Just the two children?'

'Annie and Luke,' she said.

'And they're your husband's?'

She was shocked. 'Of course they are!'

'No *of course* about it,' he said, sniggering. 'Go on, then. Get out.'

She grabbed Annie's hand again and walked on quickly, before he changed his mind. She wondered what was going to happen to those poor souls who didn't have family here waiting for them. Were they to be sent back to Ireland? If so, many wouldn't make it.

The area beyond the dock was huge, heaving with people. How on earth would William find them? She walked away from the mass of people to where there were some crates and lifted Annie up, before hoisting herself and Luke up to sit beside her. From here, at least, she could see over the shoulders of the people milling about.

Here and there were shouts of glee as family found each

other for the first time in months, if not years, but there were also those searching eagerly, not finding the person they were looking for. She knew that those who had died on the ship would be listed and guessed that some of these men would be scanning that list before the day was out.

But she didn't see William.

Dusk was drawing in, and she began to worry. A night out in a strange country, with no food and water, no shelter, was frightening, but William had said, in his letter, that he would be here, and she trusted him. Maybe he wasn't sure exactly what day the ship would arrive. No one could have been sure about that, after all. Ships were at the mercy of the weather and could come in two, three, four weeks late, or not come in at all.

Gradually the throng of people thinned, and Nellie still found herself searching the faces that were left. Perhaps William was here, and she just didn't recognise him. Or perhaps he didn't recognise her. It had been nearly two years since they had seen each other, and she knew the bloom of health was long gone from her own cheeks as well as Annie's. Luke, small, moved restlessly in her arms. He was hungry. The ship hadn't provided enough food and water, and her milk was drying. His suckling had become desperate and painful, and she hoped that when William arrived, he would have food with him.

Annie suddenly slid down from the crate and, with more vivacity than she had shown on the whole journey, cried, 'Dada,' and ran, with her arms out. Dusk had fallen. Nellie couldn't see William, but surely Annie had recognised her father? She heaved herself awkwardly from the crate, with Luke in her arms, and thrust her way through a group of working men who were blocking the path. One grabbed her arm, stopping her short. He pulled her around, leering, 'Hungry, are you, darling?

I know how you can make a bit of money. Find you somewhere to stay, too.'

Nellie gasped, 'Let me go!'

'Suit yourself,' he said, and she yanked her arm from his hand, ran a few steps, then stopped abruptly and swivelled in a full circle. She couldn't see Annie anywhere. Nor could she see William. 'Annie,' she screamed.

People turned to look then turned away again.

Nellie was frantic. She ran the length and breadth of the dock, zig-zagging through the rapidly thinning crowd, calling Annie's name over and over. She began to grab at arms, pulling people around to face her. 'Please, have you seen a little girl with red hair, six years old...'

Her desperate pleas generated a few pitying looks but even more irritated exclamations and even some fairly crude comments. And in all this time she hadn't caught a glimpse of William, either. Hadn't Annie cried out for her dada just before running? Hadn't she seen him?

Luke was crying at being jolted, and finally Nellie just came to a complete halt, numb, swaying from exhaustion. It was all she could do to stop herself from sinking to her knees. Then, in the encroaching gloom of evening, she caught sight of a mop of bright red hair and gasped with relief. It was William! Surely Annie would be with him. She found a new burst of energy and pushed people aside in her haste to get to him. 'Is Annie here?' she demanded in her native tongue, grabbing his arm.

'*Gabh mo leithscéal*?' The man responded automatically in Irish. 'Pardon? Lady, are you all right?'

He turned around, and she was shocked to find it wasn't William at all. 'My daughter,' she gasped. 'I can't find my daughter.'

He was probably wondering if she had lost her mind, whether her daughter had died on the boat. His expression softened. He said sympathetically, 'I'll bring you to the office, and you can let them know. She's bound to turn up. What's her name?'

'Annie O'Mahoney.'

He seemed to grow still for a moment. 'You're William's wife, Nellie? I was looking for a woman with a little girl, not a baby.'

She nearly burst into tears. 'Yes, yes! Where is he? He said he'd be here. I thought you were him. I thought Annie was with you.'

'I'm Danny,' he said. 'William was working with me on the railway. I came to find you because I knew William would have wanted me to. He was so pleased you were finally coming over.' There was a long pause while it seemed as if he was trying to find words to soften the blow she already knew was coming, but he found none. 'I'm so sorry. He died in an accident some three weeks ago.'

Nellie felt things growing distant. Her mind became a fog, all her mental strength fleeing beneath a darkening cloud. Her husband gone? She had made that dreadful journey to a foreign shore, and there was no husband to greet her? She had no food, nowhere to stay and her daughter was lost.

It was all too much. Strength failed her, and the man called Danny reached out to support her and stopped baby Luke from sliding from her loosening grasp.

'Come,' he said, drawing her to some wooden crates, stacked to one side. 'Sit down here a while.'

She collapsed mindlessly onto the seat, folded over briefly and took deep breaths.

'Now,' he said after a few moments, 'can you tell me what happened.'

'She was with me getting off the boat and through immigration. We were looking for William. She shouted and ran. I thought she'd found him.'

His lips compressed. They both knew she hadn't.

'It must have been you,' Nellie said listlessly. 'I thought you were William, too.'

'I didn't see her,' he said. 'But surely by now someone will have taken her to the immigration office,' he said calmly. 'Let's go and find out, shall we?'

She responded to his calm voice, the soft Irish accent so like William's, yet subtly different. It was easy to let him take control; she was just so tired, drained by hunger and fear and this latest shattering news. It would have been so easy to just give up, but her children needed her. She closed her eyes briefly then opened them again with determination. He was right. Annie would be found. She must be here somewhere.

Nellie allowed Danny to lead her to the office, where a man in a tweed suit told her Annie wasn't there and hadn't been reported, either, or there would have been an entry to say she'd been taken to the orphanage. He took her details but didn't seem too bothered. It was just another destitute Irish child, and there were enough of them, God only knew. 'Come back and check each day,' he said. 'No doubt someone will bring her in. Does she speak English?'

'No,' Nellie whispered. 'She only has the Irish.'

The man gave a grimace and shrugged. 'Why don't you people learn proper English?'

'Well, she knows her name, so,' Danny said, obviously irritated by the man's lack of compassion.

William's friend stayed by her side, and together they scoured the docks, until night fell in earnest, until even the dockyard ceased its cacophony of sound, and all that was left was the gentle thudding of ships moving against the harbour walls as the tide rocked everything to sleep. They called her name, over and over, until an irritated voice out of the darkness suggested they quiet down and go away – some people were trying to sleep.

If Annie had still been there, she would have heard.

'Let me get you back to our room,' Danny said gently. 'You can have William's bed for now, until we decide what to do.'

'I can't,' she said dully. 'I have to stay here. I can't leave her out here on her own.'

'You must come with me.' Danny's voice attained the hardness of necessity. 'You have a babe in arms. You have to think of him tonight. William didn't tell me he had a baby, too.'

'His name's Luke,' she said in a voice tiny with exhaustion. 'William didn't know.'

'Well, come back and eat at least. The child needs to eat, too. You can't stay out here. If, ah, *when* someone finds Annie, they will take her to the office, you'll see. We'll come back tomorrow and fetch her home.'

But Annie wasn't brought in that day – or the next.

They asked, frantically, as the weeks crawled by, *Has anyone seen a six-year-old child with blue eyes and thick, long hair, red as a fox?*

But no one had.

Annie was gone, disappeared, as if taken by the little folk.

Nellie grew thin and pale, and her looks started to fade. She could not sleep for wondering what her child had suffered, was suffering even now. Had some man taken her? Had she fallen into the water and drowned, unnoticed by the hundreds of people busying themselves on the dock?

She was sinking into an almost catatonic state when Danny took her by the shoulders and shook her. 'Nellie, you must stop. Annie's gone, but Luke needs you. Do you think William would want his son to die, while you're searching for Annie? I can't keep feeding you both. I'm working as hard as I can, but you must find work.'

For the first time since meeting him, she focused fully on Danny. He was looking exhausted from the long hours of work, from before daylight peeped over the horizon to the evening when he dragged himself home, caked in mud, to wash at the barrel before eating and sleeping like the dead. It was in that moment she realised he was right. None of this was his fault. He was looking after her and Luke out of the goodness of his heart, and she was giving him nothing in return.

Back at home, in Ireland, people had been dying all around her, and she had shut herself off from the world, trying not to see the horror, and she had to do the same again. William was dead, Annie was gone, but her son was alive, and he needed her. So she did what she had to do and closed the door on her grief. She would make sure her son, hers and William's, had a good life, here, in the new land. And in so doing, she would help Danny to make a new life, too.

16

ERIN

It was liberating to walk out on my overprotective parents, to actually end up in the town that had been no more than a name on Grandpa's lips. My brief interactions with Finn and Livvy have made me feel – however fleetingly – that I belong, that I am involved in the community, but they've both vanished from my horizon for the moment. The hotel is like a ghost ship. I catch the occasional glimpse of Grace or another young man sliding through doorways in the distance.

The tall, thin lady, usually wearing a nylon housecoat – presumably Noel's housekeeper – produces a meal every evening for me. I've told her I can help myself to breakfast and a snack at midday, for which she seems grateful.

Rather than sit in my room and nurse my loneliness, I've taken to sitting in the spacious, airy lounge to read, snatching glances out over the Atlantic from time to time. I'm getting to know her moods. Finn has made me think of the sea as a woman, maybe a teenage girl, tripping from sleepy self-aware-ness to raging full-blown tantrums in a moment, each day a surprise.

I brought a portable tape player with me and some recordings of the music I once enjoyed, so today I'm going to cross another bridge. I wasn't sure I would be able to listen to them, but standing outside Nancy's bar the other day, hearing real music played by real people, made me realise that music itself isn't the cause of my grief, that I shouldn't lose something else I used to love.

With trepidation, I take the first cassette tape out of its plastic box, insert it into the machine and press play. There's a moment of intense anticipation, then the orchestra softly begins the first strains of the 'William Tell Overture'. After a while, I find tears sliding down my cheeks at the raw emotion Rossini injected into his music. What an imagination! I've never understood how someone can write all those parts, for all those instruments, and blend them into such a magnificent whole. When he wrote this piece, he was not much older than I am now, so every time I hear it, I'm newly amazed at his brilliance.

Gradually, the music fills my soul, and as it rolls through its moods, from the slow *Dawn* section into the raging *Storm*, I become engrossed. The overture is like the sea I'm staring at, and I slowly awaken to the knowledge that my tears are not the angry tears of grief but are somehow cleansing, as if another dark area of my soul is finding its way to the light. Kenny would want me to enjoy music. If he's up there, watching, he'll be grinning with pleasure. I'm sure that each time I listen to music it will get easier. The smothering compassion of my family was holding me back, stopping me from giving my grief the rightful space it needed to expand and, hopefully, in time dissipate a little.

I was right to leave home and come somewhere I had never visited with Kenny, so that I could process things in my own way, in my own time, without interference, and escape my parents' matchmaking attempts at the same time.

I catch a movement reflected in the window. Becoming aware that someone else is in the room, I hastily stop the music, mid-flow, thrust the headphones behind my neck and turn abruptly. Noel is sitting a couple of tables away. When he sees that I'm aware of his presence, he heaves himself to his feet and says, 'You looked so intensely involved, I didn't want to disturb you. Do you mind me asking what you're listening to?'

'The "William Tell Overture". Do you know it?'

He shakes his head. 'I'm ashamed to admit that I never got into classical music. I'm more of a Joseph Locke man, myself. Irish tenors, our old songs and the old diddly-do Irish dance music.'

'Well, that's not something to be ashamed of,' I say. 'It's laudable, in fact. Better to enjoy the music of your own people than be a popular music groupie. In my opinion, I mean,' I add hastily.

He grins and sings out the first line of 'Love Me Do' in a surprisingly high tenor, making me laugh. 'You have to admit, the Beatles have something, too?'

'They have,' I agree, but I'm aware of that in a kind of distant way. 'I don't think I'm a music snob. I kind of veered towards classical music the moment I heard it, but I don't think I chose it; I think the music chose me.'

'Just so.'

'Did you want me for something?'

'Two things, actually. Firstly, the local teacher, Angela Daly, would like to come and speak with you about Livvy and the dreaded vile din. Is it all right for her to call on you here, after school tonight? Around four, she said.'

Grace must have regaled him with the story of my father's dismissive comment. I smile then say guiltily, 'I think she's going to tell me off.'

He laughs. 'You're old enough not to accept the old ruler tapped across the knuckles. The way I see it is, let her say her piece then discuss it. Don't predispose yourself for something that might not happen.'

Sound advice, I guess, and quite opposite to what my father would have advised. I nod and say, 'Okay,' even though I'm not really okay about it. I hate being on the receiving end of someone else's irritation. 'And the second thing?'

'A little bird told me it's your birthday in a couple of days, so I'd like to extend an invitation to spend the evening with me and my family up at Roone House. In Ireland, birthdays are family events, and I don't like the thought of you being here, alone, on your special day.'

'How on earth did you discover that?'

He winks and taps his nose with a finger.

'Oh. Well, that's very kind, but I don't want to intrude...'

'Oh, believe me, you won't be intruding,' he says dryly. 'My family love to get their teeth into other people's business. They're relentless when it comes to worming out every small detail of a person's life. So, consider yourself warned.' He pushes himself to his feet. 'You know Grace and Livvy already, so it shouldn't be too daunting. Come on up to the house at five. We can have an aperitif before dinner, and I'll introduce you to my family. We tend to eat early here.'

I'm half inclined to insist no, but Noel makes it seem as if the invitation is, in fact, an order. As he owns the hotel and the monolith behind it, I feel daunted by his presence. And yet, he's done nothing to make me feel like that. I can only suppose it's in the very bones of his nature to succeed, and that somehow permeates his whole character.

I nod and remember my manners. 'Thank you. That will be delightful.'

He grins. 'You can decide whether or not it was delightful after the event, Erin. See you then.'

He taps a salute to his forehead and leaves.

Well, he has a sense of humour, and if it's a trauma and a trial, well, I don't need to ever do it again.

The moment has been lost, though; I can't get back into the

music. I open the pages of yet another book about the famine. I discover that the blight was first noticed on the Isle of Wight, in England, causing massive concern. It spread on the wind, to Ireland and across the breadth of Europe, causing distress everywhere it landed. That surprised me. I'd always thought the potato blight was Ireland's own disaster, but the whole of Europe suffered. Potatoes being scarce, the price of grain rocketed. So, while some people were busy raising funds to help the Irish, who had been worst hit because of their over-population and reliance on the one crop, the unscrupulous were making a profit out of the crisis.

What's new? I think cynically.

Back in my room, later, I pick up Nellie's bible. It comforts me to just hold it. I wonder what she would think of me, here today, surrounded by all this luxury, when she'd been surrounded by poverty and death. Grandpa said she didn't even have shoes until the day she left, provided to her by the priest, so the story goes. I shudder, wondering what she felt about inheriting a dead woman's shoes. But then, she was a mother and a determined one at that. The kind of mother who put the needs of her children first.

I'm not going to find anything hidden in the pages, some long-lost letter that explains everything. I've already flipped through the book and picked at the bindings, so I know the bible is what it is: a book with details of lineage and birth and death dates scratched inside the cover. That was quite a common custom, there being no such things as notebooks or any other kind of book for the poor.

I can never change what happened to Nellie, but I feel I owe her a debt of gratitude. It might be a flight of fantasy, but if I can stand where she once stood and say out loud that I remember her, I will have found peace, and maybe, somewhere across the unknown dimension, she will, too.

.   .   .

Later that day I'm in my room when the internal telephone rings. I answer it, and it's Grace, saying I have a visitor in the lobby. I thank her and take a deep breath before trotting down the stairs.

Angela Daly is waiting for me by the desk. She's kind of dumpy, wearing a home-made dress with a lace-edged Peter Pan collar. Her hair is pulled into a tight knot at the nape of the neck. In repose her expression is severe, but her round face breaks into a smile as she holds out her hand. 'Erin? Angela Daly, Livvy's teacher. Have you got a minute?'

I nod, taking her hand briefly. She doesn't look cross, at least. 'Of course. I'm so sorry; I really didn't mean to interfere regarding the violin lessons. It's just that when I saw her struggling...'

She seems taken aback then laughs out loud. 'Interfere? Quite the opposite, my dear. I came to thank you. Come over and let's sit a moment. The view is stunning from here, isn't it?'

'It is,' I agree, relief flooding me.

The Atlantic is happy this afternoon. There's a faint wind, and the water is crinkled, laced with whitecaps. We stare out quietly for a few seconds, then she gets down to business.

'The thing is, I teach all the children a few tunes on the penny whistle. It's what we do,' she says, almost apologetically. 'I think the children benefit from knowing something about their national heritage. Anyway, we hosted a concert a while back, for charity, and some young musicians from Kerry came over and played. They were stunning. It's a joy to see such talent in the young, isn't it?'

I agree, wondering what this has to do with me.

'Well, the thing is, Livvy was at the concert. She took one look at the fiddle – we call them fiddles, here, you know?'

I nod. 'We call them fiddles in America, too. Unless one is playing classical, then they're violins.'

'Just the same, so. Anyway, she told her mother, in no uncertain terms – I think she must take after her father in some ways – that that's what she wanted to play! Of course, Grace went straight out and bought her one, but the thing is, we have no fiddle players in Roone Bay, and I don't know one end of a bow from another.'

'I thought I heard someone playing a fiddle in Nancy's bar the other night?'

She shrugs. 'Well, people travel miles to play the music, but most of them would have jobs and wouldn't be around to teach the children. So, I was wondering how long you'll be staying?'

Oh. I hadn't expected that. 'I don't know,' I admit.

'But maybe a week or two yet? Even if you were able to get her started, find her a book to learn from, set her on her way, I might be able to encourage her at school?'

'I don't know... I'd hate to get her keen then have to just leave her floating.'

'Oh, but she wouldn't be. We have some really nice traditional players around who can teach her some tunes. There's Tom with his melodeon, Finn with the concertina and Terry sometimes brings his penny whistle. They would all be encouraging, you know, in their own way. It's just, she needs to be taught some basics. Get it right, from the start. The bowing and everything.'

I almost laugh. As if I could teach bowing techniques in a couple of weeks! But then I recall the look of pleasure on Livvy's face as she made the first strains of 'Twinkle, Twinkle Little Star' sound almost tuneful. 'I'm intending to be here for another month, at least,' I admit. 'I'm trying to trace my family. Nellie O'Mahoney, who left in 1847 and came to Boston.'

She nods. 'Yes, I heard. I wish you luck, my dear. There are few enough records from that dreadful time, you know? But I can put word out around the community. You never know. So, will I tell Grace that you'll be providing lessons, for a little while, at least? We'll pay you, of course.'

I wince. 'I don't want paying, really. But yes. I'll teach Livvy for now. Whether she'll be able to keep going after I leave... Well, it would take some serious determination on her part, even if the local musicians are encouraging.'

She smiles and nods. 'Well, you arrived in her hour of need. I'm sure God will provide. I must be going, so. Will I leave you to arrange everything with Grace?'

'Sure,' I say as we rise.

'Thank you so much, my dear. God bless!'

She traces a quick cross over her front as she speaks His name and hastens away in a whirlwind of determination, having fulfilled one task and off, no doubt, to the next on her list. I know nuns don't have to wear robes any longer, though some choose to. I wonder if she's one, or whether she's just a devout Catholic.

Kenny was a total atheist, and I was Christian when we met, though I wasn't too regular in my devotions. As we grew closer, he came to agree that there might be *something* out there, and although I rarely went to church, I retained my belief in God without trying to pin Him down through a specific religion. We were comfortable with that compromise. There's no way Kenny could paint such intensely beautiful depictions of the raw elements of nature and not believe that life holds more secrets than we know. And, despite everything that's happened, I hold to my belief. Life is just too *amazing* to be an accident. And also, it helps to think that life is not the end, that somewhere in This wide universe, Kenny still exists, in one form or another.

Hugging the bible to my chest, I wonder how Nellie managed to retain her faith after everything she saw and experienced.

17

NELLIE 1848

William was dead and gone – Nellie accepted that. She mourned him, but as time went by, it was hard to even recall what he looked like. When she thought about William now, it was Danny's face she saw. Danny, who had rescued them, looked after them and married her because she was living under his roof and people would talk. She didn't love Danny the way she'd loved William, but he was a good man, loyal and true. William gradually slipped away, a laughing shadow in the past, almost but not entirely real. Only when she heard a man's voice singing did she sometimes stop what she was doing and freeze, as the shadow of a lost life passed overhead.

Annie, though, was ever-present in Nellie's mind. Not a moment went by without a thought or memory of her lost child. And not a day went by that she didn't pray to God to save her daughter's soul. Sometimes, she even hoped that Annie was gone. If she had slipped over the edge of the quay and drowned, that would at least have been a quick death. Nellie would have been happier knowing that, if it was true, than not knowing anything.

There was a woman, Eve Donaghue, who lived near the

shack Danny rented. She had also come through some hard times to end up in this place at this time. Her husband had found work collecting mussels in the bay. Nellie and Eve helped each other out with minding the children from time to time when there were messages to be run, chores to be undertaken. It was comforting to have a country woman nearby. Eve hadn't come from Roone Bay but many miles away, over in Kerry, and had come out with her husband when the famine had already taken most of her extended family. Nellie had never thought of people from way over the mountain as being neighbours, but separated from her home country by thousands of miles, that distance seemed to shrink in comparison. In fact, anyone from the whole of Ireland was her neighbour here, be they from Kerry or Connemara, places she had heard of but never seen.

One day, Nellie heard Eve wailing and lamenting, and eventually learned that Eve's husband had drowned on the flats while collecting mussels. Eve was desperate, because who was going to support her and her three children, including the new babe in arms? Collecting mussels was better paid than being a navvy, but the work was just as dangerous. Most of those who worked between the tides couldn't swim, after all, and it was too easy to become engrossed in the collecting, reaching for those last few mussels, while the tide crept in around the bay, cutting them off. And what was one less Irish mussel collector? Like the navvies, there were always more desperate souls queuing up to take their place.

When Nellie learned of the drowning, memories of Annie threatened to destroy the fragile hold she had on her sanity. She recalled Annie's smooth, white skin, her red hair, her blue eyes that silently contemplated all that was around her. Every day she berated herself for the loss. She had let go of Annie's hand.

It was her fault. Even if others could forgive her, she could not forgive herself. The chasm in her mind that was Annie's fate was shrouded by nothing more than a flimsy veil of determination. If she let it slip, she would lose herself to grief, and then what would become of Luke?

She steeled herself. She must live, for Luke if not herself.

Nellie didn't want to leave her son with another woman, but he was no longer a babe in arms, and while he could have walked on his sturdy little legs up to the potato patch at home, here, in Boston, she did not dare let him wander. She was afraid to lose another child, her last tie with William and the old life. But no one would give work to a woman who had a child hanging on to her skirts. So, Nellie suggested to Eve that she should look after Luke in return for half the wages, so that she could find a job to ease Danny's burden and save Eve at the same time.

The relief on Eve's face was a joy to see. They hugged, and cried, and said the rosary together in quiet companionship. The priests they had revered in Ireland, and the rosary that had once consolidated their faith, must remain secret, for that faith was reviled in Boston. Here there was no charity for the destitute, Irish Catholics in particular. It was said they got their just deserts, being beggars and thieves all, coming to Boston to undermine the lives of comfortable, God-fearing Protestant Christians.

As if being Catholic wasn't being Christian, Nellie thought.

She found a job in a laundry. It was hard, unforgiving work, in a steamy, claustrophobic atmosphere. Her one dress was always damp, her hands red raw, cracked from the hot water and caustic soap, and the wages she brought home barely fed the two families, but she'd known real hunger, so counted her blessings and tried not to be bitter about her situation.

It could be worse.

In Ireland they would have starved to death. From the

stories coming from the ships, from the emaciated survivors of those bitter weeks at sea, she learned that the Irish situation had worsened, the black blight breezing in for the third year running, and those who survived had finally learned to grow things other than potatoes, as William had foreseen. William had forged a path for their future, and for that she was grateful. Sometimes, though, when she looked around her grimy, industrial surroundings, the thought of the clear air of West Cork, with its smattering of small homesteads dotted about the green landscape, nearly made her weep with homesickness.

The laundry owners had a big house and travelled in a carriage; she had seen it twice. Their own children were clad in fine cloth, and from the lecture she received on starting work, they made her understand that providing low-paid work for desperate immigrants was an act of charity. It was just how life had always been, Nellie knew. The rich and the poor divided by a social chasm so deep, even to dream of crossing that bridge went against everything that had been engrained in her since birth.

She was given Sunday off each week, presumably to go to church, though no one ever asked whether she did. She would gather little Luke and traipse to the docks, her eyes always seeking her little red-headed girl. Maybe Annie was looking for her, too. And if that was the case, the only place she would know to look would be the docks. Annie had gone, like a wraith in the night, but how could she stop hoping?

One day, she was dragging her weary feet home from the laundry, as the light was fading, when she was yelled at by a woman from over the street. She glanced over but didn't, at first, recognise the well-dressed woman whose shoes and hat were surely those of a wealthy citizen.

'Nellie O'Mahoney! Nellie, it's me, Kate! Catherine Kelly!'

She was stunned into silence before rushing across the road. Her childhood friend hugged her, despite the state of her clothes, which stank of soap and dirt, not having been washed for a long time. With nothing else to change into, and living as they were, in little more than a lean-to shack, it would have been an impossible task. She burst into tears at the warm welcome, then her one-time friend pushed her back, holding her still, and exclaimed. 'Nellie, *mo chara*, what has happened to you? Why are you in this mess?'

She grimaced. 'I've been working in the laundry. It was the only work I could get.'

'And William, he allows this?' She looked as if she would give William a piece of her mind. She had ever been a strong character, Nellie remembered.

She grimaced and shook her head. 'William sent me the ticket, but when I got here, he was already dead. Working on the railroad. There was a collapse... they never even recovered his body.' Her memory drifted, and she fell silent.

'Oh, you poor darling,' Kate said. 'How did you manage? And little Annie. She must be six or seven now? How is she?'

Nellie couldn't help tearing up. 'Annie is lost,' she said, her voice filled with grief. 'When we arrived, there was so much noise, so many people, we got separated on the quay, and I never found her. We looked for days...'

'We?'

'William's friend, Danny O'Brien. He found me, to tell me about William.'

Kate's eyes widened at the news of her tragedy.

Nellie hiccupped; pulled herself together. 'He supports us and even now pays the rent. I had little Luke to care for. William didn't know he'd left me with child. Luke is eighteen months now, growing so fast. I think he will be tall, like William, one day.'

Kate was silent for a moment, but Nellie saw her tears echoed in her friend's eyes. Kate had come here on her own, the year before William left, determined not to be married to a poor farmer in Ireland, forever scratching a living. Nellie had thought she would never see Kate again, and thought it a very foolish thing for a girl to do at the time, but it seemed that her friend had done well for herself. She smiled slightly. 'And you, dear Kate? Are you married, to look so well?'

'Me, married?' She gave a gurgle of laughter. 'Maybe, one day, but I'm not going to be burdened with children – not yet, anyway. No, I'm the lady's maid for Clara and Margarethe Becker, Mr Kurt Becker's daughters. He's one of the richest men in Boston, on the council and everything.' She grinned. 'His factory weaves cotton and exports it, and the maids get nice fabrics to make things for the family and get to use some of the offcuts to make our own clothes, see?'

She did a quick pirouette.

'You made that?' Nellie asked, awed.

'I did, and I can show you how. The ladies get pictures sent from England, and we copy them. Of course, we aren't allowed to look grand, like them, but we do well enough.'

She stopped, taking in Nellie's worn dress once more. 'The housekeeper, Mrs Thompson, is seeking a scullery maid. I can pass you one of my dresses and tell her that I know you, that you're honest – which you are, of course.'

Nellie's eyes lit up. 'That would be good.'

'It would be better than what you're doing now, at any rate. But you must not mention priests and the Holy Communion, you understand?'

'I've learned that already,' Nellie said dryly.

'Then it's done! When do you have time off?'

'Sunday,' Nellie said. The laundry was always closed on the Lord's day, which she was sure it wouldn't be at all, if the owners weren't trying to impress the local clergy with their devoutness and their large donations to the church.

'Then you must call at the house on Sunday, early. You can wash in the scullery. I'll find you a dress and do your hair. You won't know yourself, my dearest friend. If I can procure you a meeting, you must respect her, and speak slowly and properly, and no Irish at all, mind!'

'Will it matter that I don't have my letters?'

Kate grimaced. 'They prefer it that way. If we can't read, then they're better than us, aren't they? But I learned, anyway,' she added. 'It's not hard, if only someone will show you. I can do that if you get the work.'

The following Sunday, in the scullery, Nellie was scrubbed until her skin glowed and was clothed in one of Kate's dresses, which hung loosely on her scarecrow frame. Kate proceeded to give her a thorough education in how to behave, what she must say and how to say it. The housekeeper was seeking clean girls who could obey orders instantly, keep the house running smoothly. She must walk upright, shoulders back. She must always be clean and tidy, her clothes laundered and pressed. Her hair must always be neat, managed, beneath the cap. There was to be no running, ever. The staff must not be heard moving around. She must be invisible to the owners unless tasked directly by them. She must curtsey – Kate did a little bob, lowering her head – as she answered the housekeeper or anyone above her station, which would be just about everyone. The list seemed endless. But her friend said that was how she started, and now look at her! A lady's maid, with all the perks. Cast-off dresses and shoes, time to go dancing...

Dancing, Nellie thought. As if!

It seemed a lifetime ago that such simple pleasures as music and stepping in the kitchen had been part of her family life. She welled up at the thought of the life she'd once had and the family she had lost – her siblings, her parents, William, Annie... No, she could not think of Annie in those terms. There was a dark cloud in her mind, and if she let it, it would expand

and engulf her. Sure, Annie *might* be dead, but it was not beyond the bounds of hope that her sweet child had been taken in by kind strangers and given a chance at life. She would hang on to that hope. If she had found a child wandering, alone and terrified, she could have done no less, despite her circumstances. And despite the lack of compassion that she had encountered since leaving home, there were good people out there. She had to believe that.

Despite her never-ending search for Annie, it was little Luke's need for her that kept her fighting one weary day after the next.

18

ERIN

When Finn turns up at the hotel I'm in the lounge. I see him through the glass partition and sink deeper into the chair, trying to be invisible, assuming he's come to see someone else. But after scanning the room, he comes straight to where I'm sitting. 'You don't have to hide,' he says. 'I'm not as dangerous as people say.'

There's nothing in his expression that speaks of amusement, but I know he's joking.

'Oh, hi there.' I sit up taller, as if I hadn't been trying to hide at all.

'Hi there, yourself.' He echoes my accent – badly.

'Have you found out something about Nellie?' I ask hopefully, thinking that might be why he's seeking me out.

He shakes his head and comes around to the seat opposite me. He's carrying a fiddle case. He sits and props it between his knees. I freeze, staring at it, then my eyes gravitate to his. His confidence fades at my shocked expression. 'I thought you might be pleased. It's just a loan. Because you left yours in America.'

'Why would you... How do you...' I'm at a loss for words.

'Well, the thing is, my aunt works at the school, and she knows Jane Weddows who works for Noel up at the Big House, and Jane said Livvy told Grace who told her that you're going to teach her to play, but... it's that grapevine thing.'

He gives a slight smile at my dumbfounded expression. What I can't tell him is that I didn't forget to bring my fiddle. I left it behind on purpose. I just can't play it. Not yet. That's one bridge too far. I feel guilty at being still around, enjoying life, when Kenny's dead. Enjoying life is a bit of a broad statement, but indulging in my music when Kenny is no longer able to create feels somewhat crass, disloyal even.

Finn knows nothing of this. He thought he was providing me with a gift and says, confused, 'Don't you want to look?'

Reluctantly, I pull the case onto my knees. It's one of those really old cases made out of wood, with a ridge along the top, its black paint worn thin. There's a leather shoelace tied in a bow holding it together because the catches are broken.

I pull the shoelace free and open the case slowly, as if it contains something poisonous. I'm thinking, if the fiddle is that old, it's not going to be any good, anyway, so I have an excuse to say, sorry, it's not playable.

But it's beautiful.

Made of dark wood that's recently been given a lick of spit and polish, it caresses my soul, asking to be played. I pick it up and turn it to the light. It has a patina that doesn't just suggest old but aged. It was made by a craftsman, and I'm sure if I took it to a dealer, I'd find it was made in the 1700s, either by a known instrument maker or one of his students. The back is a single piece of wood with dense growth rings, maybe Alpine spruce, another indication that it might once have been quality. Only the wealthy in Ireland could have afforded such an instrument. Maybe it had been left behind by one of the landlords who fled when things got tough. I hold it up to the light and see no gaps where the neck is joined to the body. I ping the strings with a fingernail and find it's in perfect pitch.

'Someone's set this up,' I comment.

'Yes,' he agrees, making me think it was him.

'It's got new strings.'

'Yes,' he says with a faint smile.

I pull the bow out and check the horse hair and the frog. The screw is sound. I bend the wood about. It's still got its elasticity.

'Well, are you going to give it a test drive?'

I hear a faint hint of impatience, as if he really wants to hear what I can do. I shake my head. 'I'd rather not make a fool of myself in front of anyone over seven years old.'

'I don't believe that. What kind of music do you play?'

'Used to play,' I correct. 'A bit of this, a bit of that. Classical, mostly.'

'So, why did you stop? Playing, I mean. Was it because of Kenny?'

I nod. 'I just couldn't. I don't know if I can now.' I carefully nest the violin back into its bed of green felt and clip the bow into the lid, which I close and secure with the bootlace of leather. 'You'd better give this back to whoever owns it.'

'Hang on to it. You never know, you might find the courage... It's been lying around for a while, not played. Besides which, it might help to have an instrument if you're going to give Livvy a few lessons.'

I sigh with resignation. 'That's true. And if it really hasn't got a home, Livvy will grow into it, if she keeps playing, that is.'

He shrugs. 'Who knows? She's young. She's trying things out.'

I'd heard this a lot, that children want things then don't want them any longer, and parents get frustrated.

I tell him, 'The moment I heard a violin being played, I knew that I was going to play one. Maybe Livvy's the same.'

'Maybe,' he says. 'We can all help her find out, can't we? And no harm done if it's not for her.'

What a different attitude, I think.

For a year or more, I had badgered my bewildered parents, who'd never touched an instrument in their lives. They thought music was something you purchased by the yard. It either came ready-made through the radio or was played by small groups of faceless *others* at various events. But they liked to spoil me, so one Christmas, there it was: a full-size, hand-made violin. My parents had no idea, and nor did I, that they should have bought a smaller one, maybe a cheap one from Germany or China, in case my desire to play was a fad. I had no idea how expensive the instrument was or that I would fall in love with it over the coming years. At first, I learned a few tunes with a music teacher at school. Then my teacher said I needed proper lessons, to take grades. Then the grade teacher said I needed specialist tuition as I had talent. Eventually I joined a youth orchestra and moved on to the Boston Symphony Orchestra as a first violin.

My parents were stunned. They never believed me when I said I wanted to play, least of all in an orchestra. And as for classical, Dad asked, *Where on earth did that come from?* Well, I couldn't answer that myself. I had no idea. But truthfully, 'Twinkle, Twinkle, Little Star' is the first tune I've knocked out since the accident, and I wonder if that even counts as playing.

Finn glances outside, where a weak sun is pushing through the clouds. He pushes himself to his feet. 'I said I'd help Dad fix some nets. Do you want to come for a stroll? It would do you good to get some fresh air.'

The thought of meeting a working Irish fisherman is somewhat daunting. It conjures up the image of someone tough as old boots, with no people skills. 'I'm not sure,' I say doubtfully.

'He'd love to meet you.'

'I don't know why.'

'He loves meeting people. Trust me.'

He holds out his hand. There's a quiet strength to him that overrides my inclination to retreat to my room. I let him pull me to my feet and feel a tingle of anticipation ripple through me at the contact. I like Finn. I like him a lot, but I came here to get my mind sorted not open myself to confusion.

I pull my hand free, but there's satisfaction on his face as he knows I've capitulated. He looks askance at my light blouse and skirt and says, 'It's chilly by the water. Do you want to get a coat?'

'I'd better get changed.'

'I'll wait in the lobby.'

I start to walk away, and he calls me back.

'Don't forget the fiddle.'

Upstairs, I put the fiddle case on the bed gingerly. It sits there daring me. After the accident, I had taken my violin out a couple of times, but just running the bow over the strings to tune up had set me shaking. Kenny always said we were tethered by our talents, him with his art, me with my music. Yet the ties binding us have vanished. I thought my music had died along with his art, but now I'm wondering if I was just denying myself something I loved, out of guilt and grief.

I change my skirt for jeans, pull on a jumper and slip into sensible lace-up shoes, thinking they aren't quite sensible enough for Ireland. I grab my windcheater as I leave the room. Finn holds the main door open for me, and we walk down the steep drive from the hotel, cross the main road and take the lane that dips behind the shops to the quay.

He glances at me. 'Are you warm enough?'

'I am, thanks.'

The quay is thick with fishing vessels. The churning sea doesn't seem to have realised that the wind has dropped. Tied up two deep, the boats are bumping against the fenders that cushion the sides, and small waves are irritably dashing themselves against the harbour wall, sending up small fountains of salt water. The tide is high, so the tyres that line the walls are under water. Finn takes my arm as we negotiate a jumble of lobster pots, lines and nets, and make our way towards the end of the quay. He exchanges greetings with a couple of men who are wearing bright yellow waterproof trousers hung on loose suspenders. He stops by a trawler from which the red and white paint is peeling off in thick sheets, and calls, 'Dada!'

I'm startled to hear him call his father by the childish term, but it's nice, actually. I still call my parents Mom and Dad, and never thought anything of it as I grew older.

After a couple of moments, a head pops up from behind the wheelhouse, bathed in a broad smile. 'Hey, Finny boy! Be with you in a tick. I'll just get this yoke stowed where it can't bite.'

'What's a yoke?' I whisper.

He grins. 'Anything you don't know the name of.'

'You'd think he'd know the name of everything on his boat by now!' I hiss back.

Finn casts me a sidelong look. 'Do you realise you just told a joke? Does that mean whatever's bugging you has just slipped down a notch?'

Maybe it has, I think. There's something wholesome about standing out on the end of a quay listening to the quiet banter of the fishermen behind us as they heave and pull at the yards of net, searching for holes to fix.

'Why aren't they out fishing today?' I query.

'It's the back end of the storm. Everything will be churned up. They'll be out early tomorrow, judging by the forecast.'

Finn's father makes his way nimbly across the deck and jumps down onto the quay, landing squarely on both feet. I can see where Finn got his physical shape, though his father has obviously lost a little muscle through age, and his Aran sweater does nothing to disguise a roundness that might well have been formed in a bar. He has jeans rolled up high over a pair of wellingtons, and a faded blue cotton drill cap that he pushes to the back of his head. His rotund face is smooth and double-chinned, and his blue eyes twinkle as he and Finn slap each other's shoulders in a manly greeting, then he casts a quick glance towards me. 'So, are ye going to introduce me to the colleen?'

'Erin Ryan, from Boston,' Finn says. 'My dad, Niall.'

'Well now, Finn, lad, what are you after doing down here? Don't you have work today?'

'I'm taking some time off, Dad; I told you that. I was going to help with the nets.'

Niall's face goes serious for a moment, and I wonder again what it is that I haven't been told. 'Ah, yes, sure, didn't I forget for a moment? Well, the nets will keep. And where did you find young Erin Ryan, then?'

'I'm staying at the Roone Bay Hotel.' I answer for myself, before Finn can say he found me half-dead and soaking wet on the seashore. 'I came to find out about my ancestor, Nellie Crowley, later O'Mahoney, who left Roone Bay during the famine.'

'Well, a returned Yank, eh? Sure, and I know where we'll find Nellie,' he says, adding, before my flash of excitement is betrayed on my face, 'Won't she be in the jar?'

He gives a roar of laughter, and Finn grins apologetically at me. 'He finds everything in the jar. Well, if that's the way the wind blows, what say you to a glass of porter?'

'Well, I don't—'

'Sure, she'd like a glass!'

'Just one can't hurt,' Finn says. 'Then we can get some fish and chips to soak it up. How about it?'

I didn't like to ruin the moment by saying I don't drink during the day. But I'm not driving, so I nod briefly.

.   .   .

Inside, the bar is dark; already, despite the early hour, there are several men sitting hunched over pints of back porter. The landlord sees us coming and begins to pour. 'Two for the lads? And what for the lady?'

My usual drink is a glass of white wine, but this doesn't seem like a white wine kind of bar. 'Well, I'll—'

'She'll try a glass of porter, too.' Niall says before I can answer. 'She's a returned Yank, so she is, and the girrul can't come to West Cork without trying out the local tipple, now, can she?'

I shrug, and Finn gives a lopsided smile. 'You can't fight the tide,' he says.

We slide onto a long bench behind a couple of hefty wooden tables. I'm the only woman present and feel slightly uncomfortable. The Guinness is brought over to us and deposited on cardboard beermats that are printed with amusing images of an ostrich drinking the stout, glass and all. There are two pints for the men, and for me, thankfully, a slender glass containing maybe half a pint. I take a hesitant sip. It's sort of smooth and bitter at the same time. Maybe I grimace, because Finn whispers, 'Think of it as the right medicine!'

Niall downs half his pint in a long draught, then smacks his lips with satisfaction and asks Finn, 'So? Where *did* you find her?'

He's clearly not letting that go.

'When I took Whiskey out, she was taking a night-time stroll on the beach. The heavens came down, and she was soaked and cold, so shared my fire for an hour.'

'And have you found anything of this Nellie Crowley of yours?' Niall asks me directly.

I shake my head. 'It's unlikely, too.'

I tell him what I know and see him taking it in, thinking about it.

'So, why now?'

I'm confused. 'Why now what?'

'Why are you chasing this Nellie now? What prompted you to come over here?'

Finn's dad is kind of astute, I think. The rough and ready exterior masks a quick and analytical mind.

'Grandma died a few years back, and Grandpa gave Nellie's bible to Dad, but he didn't want it. Nellie's story always fascinated me, and when I found myself at a loose end, I decided to visit Ireland, see where she'd come from. I was hoping to see the house she lived in, but from what I've learned, now, it's unlikely that I'll ever know where it is.'

'You won't be the first who's come looking and gone away empty-handed.' He shakes his head. 'Those were bad times, all right. But look – Ireland is picking itself up, now we've joined the EU. We're finally being recognised as a real country, not just some flea on England's backside. And there's promise of big financial assistance for the Irish fishing industry.'

'It'll be too late for you, Dada,' Finn says mildly, but I detect a fleeting grimace on his face. Dad always said promises by politicians are like hot air balloons: they go down when the fire goes out. I'm guessing Finn shares this philosophy.

When Finn glances at his watch and suggests it's time we left, I down the final dregs, and find, after all, that the taste has grown less unpalatable.

Niall goes back to his nets, and Finn and I visit a little hatch by the harbour and buy fish and chips wrapped in layers of newspaper to keep them warm. I find that amusing. I'd heard of it but thought it was one of those urban myths. We sit with our feet dangling over the choppy water and eat with our fingers.

Within moments we're besieged by a screeching cloud of seagulls. I'm pleasantly relaxed, surprised to find myself smiling as I throw a bit of greasy batter up for the birds to fight over. Mom would be horrified to see this uncouth display. She's all about dining rooms and good silverware.

'Kenny would have loved this,' I tell Finn.

He looks towards the horizon. 'You can tell him in your dreams. I expect he's watching over you.'

'Do you really believe that?'

'Not really,' he admits. 'But the mind can choose to override common sense with emotional needs. If you speak to Kenny in your dreams, then in your dreams he's listening.'

That's poetic, I think. As well as downright sensible.

He finally scrunches up his paper and reaches for mine. 'Let's put these in the bin and find somewhere to wash our hands. Then I'll go and help Dada with the nets. It takes him longer, these days, what with the arthritis. It's well time he retired. But old fishermen never stop looking for that last big catch.'

He bids me goodbye on the quay, and I don't look back as I walk away, though I'm tempted. I feel a connection with Finn, who becomes less a stranger every time we meet. He seems to know my thoughts, my fears, my desires. And his father defies the fisherman stereotype. He lacks the superficial culture my parents thrive on, but I can see where Finn got his ability to read people.

Back at the hotel, I sit on my bed and open a new paperback I'd picked up in the post office shop, but the story fails to engage me. My eyes keep sliding to the fiddle case. If Kenny were here, he'd tell me not to be so stupid, that I should start to play again.

'Oh, Kenny,' I whisper out loud. 'Why did you have to go and die?'

19

ERIN

On my birthday, I'm a little miffed at not receiving a card or anything at all from my parents. They know the address of the hotel and the telephone number. I'll phone them later, remind them. It's the strangest birthday ever, I think. On my own. No parents, no girlfriends from school, no Kenny – who would certainly have bought me a bunch of flowers and taken me out for a meal.

But I will soon be going for a meal with Noel Donovan and his family up at the Big House. It occurs to me that I know nothing about him, save what I read in the magazines. A poor boy who went to America – Boston, in fact – and made a killing in the world of horse breeding, which the schoolteacher, Angela Daly, confirmed. I believe the lady who's been cooking my meals here, Jane Weddows, usually works for Noel up at his mansion. I doubt she ever envisaged herself catering for the hotel guests! As I seem to be the only one here, though, in this brand new, somewhat under-utilised hotel, perhaps tonight she'll be cooking just one meal for the family.

. . .

I'm sitting in the lounge, just before lunch, daydreaming, when the front door is flung open to admit a group of four Americans who breeze in amidst a cacophony of loud dialogue. They stand around in the entrance lobby for a moment, exclaiming at the empty reception desk and the lack of attendance. They're no doubt retired and touring together, and are tired and fed up.

'Isn't there a bell, Wayne?' a woman asks, her voice reedy with exhaustion.

'Can't see one, honey,' a man replies then shouts, 'Hey, service!'

As there's no response, I suspect Grace is doing the rounds, making beds, even making dinner for all I know. Their complaints echo those I'd thought on arrival: *What, no one to bring in the luggage? No one waiting at reception to meet and greet? What kind of establishment is this?*

Now aware of the problems the hotel is facing, I find I want to defuse the situation and pave the way for these travellers to enjoy their stay. I rise and walk out into the foyer. Before I can say anything, I'm accosted by the large man wearing, of all things, a Stetson, who vents his disapproval in no uncertain terms before allowing me to speak.

'Finally. Someone comes,' he says sarcastically. 'Sweetie, can you book us in? And make us a cup of coffee, and get someone to bring the bags in from those cute little cars we hired?'

'Sure,' I say with a smile, burying my irritation. Perhaps he's not normally that rude. It's probably just tiredness and frustration.

I go behind the counter, find the book and run my hand down the near-empty page. They're the only people booked in, apart from me. 'You're on the first floor. That's the next floor up, and there's an elevator just over there,' I add hastily, pointing, before lifting the keys from the hooks. 'Rooms eleven and twelve. They have splendid views out over the bay. Would you

like me to show you up, or would you like to have a coffee while
we're waiting for someone to bring up your luggage?'

'Oh, coffee, absolutely,' the other woman whines. 'I'm dying
here! Those roads! It said in the brochure that the roads were
narrow, but they're just tracks, I swear! I nearly had a heart
attack every time something passed the other way, on the wrong
side of the road, too. And Wayne, there, put the wheel in the
ditch a few miles back. Lucky he was able to back out or I don't
know what we would have done, stuck out there in the middle
of nowhere.' She fans her face with her hand, sighing, to accen-
tuate how awful it was.

I manage to hide my amusement, though I empathise. I'd
found the driving traumatic, too, and once I'd landed here, save
for my one foray to get the lay of the land, the canary-yellow car
has been glued to the parking lot. If I'm here much longer, the
car rental company might as well collect it, for all the use it's
getting.

'If you'd like to take a seat, there in the window,' I suggest,
'I'll bring the coffee over, and someone will be down shortly to
bring in your luggage.' At least, I hope they will.

'You're a darling,' the first woman says. 'But aren't you
American, too?'

'Boston,' I admit. 'But my ancestors came from here.'

'Oh, that's so adorable,' she drawls. 'Going back to work
where your ancestors came from! Isn't it, Wayne? We're from
Wisconsin, you know, doing Europe for a couple of months. I
don't think we have a drop of Irish blood between us. But this
place! It's like going back into the dark ages.'

'I'll go and get your coffee,' I say.

Adorable doesn't quite express how I'm starting to feel
about Roone Bay. I know I'm several generations down the line
from Nellie, essentially American in everything but genes, but a
sense of belonging has started to seep into my soul. There's
something intensely personal in treading in Nellie's footsteps,

and the way I'm treated here makes me feel as though I belong, and I can't recall that happening much at home. I was always treated well there, of course. It goes with the dad territory, because everyone who's anyone in Boston knows him. I quite like the unique feeling here of just being me, not Dad's daughter.

In the restaurant area, I peruse the coffee machine, then put a couple of spoons of ground coffee in the filter and fill up the water container. I press the big green button hopefully. After a pause, I hear it gurgle and hiss, and a few drops of brown water start to spit into the glass jug. It's making the right noises, anyway. I gather the cups and saucers and put them on a tray, with some biscuits and sugar. When the coffee has finished dripping through the filter, I take it over to the table where the visitors have finally seated themselves, feeling quite chuffed with my achievement.

As I walk away, Grace comes barging through the entrance, looking flustered, with a young man in tow. 'I had to pick up Livvy from school,' she says to me. 'She wasn't well, apparently.' Her eyes fly up in exasperation. 'She looks all right to me, the little monkey! I didn't expect our guests to arrive this early, though, so when I saw the cars on the forecourt, I rushed straight over.'

She glances around and sees the four newcomers sitting by the window with their coffees, munching on biscuits. She looks puzzled.

'I made them coffee and said someone would be along to bring in their luggage,' I say and lower my voice. 'They were getting antsy.'

'You did?' She blinks. 'But you shouldn't have... Thank you so much!' She turns to the young man. 'Go and ask what you should bring in. It's rooms eleven and twelve, first floor. Try to sweeten them up a bit!'

He goes over to the guests, whose belligerence has been

eased a little by the steaming-hot coffee, and within minutes he has the two ladies preening themselves and giggling. He'll go far, I think, smiling.

Grace watches the play and scowls. 'Really, we need to get the staffing sorted. If only we could find someone to manage everything. The last manager sounded so good on the phone, with all the experience, but she just never turned up. And that chef! Once he was here, he just wanted to tell everyone else what to do. He thought he was above lifting a finger to help.' She looks guilty. 'Actually, it was my fault he packed his bags and walked out. I think I might have given him a piece of my mind.'

I grin. 'It was probably what he needed.'

'Yes, but the timing! One of the young waitresses had to go back to university, and we were scurrying about trying to make up for the shortfall, and there he was, twiddling his thumbs telling us all to get a move on...'

'I can look after Livvy for a couple of hours, if it's a problem,' I offer.

'No, it's fine, thanks. Her grandmother's back at the Big House now. You really shouldn't have had to do anything; you're a guest here, too. But I really appreciate it, thank you. We don't really need guests spreading the word about bad service before we've even got going! We'll see you tonight, for dinner. A lady is coming in to provide for our guests tonight.'

Grace is related to Noel, who owns all this. If so, I'm impressed by her willingness to get her hands dirty, so to speak, when she's possibly the heiress of what I understand to be a sizeable fortune. I know it's not my business, but I can't help being curious.

I dress for dinner with some apprehension. What should I wear? I didn't bring anything suitable to impress, which my mother would have insisted upon at a time like this, so I settle for the skirt and blouse I'd been wearing a couple of days before and add a warm cardigan. Sliding the clothes from the hangers makes me realise I should source a dry cleaner or buy some new clothes. I sniff the blouse warily. Dad used to say, *If you have to sniff it, wash it!* But he's not here and I didn't, so it will have to do.

I take my time getting ready. I shower then wrap myself in a big towel while I blow-dry my hair, turning the ends under into the pixie-cut style it's supposed to be. It's been a natural disaster since I got here, so I see a stranger staring back at me out of the mirror; someone I left behind in America. Wide-spaced eyes, generous mouth, slightly crooked nose from the accident – the pieces that make up my face are familiar but no longer feel like mine. I dab on a bit of make-up. When I've finished, I feel totally out of place in Roone Bay and wipe it off again.

I'm ready to go but slightly nervous at the thought of being a guest at the Big House. I don't know these people at all, really, and I'm thinking it might be a stress I don't need. Perhaps I should have gracefully declined the invitation, but Noel caught me off guard.

There's a soft knock on my door. I open it, and Grace is standing there, looking chic in a neat, short dress and a pair of kitten heels.

'Noel thought it would be easier for you if I brought you up to the house,' she says.

'Thank you.' I sigh with relief.

She smiles and pats my arm. 'We're only human, you know. I was once in awe, too. But trust me, beneath the wealth, Noel is still the poor boy who left Roone Bay to seek his fortune. Just be yourself. You'll be fine.'

.   .   .

The house is as posh as I expected it to be, but Noel and the four generations of women have me laughing within minutes. Grace's grandmother, Caitlin, particularly, has a knack of coming out with outrageously inappropriate comments, just the twinkle in her eye betraying her humour. Over a fairly basic but hearty family meal, I'm regaled with the bones of Noel's amazing success story and the bittersweet tale of his long-standing love for Caitlin.

'So, this is all going into the memoir?' I query.

Noel shakes his head. 'That's just between the family. The memoir will largely be about the Boston years and doing this place up when I returned to Roone Bay. Grace has most of it typed up. Now we just need to go through the photographs and brochures and choose which ones to use.' His grin is that of a teenager. 'I suspect the pictures will sell the book. Most people are voyeurs at heart, and I suspect they want to see what the inside of a millionaire's home looks like. I'm going to leave the place to the state when I die, which will bring more tourists into the hotel. It will benefit the whole of Roone Bay, I think. That will probably be the time for Grace, or whoever, to publish.'

I cast a surprised look at Caitlin, who smiles. 'Sure, what would I be wanting a huge place like this for? I'll be well provided for, if I don't go first, and that's in the hand of God. So, tell us about yourself. I understand you play the violin? You've certainly impressed Livvy.'

Olivia states, in a matter-of-fact voice: 'I can play the violin now, too. Erin showed me how.'

'You're a very quick learner,' I say.

'I know. That's what my teacher says.'

Grace rolls her eyes slightly, unseen by Olivia. 'Darling, it's not nice to brag.'

'It's not bragging if it's the truth, though, is it?'

'Sometimes,' Grace comments, 'you have to be a little bit

careful with the truth. Now, if you've finished, you can go and play with the dogs for half an hour before bed.'

Olivia pushes her chair back. 'Can we sleep here?'

'No, Dada Sean will be waiting for us, at home.' She glances at me as Olivia skips out. 'Sean is my second husband. Well, we're not married yet as my divorce hasn't gone through, so technically, we're living in sin.'

She doesn't look bothered about living in sin. I'm wondering how they get away with that in Ireland, when Caitlin gives a belly laugh and answers my unspoken query. 'It's surprising how wealth greases the wheels of acceptability. I was happy to live in sin with Noel, actually, but he insisted on us being married.'

'Less problem with probate if I go unexpectedly,' Noel states matter-of-factly. 'But we were interrogating Erin.' He turns to me. 'That's the reason I invited you to dinner, besides the fact that it's your birthday, of course.'

'Stop badgering the poor girl,' Caitlin says, but Noel ignores her.

'So, you play the violin, you told me. And Livvy told us Finn found one for you to play. Will you give us a tune some time?'

I find myself not wanting to lie to these people, who have welcomed me into their home, and admit, 'I'm not sure I can. I haven't played since the accident, when my husband Kenny died... I can't find the music, in here.' I tap my hand briefly on my chest.

'Ah, you poor dear,' Grace says and puts her hand over mine where it's resting back on the table. 'I can't imagine losing Sean. I'm sure your Kenny wouldn't have wanted you to give up something you love, though. It will probably come back when the time is right. But are you sure you're okay about giving Olivia lessons?'

I nod but add, 'I feel bad about encouraging her, though, when I'm not intending to stay here.'

'Have you made plans to leave?'

'No, I'm still hoping to find out a little about my forbears, Nellie Crowley in particular. I'd love to find out where she actually lived. Just to have the mental picture, you know?'

'I totally know, but we'll have to make sure you don't get all the details too soon,' Noel says with a faint grin. 'Not until the prodigal child has decided she wants to play the piano instead.'

Grace ignores his facetious comment. 'Her teacher asked today if you might do the lessons in school time, at the school? Maybe Friday afternoons, which is when the children have an *interest* hour.'

'What's that?'

'It basically means they can do what they like as long as it's got some educational value. Reading, music, craftwork...'

'Why would she ask me to do that?'

Grace looks too innocent as she replies, 'I have no idea.'

'Never mind that,' Noel says. 'We're off topic. I'm curious to know what you've found out about your Nellie, so far.'

I explain to him about Grandpa's stories that were handed down and about the bible containing the few dates and facts. I tell them about Nellie arriving in Boston to find William had already died and then apparently losing her daughter on the docks, adding, 'I don't really know if that's true. I wonder if she actually died and *losing* is a euphemism for *dying*. But she didn't write in a date for Annie's death.'

Grace puts her hand to her mouth, and I realise the story has touched her on a personal level. The child would have been about the same age as Olivia. 'I can't imagine...' she says. 'Oh, that poor woman. What she must have suffered.'

'And the child, losing her mother? She must have been terrified,' I add. 'It doesn't bear thinking on, does it? But I can't forget it, because it's that lack of knowledge that bothers me most. I mean, how could Nellie carry on and cope, never knowing what happened? Of course, she had to cope, for her son, Luke, but still. I'd really like to know the truth, but I'm not sure if I ever will. And I'm not sure why I thought I'd find it in Ireland, actually.'

The chatter shifted away from Nellie's story, onto more mundane and present matters, and although Noel had joked about grilling me, that was the one thing they didn't do. After a while I simply felt at ease, welcomed into their little family unit.

20

ERIN

Noel and Caitlin invite me to join them for a nightcap, but I make my excuses and leave when Grace does. It's not late, but Olivia is yawning widely, and I suspect Grace is a force to be reckoned with when it comes to arguing about bedtimes. She, I understand, is still in the honeymoon period with Sean, the new love of her life, and young enough to be enjoying it in every sense of the word.

I'd heard a little of Noel and Caitlin's haunting love story, too. They had met again recently after a lifetime apart. They betray that delicious spark of unspoken communication rarely seen in younger lovers, who are still consumed by their more physical needs. I imagine them sitting together on a sofa, their closeness all the more poignant for the diminishing years that lie before them.

I like to think Kenny and I would have been like that, growing old together in comfortable companionship. I've seen various friends bounce through partners, going from fiery attraction to indifference or even passionate hatred. They were so consumed by their need to love and be loved that they forgot to be friends somewhere along the way. Kenny was my friend before he became my lover, and when we finally realised how right we were for each other, it was a magical union, less passionate than tender. That's why I feel his loss so desperately. The friends who gathered around, trying to protect me from grief, had never known love like that.

One Christmas, we were sitting before a tree that Kenny had decorated with just red and silver – he loved an artistic theme on a tree, rather than piling on everything, as I would have done – and he asked me, seriously, if he was enough, whether I thought I might get bored with him in the end. It didn't occur to me that I might never get to find out. But at the time I searched for the right words. Our hands were linked, our shoulders touching, when I told him: *It's like everyone else, even friends and relatives, are itinerant actors, drifting onto our stage, saying their lines, then slipping back into the wings. We're alone in our togetherness, and no one will ever understand just how enough that is.*

Of course, I was a bit tipsy at the time, but there are some precious moments in life that remain glued firmly in the memory. That was our last Christmas together, and I've been alone on my empty stage ever since.

It's too early to go and shut myself in my room, and the night is clear, the darkness filled with stars twinkling like fairy lights. The shushing of the sea in the distance is magical, and I find being alone isn't so wounding now as it has been. The people here are becoming more familiar, this place less a temporary stage than an affirmation that I'm still alive.

I've wandered down the hill, and I'm halfway up the other side when I hear the faint sound of Irish music coming from Nancy's bar. I'm drawn to it, as if Kenny's ghost is quietly pushing from behind. I take a step towards the door then hesitate. What if everyone looks at me as I enter? I don't think I could bear that. Then the door is thrust open, and two youths come out, laughing as they barge accidentally into me.

'Oh, pardon me, ma'am,' one says and pushes his back against the door, holding it open. He's so polite I feel obliged to say thank you and slip past him into the semi-darkness.

The pub, dark and shadowed by moonlight outside, is heaving inside. I slide between the packed bodies and eventually stand with my back to a wall, hugging a glass of white wine. A few people glance at me curiously, and I suspect this bar is populated mostly by people who know each other.

There are five musicians: two older men with a bodhrán and a button box respectively, a woman with a fiddle, a young man with a guitar and Finn with his concertina. They're seated around a circular table laid thick with glasses of black porter in various stages of consumption. The reel they're playing is almost frantic, except that every note is clearly defined by familiarity. There's no physical signal that I see, but they move seamlessly from one tune to another, like a school of fish turning in unison. The key notches up, injecting a swirl of glee into the atmosphere.

There are a few feet tapping intermittently, but everyone is talking so loudly I think they aren't really listening. When the set comes to an abrupt end, though, there seems to be a pause in the chatter as heads tilt with anticipation. It's background music but not audible wallpaper. Rather, it's something that exists in their collective cultural psyche, comfortable and familiar as the countryside; something they see every day and wouldn't comment on unless it disappeared.

The musicians play a few more sets, some of which I recognise from my Irish connections in Boston. Jigs, hornpipes, set dances... No one claps, and the musicians snatch a gulp of drink and exchange some banter between tunes.

Then Finn tickles a few stray buttons, and something in the atmosphere changes. Anticipation. He begins a slow air that, after a few notes, sends a shiver of coldness down my spine. There are a few *shushing* whispers, and within moments, the conversation has petered out, the whole bar like deep, still water. Glasses hang on lips, feet stop moving, dialogue drifts away. The tune Finn plays is haunting, beautiful and heartrending, and it seems to speak of tragedy.

The guitarist joins in softly. Where, before, he had been thrumming a rhythm, he now picks out lone harmonics. Then the woman starts to sing, softly, in Irish, her voice high and sweet, and time is suspended. There's a hint of melancholy and pathos in her voice, and something about the soft almost *shushing* sound of the words makes me truly wish I spoke the language. I thought Irish wasn't spoken much any longer, but from the expressions of sadness around me, I must surely be wrong.

Finn has his eyes closed, but as the final notes hang on the air and fade, they flick open, and a smile of satisfaction hits the corners of his mouth, his unspoken applause directed at the singer.

As his eyes stray around the bar, they find mine and widen.

He puts his concertina down and stands. He leans over and says something to the girl, who nods and picks up her fiddle. As she takes another tune away, he weaves through the crowd towards me. It's then I realise that my face is wet with tears. I don't know if I'm crying because the music was so beautiful, because I miss playing or miss Kenny. Perhaps it's all these things combined.

I put my nearly empty glass onto the bar and swipe my face with the back of my hand. Without a word, Finn takes my arm, pushes open the door and steers me down the road towards the harbour, where we stand in silence for a moment.

'I'm sorry,' I say. 'I didn't mean to make a spectacle of myself.'

'Don't be. Yours weren't the only tears in the bar, and emotion is the best tribute of all for musicians.'

'I couldn't understand the words, but I knew it was sad.'

He nods. 'That song was "The Lone Rock",' he says eventually. '"Carraig Aonair" in Irish. The story is: two brothers and their brother-in-law went out fishing in their little boat a few days before Christmas to get fish for their Christmas dinner. It was a deceptive calm, and a storm struck unexpectedly. Their boat was dashed to pieces and they swam to the rock, out there.' He points across the dark flood of water, towards the faintly blinking light of the Fastnet Rock lighthouse. 'There wasn't a lighthouse on it then. The men managed to clamber up onto the rock, but the tide was coming in. No one knew what had happened to them, until the rudder from the boat was washed ashore a couple of weeks later, and on it one of the men had scratched the tale of how they had waited, hoping for rescue, but no one knew they were there, and no one came.'

'That's a really sad story,' I say.

'It's a true story. Someone wrote it into a poem, and another set it to a tune,' he says quietly. 'Though it was a hundred years ago, everyone in that room, just now, has grieved for the death of those men over and over, and for the father who would never see his sons again. The song is, in fact, a lament sung by the father of the two boys. He tells his daughter to put her grief aside, as she'll one day find another husband, but his grief is forever as he will never have any more sons. You wept, hearing the tragedy in the music, and now you know why.'

I shiver and clutch my arms around me. Tragedy seems to permeate this place, and it resonates. We stand in silence for a moment, imagining the last, dreadful hours of those men, united by love, waiting for the sea to engulf them, scratching a message for the uncaring water to take home to their family. I wonder, then, whether it really was better that they knew what happened than to remain in ignorance. Finn's arm is strong, lending me comfort, and I realise how much I've missed the physical comfort Kenny used to provide.

'Irish music isn't just "fast diddly stuff" as some say,' he explains after a long moment. 'It tells stories. It immortalises Irish history: the legends of the fairies; the ancient tales of Cú Chulainn, the Irish hero; stories about death, famine and emigration; and also love and the overwhelming joy of being alive. The Irish have an enormous capacity to keep going in the face of great odds. You felt that. I could see it written on your face.'

His words hang on the cool air.

'Can I tell you something?' I ask. 'About the accident, when Kenny died?'

'Of course.'

'The last thing I remembered before waking up in hospital was the overwhelming physical thumps of other vehicles slamming into us, again and again. I was shaken like a pinball in a machine. I remember my head banging into Kenny's, then into the side window, the cut of the seat belt as I flipped forward and smashed into the dashboard, before the explosion of impact knocked me out. There was never any doubt that the semi-truck was going to slam into us; I just prayed to God that, somehow, we would survive.'

I felt as if the universe was silent, listening.

'When I awoke in the hospital, my mother was sitting by the bed, dozing. I must have made a noise, or moved, because she jolted and shouted to the nurse: *She's awake! Help, someone, she's awake!* I thought that was a strange thing for her to say, at the time, until I learned that I'd been in a coma for over a week. Then I was told that Kenny was dead, and I knew that my life would never be the same again. But I think I already knew. There was a kind of silence around me, a profound emptiness in the space where he had been.'

I shiver. Finn puts his arm around my shoulder and exerts a tiny pressure, sharing my pain.

'My father wanted to sue the haulage contractor, but after the inquest we learned that the driver of the semi-truck had had a massive stroke and died at the wheel, so really it was nobody's fault. There were two other deaths and about thirty people injured. It had taken the police and firemen the whole night to extract everyone from the crumpled wrecks and get the traffic moving again.'

'I can't imagine,' he says softly after a moment.

I carried on, getting it all out into the open as I have never done before. 'I was in the hospital for a while, but when I was discharged, I couldn't go back home to our empty house. I went back to Mom and Dad.' I give a little laugh. 'Mom tried to cheer me up. She said, *Well, at least your hands weren't damaged.* She didn't know, but it was those words that stopped me from playing again. It just felt so unfair. There were many times I wished it had been me who had died, not Kenny.'

'But then Kenny would be struggling to rediscover a future without you, and that wouldn't have been fair on him,' Finn commented.

'No, and Kenny didn't even have family to support him, as I had. Anyway, I had nightmares. That's why I went on the happy pills. Every moment I wasn't actively engaged in thinking about something specific, the moment of seeing the semi-truck sliding towards us wound into my mind on endless replay. I relived it, over and over, wondering what I might have done that was different but always came back to the knowledge that I did exactly what I could do, which was brake hard and watch the tragedy roll towards me.'

'It was just one of those things. An accident of fate. Being in the wrong place at the wrong time.'

'But I blamed myself, don't you see? Because I was driving. And I wasn't the only one. The truck driver's wife had a breakdown when she learned that not only was her husband dead but he'd ruined the lives of other families, too. She felt guilty on his behalf because he wasn't there to be guilty for himself. Stupid, eh?'

'She must have been a good woman.'

I take a deep breath. 'It was Dad who told me to pull myself together. He said I'd wallowed in my grief for long enough, I was lucky to be alive and it was an insult to Kenny if I didn't get on and make the most of it.' I laugh lightly. 'He made me furious at the time, but a few days later I realised he was right. My time with Kenny had been a gift, and I should remember his life not his death.'

'That took courage. It can't have been so simple.'

'Not simple at all but necessary. One day I threw the anti-depressant pills away and sacked the therapist. I boxed up Kenny's paintings and put them into storage. I might be able to look at them one day, but not yet. And then I told my family I was going to Ireland.'

I sense Finn smile. 'And that went down well?'

'Not at all! But I had to get away from everywhere I had been with Kenny. I needed to be able to walk out of the house without all the little memories driving in to haunt me.'

'That was brave.'

'Or stupid,' I say, remembering that night, on the beach. 'I'm getting cold. I should go back,' I say eventually.

He turns me to face him, his hands on my shoulders. He bends his head towards me and kisses me gently. And as if he knows exactly what I was thinking, he whispers against my lips, 'You chose to live, Erin.'

I close my eyes, thinking about Kenny watching. 'I think I have, after all.'

A faint trickle of interest stirs inside me at Finn's touch. I'm needy, starved of physical contact and jolted with desire at the merest breath of a kiss. I wait for guilt to flood in, but it doesn't.

When I open my eyes, his are staring straight into mine, maybe reassured by what he sees there. He smiles, takes my hand and we head up the road in companionable silence.

At the door of the hotel, he says, 'I want to hear you play, Erin. If you have music in your soul, don't let it die for want of sustenance. Kenny wouldn't want that. Sleep well.'

21

ERIN

I sleep like a log, in fact, and wake late, feeling as though a little of the weight of grief has been lifted from my shoulders. I touch my lips with my fingertips and wait for the feeling of guilt to flood in, but it doesn't. Finn kissed me, and Kenny's presence is growing fainter.

I didn't come to Roone Bay seeking a new relationship. If anyone had asked, it was the last thing I was seeking. But perhaps not looking for love is the best way to discover it. I'm not going to convince myself that that's what it is with Finn – it's far too soon. But the barriers have descended enough to allow for the possibility. It is time I let go of Kenny, and I think he would approve. He wouldn't want me to die of love, like women do in the old ballads. He would want me to live life to the full.

Maybe I've negotiated one of those mystical hurdles my therapist mentioned. *One hurdle at a time. You'll be surprised, one day, when you wake up and find that you still have something to give, something to live for.* That was all the help she ever gave me, actually. Mostly the therapy sessions were me venting about the unfairness of life, and leaving without any hint of how I was supposed to move on.

Grace looks happy when I bump into her downstairs.

'Did you enjoy meeting my family yesterday?'

'Absolutely,' I say and mean it.

'I have to apologise for the third degree. It's what people thrive on down here. There's little enough to do except gossip.'

'You're not Irish yourself, though?'

'Born and bred in England, but all four of my grandparents were Irish, so I've got an Irish passport. Apparently, that makes me Irish, but I'm going to marry an Irishman when my divorce is finalised, which kind of seals the deal!'

'I guess I'm American through and through, despite some of my forebears coming from here.'

'It's not always in the genes. We have people drifting in from other nations, England, Holland, Germany and further east, who come here for a visit and stay because they feel that they belong.'

I can understand that. I felt like an absolute alien when I arrived, but in just a short time, this place has its claws into me, and I don't think it has anything to do with my somewhat diluted Irish ancestry.

She changes the subject. 'Well, actually, I came to tell you some good news. 'Yesterday we interviewed a young woman from Cork. We all liked her instantly, and Noel asked her to start in the hotel after Christmas. She has to work her notice, and we're already heading towards November.'

'As manager?'

'No, unfortunately. She's keen but doesn't have that kind of experience. She'll be an administrative assistant and general dogsbody, so can at least take the pressure off my mother and myself, but who knows where that will go? And I have a chef coming in to interview next week. Again, he's young and worked in a restaurant, so he's inexperienced in managing a kitchen this big. But he's keen too and has all the right qualifications. He won't have much to do, though, until the spring, as we have very few bookings this side of Christmas.'

'Maybe you could offer cheaper meals to the locals for a few months, give him a chance to practise? I'm sure the residents of Roone Bay would love the opportunity to come in and check the place out. You could do tours. Explain how the hotel is going to help local businesses, offer it to them as a venue, maybe. What about a pre-Christmas party? Have a bit of live music? You could open the bar, and the restaurant is big enough if all the seating was pushed back.'

Grace freezes for a moment then says, surprised, 'I never thought of doing any of that. Perhaps next year, though. I was just seeing this place as a hotel not a venue for functions. I'll put it to Noel. Meanwhile, we do have a party arriving this afternoon. They were supposed to arrive yesterday, but apparently there was a problem with the flight, and they're driving down from Shannon as we speak, so I'll need to be here for when they arrive. Will you be around later?'

'I don't have any plans...' I say questioningly.

'Well, after school, Sean's going to drop Livvy here, so maybe I could tell him to bring her violin? She's really enjoying her lessons.'

'Sure, absolutely,' I say, surprising myself by meaning it.

'Oh, and Noel usually pops over in the afternoons. Maybe you'd like to put your suggestions to him yourself?'

'It was right off the top of my head. I hadn't really given it any thought.'

'Well,' she says, with a bright smile, 'you have time to give it some, then! But only if you want to, of course.'

I laugh and shake my head. 'I'm popping down to the library, see if anyone has responded to my plea for information. I'll be back after lunch.'

'Didn't you say Finn was helping with your search?'

'Well, I don't really know if he's interested, and I don't want to pressure him into helping me.'

She nods. 'That's kind. He's struggling at the moment, after what happened, you know.'

'What happened?'

She flushes a little. 'Oh, I assumed you knew. Well, I've said that much now, and it's no secret, after all. You know he's a coastguard and also a volunteer on the lifeboat? He might not have told you, though, that he's also on the dive rescue team. It comes with the territory, I guess. A yacht foundered off the coast a few months ago. There was an unexpected summer squall that raged inward from the Atlantic like a steam train. It only lasted an hour, but it flattened everything – crops, trees, even roofs went. It was dreadful.

'It had been broadcast, and the couple on the boat were trying to get to safe harbour but were inexperienced, from what I understand. They broadsided onto the rocks at Baltimore Beacon. Before the lifeboat could even launch, the keel hit the rocks and the yacht foundered. The mast broke, and the boat turned turtle. That close to the shore, the waves were terrific so the lifeboat couldn't get near them until the blast faded out. The couple drowned. Finn was one of the team who dived down to see if the yacht could be recovered.' She grimaces. 'When Finn accessed the cabin, he found a child. A little boy. It hit him hard.'

'Oh, for pity's sake,' I exclaim. 'Poor Finn. No wonder he's distracted! That would hit anyone. It must have been devastating for him. And that poor child, all alone in the cabin...' I'm nearly choked with an onslaught of emotion. 'Those poor parents, struggling to survive, knowing their child was below. What a horrible tragedy all around.'

'It was. It affected everyone, for miles. People buy these expensive yachts as if they're motorhomes and haven't a clue how dangerous the sea can be.'

'Isn't there some kind of, like, boat driving licence?'

'No. There are rules about having a radio, what to do in harbours and all that, and which side to pass on, but in reality, anyone can buy a boat and just take it out.'

'That's crazy!'

'I think so. It puts the lives of so many others in danger when they get into difficulties.' She shakes her head. 'Finn said he was all right at the time, but the next time the lifeboat siren went, he was shaking so much that the captain didn't let him go out. The coastguard service gave him time off and marked it down to post-traumatic stress.'

22

ERIN

I walk down to the library to return some books and find that last night's calm has spread into the day. The sea, which had looked black under the stars, now reflects a clear blue sky. When it's mild, as it is today, it's difficult to imagine storms and rough seas sending cascades of waves exploding against the shore. It's like trying to imagine the chill of winter snow when you're dressed for the beach in summer. I never used to be so concerned about weather, but the tragedy that consumes Finn highlights the very real and present danger of the Atlantic and her unpredictable temper.

I'd read about dreadful tragedies in the past, when mussel collectors in Boston Bay were drowned by the incoming tide, but it was like ancient history. Thinking about it now, I'm sure people must still collect mussels there. I feel guilty for eating mussels in fancy restaurants without a thought to those people. I was living my magical life with Kenny, consumed by our respective arts, planning a safe future that never happened.

The lady at the library smiles as I enter. The severe look she'd given me when I arrived in Roone Bay has given way to one of recognition.

'I put your notice up,' she says, indicating the board, 'and it's generated some interest, but no one, so far, has offered any clues at all. But I saved these for you.' From under the counter, she pulls out a few small publications. 'These are of local interest, for background information, even if it's not what you're looking for. They were written many years after the famine, in the early 1900s, but the photographs are fascinating, if nothing else. They still show what it was like here back in the day. Things didn't change so fast, then.'

'Thank you,' I say, flicking through one. The grainy images are of women and girls in ankle-length dresses and stout boots, all wearing beribboned hats, and men and boys in jackets, waist-coats and flat caps, leading donkeys and carts. There are no pavements. The shopfronts sit straight on the side of the road. 'Wow. And is that Roone Bay harbour?'

She peers closely. 'It is indeed. And see how tiny those fishing boats are? With oars, and nets to throw over the side.' She shakes her head again in bewilderment, as if this has all happened in her lifetime.

'Anyway, how's your stay going so far?'

I tell her about having dinner with Noel and his family up at the Big House, and her brows rise. I don't think I'm so far out in my suggestion to Grace that the locals have doubts about Noel's enterprise and that something needs to be done to change that perception. I add, 'I honestly think my forebears' history is going to remain out of reach, but I've met so many wonderful people, it doesn't seem to matter.'

She nods, taking the compliment as her due. 'Well, I'm pleased to help if I can. If anything turns up, I'll let you know.'

'Thank you.'

I walk back out into the morning. There's a clothes shop in the high street, where I buy some jeans and a fleece for warmth, but the rest of the clothes are so dated they look as if they've been there for twenty years. I'm not as concerned about fashion as my parents, but modern fashions certainly haven't found their way to Roone Bay. But then, that's part of the charm of this place. It's like stepping back in time.

I'm enjoying being out and about. I spend too much time in the hotel, so I order a solitary cup of coffee in the local café, while perusing one of the publications the librarian gave me. People – strangers – nod to me as they pass the window, which is strange. In Boston, I wouldn't make eye contact with someone I didn't know. But then, everyone here probably knows who I am as I'm possibly the only foreigner in the place.

Then the bell rings, and Finn comes in.

I beam a welcome, and he responds with a lopsided quirk of the lips. 'May I join you?'

I wave at the empty seat and smile. 'Of course.'

'How are you this morning?'

'Fine. Really.'

He orders tea and scones, and pushes one in front of me when the girl brings them over. 'Carbohydrates are better than happy pills. You're less likely to get hooked on them, too.'

'I don't need happy pills.'

'No, actually, today you just look beautiful.'

Woah. Where did that come from? I flush a little and bend to scrabble in my bag, hiding my face for a moment. I pull out Nellie's bible. 'I was hoping to see you, actually. I told you about Nellie's bible. I've been carrying it around with me just in case. I thought you might like to see it.'

He wipes his hand on his jeans and takes it, reverently, and opens it to the family tree in the front.

'That's all there is, really. Everything else is verbal, stories from my grandpa.'

'Stories are history come to life,' he says, responding to my apologetic tone. 'Never mind the politics. Real history is made by ordinary people, like you and me. Your Nellie actually lived. This bible was in her hands. That makes it special.'

He runs a finger down the list.

'That shows the direct male line, from Nellie, who was born in 1824, then Nellie's son, Luke, all the way down to Dad,' I say unnecessarily, because it's obvious. 'The bible was given to her by a Mrs Becker, in 1849 – see the inscription? She must have backtracked a little, to put her parents in.'

He nods, agreeing, then says thoughtfully, 'But that's strange...'

'What's strange?'

He taps the faded ink. 'I assume that's Nellie's handwriting. It's a little immature, as if she learned to write later in life. She's entered her parents' births, marriage and dates of death, and below her name, she's put in her children, Luke and Annie. Then she notes Luke's marriage in 1863, to Sarah. See, she'd got better at writing? Then Patrick, her grandson is born also in 1863, and Luke dies two years later, in 1865, at only nineteen. That's tragic! There are no further dates for Annie, which is understandable. Then the births of your grandfather and your father are entered in by a different person – see the handwriting changes? It's the same hand for Nellie's death in 1894, which is the last entry.'

'No one bothered to keep it up,' I say.

'True, but I wonder why Nellie didn't note Gabriel's birth, because she still would have been alive then. You'd think Nellie's death would be where the handwriting changed.'

'Goodness,' I say. 'I've looked at this so many times but never noticed! You're right.'

'That means Nellie was alive for ten years or so after ceasing to make entries.'

'Maybe she had gone blind. That wasn't so uncommon, what with cataracts and the like,' I suggest diffidently.

'Or maybe she'd simply lost the will to keep doing it,' Finn suggests.

'That would be sad. But it doesn't sound like the dauntless

spirit I'd come to accept as Nellie's. It's not a complete record, which is a shame, but they ran out of space on the page, I guess. Grandpa had siblings, and none of them are in there, either. Just the direct male line to Dad.'

'It was a time when only the male line was important – for inheritance purposes.'

He closes the bible and pushes it towards me. 'Better put it away before we get butter on it. I think your grandfather would be pleased to know it's ended up in your hands. Complete or not, it's something to treasure.'

I nod. 'It's amazing that Dad didn't throw it in the bin. I suspect he's wishing he did now!'

'Well, if it's the bible that brought you here, I'm glad he didn't.'

'It wasn't just that,' I admit. 'My grandpa was good at telling stories. Too good. Sometimes I wasn't sure whether he was making them up. But he wasn't making up the story about Nellie emigrating and William's death and Annie getting lost. He told me several times, like he was wondering what happened, too, and it was almost the same words each time.'

'I think I would have liked your grandpa.'

'I think you would have liked him better than my dad,' I say wryly.

'Well, if push comes to shove, I'm interested in you, not your dad.'

'Oh,' I say, at a loss for words, and warmth floods my cheeks again.

'So, let's demolish the scones,' he says, extending an arm and twisting his wrist to check his watch. 'Because I have to go to the city for work. I don't know how long for.'

When we leave, we stand outside the tea shop for a moment. I feel a little awkward, not quite knowing how to say goodbye. Then Finn's eyes meet mine intently. 'Look after yourself, okay? Don't go getting depressed when I'm not here to help.'

'I'll try not to,' I say, laughing.

Then he bends his head and kisses me again. It's not fleeting, as it had been last night. His lips are warm and soft, lingering just a little before he steps back to assess me quizzically, deciding, perhaps, that as I didn't back off, it was okay.

It was.

23

ERIN

When I finally head back up to the hotel after lunch, there's a big car out the front, almost a small bus. I assume Grace's guests have arrived.

Grace is at the desk, and she's on the phone but frantically waves to me. I stop and wait. 'It's your parents,' she hisses. 'They wanted to surprise you, but I'm thinking you'd rather be forewarned.'

'My parents?' I repeat, shocked. 'Here?'

She nods. 'I'm to tell them when you come back in and bring a tray to the table, over there, by the window.'

'Oh, good Lord,' I mutter. 'What on earth are they doing here?'

'Apparently, they were going to come for your birthday, but the plane was delayed.'

I give a faint smile. 'Well, thank goodness for small mercies.' She grins conspiratorially as I add, 'I got to spend my birthday with your family, which was so nice!'

'We enjoyed it, too. Grandma likes you, which is always the clincher around here. So, shall I put the call through?'

'Give me half an hour,' I say. 'I'll go and freshen up and try to get myself psyched up for the event.'

'That bad, eh?' she commiserates.

'I love them to bits, but...' I hesitate and tell the truth. 'To be honest, I came here to get away from them. They were fussing over me, wrapping me in sympathy because of Kenny, you know, and it wasn't helping.'

'No,' she says ruminatively. 'No, I guess it wouldn't have. Come down in your own time, and I'll call them when you give me the nod. I think your mother is sleeping, anyway. Jet lag, she says.'

'That would be about right. She never travels well. Give it a couple of hours. Will I be able to order a pre-dinner drink?'

'Of course. Anything to grease the wheels.'

I laugh and head upstairs. I lie on my bed for a bit, read, then shower, dry my hair, make up my face, and put on the skirt and blouse I'd worn the other day, wishing I'd brought something a bit smarter. I'm startled by the thought. I hadn't felt the need to dress to impress for Noel's birthday dinner invitation, but I do for my own parents. How strange.

When I'm ready, I look at myself in the mirror and see a stranger. It hits me that I didn't look like this with Kenny, at home, either. The person I see is the one my parents want me to be, not the one I rediscovered here in Roone Bay. I'm almost tempted to change back into jeans and scrub my face clean, but envisage my mother's disappointed remarks about keeping up appearances. It's just not worth the aggro.

I'm dithering, when I suddenly recall Livvy and the violin. I don't want to disappoint her. I rush downstairs to find her sitting quietly, waiting, the case beside her. She beams as I come in, then her jaw drops. 'Oh,' she says. 'You don't look like you any longer.'

I see Grace about to reprimand her, so I say quickly, in a

pretend whisper, 'I don't feel like me, either, but you see, my mom and dad are here.'

She nods seriously. 'My daddy in England always made me dress nicely, but Dada Sean says dirt is good for me.'

'Dada Sean is right,' I say. 'But perhaps we won't tell my parents that I agree with you? So, will you play for me?'

While she tightens the bow and rosins it, I check the tuning then hand the violin to her. 'So, show me what you've got, buster!'

Grinning, she tucks the violin under her chin and starts to play. But she doesn't just play the first two stanzas; she plays the whole tune, scraping the bow its full length for each note, the timing perfect, the level of sound ear-bending.

I clap, my brows rising with pleasure. 'Wow, you clever thing! You worked it out!'

'I did,' she says. 'All on my own. The middle bit is the same, two times, then the first bit again. Now I want to learn another tune.'

I hadn't thought we'd get there so soon. I rack my brains.

'Do you know "Hush Little Baby, Don't You Cry"?'

She shakes her head.

'Really?' I thought all children knew that, but perhaps not here, in Ireland. 'How about I play you the tune first, then we can learn it. I can write it all out for you for tomorrow. Your teacher wants me to come to school for interest hour.'

'Yes, I know. And Bobby and Colm are bringing in their daddy's fiddle to learn.'

Ah. Mrs Daly's request for me to go into the school begins to make sense. I'm not sure I like having been manipulated, but Olivia, and presumably the boys too, will be disappointed if I don't turn up. I sigh. 'Okay, so this is the song.' I play it through slowly a couple of times, singing the words as I play.

Hush little baby, don't say a word

Papa's gonna buy you a mockingbird

'You can sing and play at the same time,' she says, impressed.

'It just takes a bit of practice, that's all.'

'I'm going to do that.'

'Great. I can write the words down for you to learn, too, but we can just do it with the first two lines, because the rest are all to the same tune.'

'Yes, but what's a mockingbird?'

'It's a bird that imitates the sound of another bird, like making fun of it, or maybe just because it likes the tune.'

'Okay.'

I talk her through the simple two-line melody. 'D, A, A, B, A, G, G. Open string, first finger...'

She's a quick study and after a few tries has both lines.

'It's a great tune to learn with, because once you know where to put your fingers, you can play the tune starting on any one of the first three strings. That's G, D and A.' I point at them as I'm talking, then take the little fiddle off her and show her each of the variations. 'That means you can practise making the same tune on all the strings.'

A slow clap starts behind me, and I swivel to see Dad clapping, and Mom and... *Oh, shit.* Scott. What on earth is he here for? Scott is more handsome than ever, with his clean-cut all-American-boy appearance that I find just slightly too plastic. He's never got a hair out of place, or a zit or a scratch from shaving, like a model who has just stepped off the podium. Dad is leading the way, Mom and Scott trailing in his wake like ducklings, all wearing professional smiles, as if auditioning for parts in a film.

'Right,' I say to Livvy. 'You had better pack that away and practise at home, eh? And when I come into school we can go through it again together.'

'Okay. But is that your mum and dad?'

'It is.'

'Your dad's got a very posh suit. Like my first daddy wears. Your mum is very pretty.'

'Yes, she is.'

Overhearing, Mom preens slightly.

'And who is that other man?'

'Scott Freel.'

'Is he your husband?'

I flush slightly. 'No, he's not. He works for my father.'

'With your father,' Scott corrects gently.

But in my book, when Dad does the hiring and firing of his employees, I don't think I'm wrong. Scott's not a partner yet, even if he's got his eye on the ball. He takes my shoulders and leans in, presenting his clean-shaven cheek to mine as if he has the absolute right to do so. His aftershave is overwhelming. I perform an air kiss and take a minute step back as soon as I can.

I give Mom a hug. 'Great surprise! But what on earth are you doing here?'

'Well, honey,' Mom says, 'we should have been here for your birthday, but the plane was cancelled, so we spent the evening in a hotel rather than drive home again. What a bind! I didn't call, because I wanted to surprise you. I expect you thought we'd forgotten!'

'As if, darling,' Dad says, patting me on the shoulder before turning to Olivia. 'And who is this charming little lady?'

He sure knows how to butter people up.

'I'm Livvy Adams, but when Mummy marries Sean, I'm going to be Livvy Murphy,' Olivia states.

'How very Irish,' Dad says, sarcasm barely audible in his voice.

I love my father, of course, but sometimes I wonder why.

'Yes,' Olivia says. 'And Erin is teaching me to play the fiddle. I'm going to be good, like her, one day.'

'Are you now,' Dad says and turns to me with a slight crease between the brows. 'And how long will that take?'

'Oh, she's a quick study,' I say with a faint smile.

'So, honey, how are you doing, really?' Mom asks, meaning, am I over Kenny yet.

'I'm fine, Mom, really. I've met some lovely people. Grace here' – I point to Grace, who is hovering behind them – 'brought me up for a meal at the Big House last night so I wasn't alone for my birthday. They're all very kind.'

'The Big House?'

'It's what they call the manor, up behind the hotel.'

'And who are *they*?' she asks pointedly.

'Noel O'Donovan and Caitlin own the hotel here and Roone House, up behind it. Grace is his granddaughter, and Olivia here is his great-granddaughter.'

Mom does a double take at Grace, immediately understanding the implication that this pretty woman should be treated with a little more respect than a mere employee. 'Hi, Grace,' she says, holding her hand out regally. 'We're so pleased to meet you.'

I want to cringe, but Grace isn't fazed at all. 'Pleased to meet you, too. We're really enjoying having Erin stay with us. Now, let me get you all some refreshments. Will it be coffee or an aperitif?'

'Martinis all around,' Dad says before Mom can open her mouth. 'We need to drink to Erin's future, don't we?'

Grace's eyes hit mine briefly, then she hands over a menu. 'And if we could take your orders for dinner? We're a bit short-staffed at the moment, so if you'd indulge me?'

What could they say but 'of course'?

Grace fetches the drinks, puts a dish of nibbles on the table and holds out her hand to Olivia. 'Come on, Livvy. I'm going to take you up to stay with Grandma until Dada Sean can pick you up after work.'

Olivia casts an irritated glance at her mother, but even as her bottom lip starts to jut out, she realises the futility of arguing and does as she's told.

'What an obedient child,' Dad says after the door has closed behind them. That, in his opinion, is high praise.

There's a brief silence as none of us can think of anything to say, then Mom exclaims and reaches into her handbag, pulling out a present wrapped in silver paper. 'From all of us,' she says.

I open it to find a pair of exquisite diamond earrings.

'Put them on, then,' Mom says gleefully. I do, and she preens towards Dad. 'I said they would suit her. Didn't I?'

'You did,' he says complacently. Then, to me: 'So, tell us what you've been getting up to?'

I briefly outline my search in the library and on local gravestones, and explain my curiosity about the strange stone Finn showed me. I pull out the transcript from my purse and read it out. *'Thomas and Mary Crowley, d. 1846, who sacrificed themselves that my children could live. Your loving daughter, Nellie, 1885.'*

'Did this Thomas and Mary have other children?' Mom asks. 'Might one of them have put it there?'

'I don't know, but it's signed Nellie. That's the strange thing. It's a mystery, eh?'

'And you're sure she never came back to Ireland?'

'No, I'm not sure. But if she did, I can't find anything about her locally. And you saw the diary. She stayed in Boston until she died, from what I gather.'

'Well, it's all in the past,' Dad says, as if that's the last word on the subject, but Scott seems interested.

'Did you bring the bible with you? You've never shown it to me.'

'Oh. Yes. It's up in my room. I'll go and get it.'

'I'll come with you,' he says.

Mom and Dad exchange a knowing smile, but actually, I'm

pleased. It's the first time Scott has shown any interest in the subject of my ancestry.

'We can take the stairs,' I suggest as he heads for the elevator. 'It's only two flights. I'm at the top.'

I lead the way and open the door to my room. We're hit by a blast of fresh air. I love the Juliet balcony and the scent of the sea, but Scott goes straight to the window and pulls it shut.

'It's like the Arctic up here,' he complains. 'Good view, but our rooms are better appointed.'

'Bigger, you mean? I like it up here, and it's not as if I need more space.'

I reach for the bible, which is beside my bed, and hand it to him. I don't read it at night, but I keep it there because Nellie feels closer to me, as if she's willing me to find her story and expose some long-kept secret. I wonder if she was ever able to read the good book herself. From what I gather, poor people of her generation in Ireland mostly spoke Irish first and English second, and often weren't literate in either language.

'Well, if you're happy, that's all that matters,' Scott says.

He's looking a little uneasy and doesn't so much as glance at the bible, so I say, 'Come on, Scott. Spit it out. Have you fallen out with the parents or something?'

He's startled. 'Absolutely not. It's just, well, I spoke to your father recently.'

He pulls out a small box and proffers it to me.

Now I understand why Mom bought the diamonds, which are a perfect foil for the ring.

'Darling, will you marry me?'

24

NELLIE 1850S

After Nellie had arrived to work in the Beckers' home, Kate had spoken to Mrs Thompson, the housekeeper, who had told the mistress, who had begged her husband to enquire about Annie to the authorities. He did so, but his enquiries proved fruitless. But that, too, was useful as the mistress discovered a slight compassion for the new scullery maid who had lost her husband and her daughter, and instructed the housekeeper to elevate her to kitchen maid, which provided her with a few more pennies – as if that could compensate her for the loss of her child! But it was a kindness that Nellie would store away in her mind like a treasured gift as she worked and watched and learned.

All the same, it was hard to be in the posh house, cleaning, doing chores, saying little to anyone except *yes ma'am, no ma'am*, when occasion demanded, bobbing humbly as she had been taught. She felt guilty that Danny was still doing hard, dirty work, building railways, and that her own son was living in squalor with Eve, while she had a proper bed to sleep in.

Danny eventually found lodgings with two rooms, into which he moved with Eve and her children and Luke. As the years passed, Nellie watched from a distance as Eve and Danny became more like husband and wife every day. Eve was a good woman and cared well for little Luke. Nellie spent her one day off a month with them, and looked out for him on the other Sundays when Eve took a detour to church so that they could exchange a discreet smile in passing. She hated feeling envious of Eve, that she got to spend so much time with Luke, but determinedly buried her anguish because any other course of action meant all of them receding back into the squalor they had known before Kate had recognised her, despite her filthy state.

Many hundreds of her Irish countrymen who had been packed into the dockyard slums where she had first lived with Danny had succumbed to the cholera. It had raged through the community, cutting a swathe of death through the desperate families who inhabited it. The newspapers were full of the 'dirty Irish' getting their just deserts, as though the conditions they were forced to live in were somehow their fault. She had to bury her anger when she heard one of the master's friends laughingly say: *A few more epidemics like that, and perhaps the docks can be cleared of vermin.*

She was grateful that she'd been able, through a chance meeting with Kate, to remove herself, Danny and Eve and their children out of the slums before that happened, though she did wonder whether Annie had been there with some other family and had succumbed to the dreadful disease. Thoughts of Annie rose unbidden whenever she let her guard down. It was the unknown that consumed her. At times like those she hoped Annie had died. She crossed herself discreetly and asked for forgiveness for her thoughts, which were, maybe, selfish, because even if Annie had died in her arms, she would not be living with this empty desolation of unknowing.

Kate remained a good friend and kind, but she was, in Nellie's opinion, more interested in dances and young men than

Nellie thought appropriate, especially as she had no intention of being married. But that was Kate's character. That was why she had left Roone Bay in the first place, not just because of the hardship of rural life but to be free of the conventions that ruled small towns in Ireland, particularly for women, whose lives were still very much constrained by the rigid guidelines of the Catholic Church. She suspected that Kate was careful enough, though. Becoming an unmarried mother, and losing her cherished position as lady's maid, wasn't part of her plans.

Always, when running errands for the family, Nellie's eyes sought her little red-haired daughter. Annie would, by this time, be eight years old. Even flaying herself mentally with guilt, she could not really accept that Annie was dead, and every day her wandering mind painted wishful pictures of what her little girl might look like now. At odd times she would be missed in the house, and everyone turned a blind eye, knowing that Nellie was hurrying down to the docks, back through the old quarter, searching. She knew every street, every building, and many Bostonians knew her as the mad Irishwoman who was always asking after her child, as if it wasn't obvious that the girl was long gone.

In the flickering candlelight, when the daily chores were done, Kate taught Nellie how to sew, and she now had a dress suitable for wearing out, but she always declined to go to dances with Kate, not least because every dollar she earned was being sent to Danny, to help him and Luke. And also, how could she go out enjoying herself when her Annie remained lost? Kate also taught her the English writing, and gradually she was able to decipher words on packages and make out the headlines on the newspapers that were delivered to the master.

From the newspapers she learned that America was minimising immigration, making financial stipulations that few Irish could meet. She learned that the famine in her homeland was abating, not because the blight had been eradicated, but because the families who had survived were planting different vegetables, as William had. The massive emigration and death toll had left more land available to those still alive, and as there were fewer people left in Ireland to provide labour, they were beginning to dictate their own terms to landlords, or leave fields untilled and rents not paid. In wonder, she read that the Irish were rising in rebellion, intending to oust the English occupiers and overlords from the country. With a brief flash of insight, she realised that had William been alive, he would have been filled with zeal, wanting to return to Ireland to help lead the oppressed Irish people towards a new state of self-governance.

Personally, she thought it highly unlikely that they would succeed against the might of England and prayed for the souls who were going up against the English army like sheep attacking wolves. Living in Boston had taught her a truth William had not known: it wasn't just about peasants rebelling against the titled ruling class. It was also about the wealthy holding on to their privilege with all their might. In America there were no fiefdoms with landlords demanding rent by ancient right. It was said that in America every person was equal under the law, but in truth, the power of money held sway, there, as everywhere.

When Mrs Becker's personal maid left to be married, Kate was appropriated for that job, and Nellie, who by now had almost eradicated her Irish accent, slipped quietly into her place to become lady's maid to the two daughters. She learned to dress hair, mend rents in lace, and freshen the girls' wardrobes with lavender and mint. She cleaned stains from gowns, which she would press and slip over the girls' heads without disturbing their hair. She learned to trim hats and present the daughters to their parents in a manner that sometimes earned her a small glance of approval from the mistress.

Ireland, Roone Bay, her parents' small farm, even the great

hunger and the dead lying scattered in the boreens were fast receding into the mists of her memory.

Nellie showed no interest in dances or young men, which her employers saw as a bonus. Her unsmiling face had been hardened by her troubles, her youth overwritten by trauma. Indeed, it had been another life, like a half-remembered dream, sowing potatoes in the lazy beds, piling the soil up on them from the trenches and waiting for them to flourish; walking to church in her bare feet; meeting and falling in love with the beautiful, gentle, red-haired William, her romantic heart filled with the promise of a long life and a string of children. Sweet William had been ahead of his time, she realised now. He had been a dreamer but a thinker, too, and it was clear where Luke's questioning mind came from. She felt guilty that she could no longer recall his face with any clarity but accepted that though her life in Boston was not what she might have envisaged while growing up in rural Ireland, she had a better life than some.

And she was determined that Luke would have every opportunity to better himself. She missed him desperately. Her arms ached to hold him, and each time she saw him it seemed as if he had grown another inch. Her thin, contemplative child, who took in everything around him with a serious perception she found slightly daunting, was now nearly as tall as her. He made no complaints, understanding that Nellie was providing for him and Eve's family; that it was a necessity.

'One day,' he said solemnly, 'the tables will be turned. I will provide for you, Mother. I will buy you a house of your own and fine dresses, and you will have your own maid.'

'What will I be wanting fine dresses and a maid for?' she scolded, laughing.

But at the same time, it was nice to be wearing clean clothes again, and soft leather shoes, which she'd never had before.

. . .

One day, when Nellie visited Luke, it was obvious that Eve was pregnant. She must have been pregnant for some time, but now there was no hiding it. Danny, she learned, had found new work in a brewery, heaving barrels of liquor onto the wagons that moved it around the country. He was better dressed than when she'd first met him, and he looked handsome, though his red hair was slightly dimmed, touched with grey at the temples. She was pleased for him. They were about to move into a normal house, he said proudly, with a bedroom and a scullery.

She sensed that Danny was on the verge of speaking a few times, that he was nervous. Finally, he found the courage. 'I need to ask you a favour, Nellie,' he said quietly. 'No one knows we were ever married, and in the eyes of the church, we never were, not if a body wanted to contest it, that is.' He flushed slightly, referring to marital relations that had never taken place. 'I'm a man, with needs. Everyone thinks Eve is my wife. We can't have people calling our new child a bastard.'

She grimaced at Danny's words but nodded in acquiescence. She had been brought up as a Catholic in a land where divorce was simply not allowed, and the word of the priests was, she had believed, God's word uttered through their mouths. But that was before everything changed.

Her few years in Boston had taught her that people could belong to any religion, yet God didn't smite them as the priests would have had her believe. Instead, the poor and the innocent died in droves while the rich thrived, as it had always been. Danny was right: he and Eve were married in every way, except by the church. It was obvious that they had grown close in a way she had not been able to with Danny. Her love for William had consumed that part of her heart and would never let it go.

'Go and marry quietly,' she said, 'so that you have the certificate for the children. No one need ever know the truth. And I'm sure God will understand.'

Eve hugged her. 'Without you, we would have died, Nellie,

my love. Me and my children. We're bringing Luke up right, but he knows he's your son, that you love him, and he knows you're working for all of us. We don't lie to him.' She flushed slightly, glancing at Danny with a quick smile. 'Well, excepting that you married Danny, of course.'

'That will be our secret,' Nellie agreed.

25

ERIN

I don't recall Kenny formally proposing to me, in all honesty. I just know we were so good together that one day he said, 'Should we set a date?' And we both looked at the calendar, knowing what he meant. I didn't even think to say yes, because there was an unspoken understanding that we wanted to make this commitment, even though in this day and age it's not strictly necessary. We rejected Dad's plans for a stunning society wedding, which put him out, because he and Mom had always enjoyed splashing out on a social event.

So, when Scott proposes, I freeze for a moment, grateful only that he doesn't sink onto one knee. Then I ask, very quietly, 'You asked my father's permission? And he said yes?'

Scott seems to find this encouraging. He nods happily. 'He said it would be perfect for everyone. We agreed that enough time has gone by and that I should pop the question. I think you're absolutely gorgeous, which is why I've flown halfway across the world for you.'

He says that last bit as though it's the clincher and takes a step closer, so that I can take the ring from the box.

I take a step back. 'You think I've grieved for long enough, do you? And you discussed with my father that you would be a suitable match for his daughter? You presumably think we'd look good together in the wedding photographs?'

'I, ah—'

He was about to agree! 'What is this, 1876? Just because my father values your skills as a lawyer doesn't mean we have anything in common. What do you even know about me? Do you know what my favourite colour is? Or my favourite flower? Do you know that Kenny bought me opals because I don't like diamonds? Or that he asked me to choose a ring for myself as I was the one who would be wearing it? Do you know that I'd prefer flowers as a birthday gift rather than these... these *baubles*?' I rip off the earrings that Mom gave me and throw them onto the bed. I see the light-bulb moment, where he realises that he's got something a little wrong but isn't quite sure what.

'Sweetheart, I don't understand. I thought you liked me—'

'Do *not* call me sweetheart! I was polite to you because Dad likes you. I don't love you. I don't *like* you enough to marry you just because I'm lonely. What do you even know about me other than I own a brownstone and my dad owns rather a lot more than that?' Hot tears spring. 'Kenny knew I loved gladioli and roses, and he made a little garden for me in the yard, and you're not even worthy of licking his paint brushes clean, you... you clothes peg!'

'But it makes sense,' he perseveres. 'We feel that—'

I roll my eyes as I interrupt. 'Go home, Scott. Go and find someone who is attracted to your looks and your ability to make money, because I can't see that you have anything else to offer.'

'You can't mean that.'

I sigh, calming myself down. You can't argue with a brick wall. 'Scott. Listen. I don't want to marry you just because you think I would be a *suitable* wife. Trust me, I would not be a suitable wife for you at all. I hate social functions. I hate being nice to people for business purposes. I hate fashion. See if you can get a refund on that dreadfully ostentatious ring. I suspect it cost quite a lot.'

'Of course it did.'

He's looking peeved now and probably thinks me ungrateful, but I think he finally understands that I'm saying no.

'What on earth am I going to tell your parents? They think we're going to come down engaged!'

'More fool them,' I snap. I pace a little more and throw the windows open again.

'But what should I say?' Scott asks, looking like a rabbit caught in headlights.

I pick up the earrings and slip them back on. 'I don't want to ruin their break. Go on down. Tell them I said it's too soon, and I want to wait until I come home to make any plans for the future. Then I'll let them down gently. I suspect Mom's already been planning the wedding.'

From the way his cheeks colour, I suspect they all have.

I shake my head and open the door. 'Go on, and say I'm overwhelmed. I'll meet you for dinner when I've calmed down. Oh, and take the bible down, and try to find something to discuss. After all, that's what we came up to collect.'

I thrust it at him and open the door. He looks as if he's going to say something, then thinks better of it and sidles out.

After lying on the bed and stewing for half an hour, I see the funny side of it and tell Kenny all about it, as if he isn't up there watching it all. He finds it funny, too, I know.

Scott looks worried as I come into the dining room, but I've redone my hair, touched up my make-up and am able to kiss Scott on the cheek with the distant familiarity they are used to seeing.

Dinner went well. I enjoyed it, in fact. Dad told us about his latest success in the world of corporate law, Mom told me about a fashion show she'd been invited to and Scott did exactly what I'd told him to do, and talked about Nellie and the bible, but only to the extent of his limited interest.

As usual the conversation soon enough turns back towards Dad's latest high-status case and Scott's involvement in it. Mom manages to look interested for a while, then I notice her gaze go a bit hazy and drift towards the impressive swags and tails that frame the dining-room windows. I suspect that she's mentally updating her lounge with William Morris designs.

I try hard not to yawn, but I'm pleased when I can finally justifiably excuse myself, and take myself off to bed and unwind with a novel I'd picked up from the library.

I walk with Mom and Dad through the town and take a stroll on the quay. I tuck my arm in Scott's as we walk in two pairs. I don't want to marry him, not at all, but I've forgiven him. He can't help having absolutely no idea about women, after all. It's probably something he was born with, or without, as the case might be. I'm sure he'll find some pretty socialite to hang on his arm when he gets back to Boston.

I talk enthusiastically about Roone Bay, about its history, about Noel and the new hotel, and how I came to be teaching Noel's great-grandchild the fiddle. As I speak, I realise how familiar it all feels to me. I don't feel like a stranger any longer. I show them the tiny quay, with its worn-out fishing fleet, the tiny post office and library.

I try to enthuse them and realise I've failed dramatically when Mom flicks an eye over her watch. 'Isn't it time to get back to the hotel? I'm getting chilly.'

We all swing around and walk the other way. They'd run out of interest in this tiny town and didn't care that Dad's forebears had emigrated from here. One hick Irish town is much the same as another.

'So, sugar, when are you coming home?' Dad asks. 'Geoff from the orchestra has been asking when he can expect you back.'

'I still want to find out about Nellie, remember?'

'But, really, does it matter?' Dad says. 'It's all water under the bridge. Are you sure you don't want to come on to London with us?'

Mom backs Dad in his invitation, 'Yes, do, sweetheart; it's so nice seeing you and Scott together again.'

'Thank you, but I'd rather stay here awhile,' I say.

Scott and I managed to keep our faces pointed religiously towards the hotel.

After fishing unsuccessfully for an invite to the Big House, which, of course, is something I can't offer, and trying, also without success, to persuade Scott to stay here with me, Mom gives a theatrical sigh. 'It would be nice if you two lovebirds could spend some time together.'

'There's plenty of time,' Scott says.

I cast him a grateful glance as Mom wonders to Dad whether they might cut their visit short and go on to Dublin. After all, there isn't anything to do here.

They're very sorry to let me down in not staying for the full five days, Mom says, with a final hug and a kiss. I don't remind her that I hadn't expected them to come at all. If they had mentioned it to me, I would have done my best to dissuade them.

At the side of the big car, I give Scott a hug and a kiss too, and whisper that it in no way changes my mind. Scott is to drive them up to Dublin, where Mom can spend a couple of days shopping before hopping over to London. I'm invited to join them on this, too, but decline. I've never been to Dublin, and might one day, but the thought of spending two days with Mom trawling fashion boutiques isn't my idea of fun.

As they drive off, Grace comes and stands at my side. She glances at me, and I grin. 'I'd like to say good riddance,' I comment. 'But they're my parents and I do love them. I think I must have been a cuckoo in their nest, we have so little in common.'

'And Scott?'

I grimace and shrug. 'My parents are planning the wedding. I'll deal with that when I'm up to it.'

26

NELLIE 1860S

By now Nellie was a stable and solid employee for the family. Her free day once a month was spent with her darling Luke, a reserved boy who looked out at his world contemplatively and analytically. She felt endlessly guilty for not being able to be a full-time mother to him, but whenever they met, she hugged him close and whispered that she loved him no less passionately than she loved – and mourned – her lost Annie, and that circumstances alone conspired to keep her from both of her children.

As Luke grew older, she talked to him of her early life in Ireland, painting a somewhat wistful picture of his grandparents, the little cottage with the well above, the altar stone high on the hill from where she had watched William's ship disappear over the horizon. He understood the sheer desperation of the dreadful journey she had undertaken to be reunited with her husband, only to find that he had died weeks earlier.

She was sad she didn't have an image of William and could only recall him as a whisper of memory: his stature, his hair, his song and ready laugh, because the finer details had faded behind the mists of her memory.

Their days together were spent catching up with the minutiae of their everyday lives, while enacting the never-ending search for little Annie, who – if she was still alive – would no longer be so little, after all. Luke knew the story of what had happened and offered his mother unconditional support in what he, and everyone except Nellie, knew was a pointless search. He wouldn't recognise his own sister and doubted even Nellie would by now.

Nellie, though, saw Annie at every turn – the brief glimpse of a face, the hint of red hair – but every time she chased after the elusive hint, the girl who turned to face her was a stranger. She knew, in her heart, that when she saw Annie again, she would know her. There would be no doubt, no moment of confusion. She would just know. Her employers knew of her continuing search for her lost daughter and generously made allowances for the occasional moment of detachment, rather than lose such a virtuous, hard-working and honest servant.

When Luke was twelve, Nellie obtained him a job as a boot boy for the Beckers. His job was to clean the silverware, polish shoes, bring in coal, or any other job the other manservants felt was beneath them.

Luke made his tearful farewells to Eve and Danny and moved into the stables, where he was given a straw mattress of his own. Danny and Eve had been as parents to Luke, and he visited them whenever he was able. Thankfully, he had no recollection or knowledge of Danny's marriage to Nellie. If that came to light, Danny would be imprisoned as a bigamist and the children Eve had borne with him labelled bastards.

Nellie was thrilled to finally have her own son living with her, in the same household. Rather than see him once a month, he was there, on the same property. They caught each other's glances from time to time, but when she gave him the tiniest of winks, he would do the same back.

Luke proved his worth, in reliability and willingness to do

anything he was asked without complaining, and because he was good-looking and most particular about his appearance, two years later he was promoted into the house as a manservant. There, he rid himself of the remnants of the Irish accent he'd picked up from Eve and Danny and watched carefully how Erich, the master's son and heir, behaved and dressed. One day he was going to be like Erich: rich and in control of his own destiny.

Luke grew into a tall, thin youth with a shock of flaming red hair, and Nellie saw William's shadow reflected in his every move. He was a quick study, and his washed-out-blue eyes, so like William's and Annie's, gazed avidly out at life, absorbing everything they met. He had decided, fairly early on in this new household, that he was not going to remain a servant all his life. He was one day going to be the man employing others; though, in what capacity, he didn't know. But in Boston, having broken free of the stain of the destitute immigrant, there were opportunities for a man to better himself and move into the echelons of the professional.

In time, the two daughters of the household, Clara and Margarethe, were betrothed, married and moved out into their own houses, and Nellie, a quiet and reliable soul, obtained the highest-paid position in the house – that of housekeeper. Wearing her smart uniform – black shoes and a black dress with a starched white collar – she sometimes thought back on her early days in Ireland, barefoot, tending to the lazy beds of potatoes for her parents. How strangely her life had changed, with its tragedies but also its unexpected benefits. In Ireland, Luke would have forever remained the poorest of the poor, but here, at sixteen years old, when he wasn't dressed suitably as a manservant, he was able to wear suits and a watch chain, like a gentleman, and no one took him to task for it.

In this presentable guise, and able to read and write as well as any wealthy American, Luke obtained a job as the scribe to a lawyer and left the Becker household. This meant long hours copying documents by candlelight, and Nellie saw him rarely, but she was thrilled for him. She was amazed that she had produced such a talented and determined son, and only sometimes, in the quiet of her own space, when she was feeling particularly low, did she shed the occasional tear for sweet William's lost life, for she knew Luke's determined yet generous character had come directly from him.

As for little Annie, Nellie just lived with the hope that someone good had rescued her, that she had grown up loved and cherished, and would one day marry and have children. She invented many idyllic scenarios in her dreams, because any other thoughts would lead to madness and grief. She had never totally lost her faith in God, and if a hint of grief sometimes trickled into her mind, she pushed it firmly away, knowing that one day, in quite a different realm, she would be reunited with her little girl.

Nellie would still sometimes visit Eve, who was having yet another child; hopefully the last, she admitted wistfully. She also visited Kate, who was ostensibly happy, having very sensibly married a man with means. She secretly admitted to Nellie that she respected but didn't love her husband. She whispered nostalgically of the footloose and fun life she'd enjoyed as a lady's maid, but stoically did her duty by her husband and children as the alternative would have been to remain a servant all her life, like poor Nellie.

Nellie's friendship with Kate never wavered, but she never knew what to expect from her somewhat volatile childhood acquaintance. There would be days when Kate was a whirlwind of excitement over some social event or another and times when she cried on Nellie's shoulder, wishing she had never married her husband. Nellie took it all in her stride, as they both knew that Kate would never have been happy poor, and such regrets were pointless.

When Luke was seventeen, in the Year of Our Lord, 1863, he married Sarah, the daughter of his employer's brother, another lawyer in the firm. Sarah had already been married and widowed in the same year, and had a child from the union and a small inheritance that Luke now controlled. Luke's new wife was three years older than himself and quietly confident of her own place in society.

He moved into her parents' home, and his status was elevated to that of a legal assistant. Within the year, Sarah bore him a son, whom they called Patrick. Nellie found herself a grandmother at thirty-nine years of age. She was given leave to visit her son and his family once a fortnight, and was quietly impressed with the house and the upmarket situation Luke had moved into.

She was never fully accepted by her son's new family, being in service, but was happy to stay quietly in the background, playing with and adoring her grandson, and being pleased that her son and his family were able to live a life that had been undreamed of twenty years previously.

27

ERIN

The school at Roone Bay is cute, with just two classrooms, both painted in bright colours and decorated with the children's art. I can't imagine anything that small back in Boston. Maybe out in the boondocks, but not in any place I've ever visited. I was terrified of walking in through the door, of course. I haven't had much to do with children, and was afraid of the hurt I would experience. Kenny and I had planned to have children, but the accident meant that the rooms in my heart where our children were supposed to reside will be forever empty. But as with many things, the fear of doing something is worse than the act. These are not my children, and their enthusiasm is almost overwhelming.

They want to know, almost in a single breath: Will I be taking over from Angela Daly, teaching the penny whistle? Will I be teaching the button box because Grandpa has one in the back room?

'Woah, one at a time!' I say, laughing.

They want to touch the violins, run the bow over the strings with curiosity, or tell me that their respective granddads, aunts or cousins 'play the songs'. I'm fascinated by the fact that playing music rather than just listening to it is engrained in their culture.

Olivia doesn't give me a chance to become maudlin. She takes charge of the music lesson, which is amusing and quite charming. I'm her find, and she milks it dry, presenting to the whole class, with the confidence of a maestro, the tunes she's learned.

As I walk back to the hotel, I wonder about my relationship with Finn. Is it even real, or is he just being kind to me, helping me to cope with my overwhelming grief? He said he would be away for a while, and I'm curious to discover what will happen when he returns, whether his interest in me might have cooled with distance. Call me old-fashioned, but I kind of think it's the man's job to make the moves. I've never been one to chase; if two individuals haven't worked their own feelings through and come to the same conclusion, then it isn't right.

But I know that Finn is a troubled soul.

Should I get over my fear of being rejected and expose my emerging interest? If it makes him run a mile, then at least I'd know. The last thing I want is to be mooning like some lovesick teenager over someone who doesn't respond to my overtures.

When his arm had gone around me on the quay in the early hours, when his lips brushed mine, in that magical instant the tight band of grief that had kept me in thrall for two years had eased. Like a Viking burial, the burning light of my love for Kenny had flared brightly then floated out over the dark Atlantic, leaving a shadow of regret that will remain quietly within me forever.

Scott was right when he said it was time for me to move on, but I already have. It had just taken his lack of empathy to make me realise it. I've never believed I'd fall in love again, but without a doubt, Finn has touched that sweet chord inside me. He reminds me so much of Kenny, but not in any way that I can elucidate. Maybe it's his bohemian spirit, his love of the more basic things in life, his sensitivity. I feel that something deeper than friendship has reached out to connect us. But his absence bothers me. Is my impression one-sided? Have I read more into it than I should? Has the exposure of my own still-raw experience sent him running the other way?

I've been here for two strangely confused months, feeling both lonely and also embraced by the community. It's not just my quest for Nellie that binds me to this place; nor is it my unexpected discovery of Finn. Even if that doesn't turn out to be what I hope it is, I still have the feeling that I'm meant to be here. Like a pigeon that lost its bearings and finally scented home on the breeze, I feel as though I've landed in the place I was always meant to land in.

I wonder if Nellie's genes have somehow settled down the male line, through Luke, and Patrick, and Gabriel, and my father, to finally emerge in me. Maybe she didn't come back to Ireland at all, but if not, I feel as if I've brought her back with me, inside my soul. If so, I hope she's happy now.

I doubt my parents will be happy. I can only imagine what they will say when I tell them I woke up one morning with the knowledge that I actually don't want to go back to America. I'll leave that revelation for later, after they've gone home, from London, or Paris, or wherever they end up, or I might find them turning up here with a psychiatrist in tow. I'm hoping Scott has the sense not to say anything too soon.

Did I just decide to stay here, after all?

With that epiphany, I phone up a realtor in Boston from the hotel and put my brownstone on the market. I'll need that money if I'm going to buy a house here. I'll ask them to arrange for my belongings to be put into safe storage. I can go through them at my leisure somewhen in the future.

In the meantime, I'll find a place to rent.

I can stay in the hotel for now but, to echo Scott's words when he visited my brownstone a while back, I have a nest-

building instinct and like to surround myself with clutter. I
don't think he meant it as a compliment, but the last place I
want to live in is an impersonal showpiece like the house I grew
up in.

Mom gets someone in to do a makeover every few years, and
everything has to go. Maybe my need for friendly objects is
because I never grew up with anything that survived Mom's
blitzes long enough for me to fall in love with it. She doesn't
understand the meaning of memorabilia, and I'm once again
grateful that Nellie's bible didn't end up in the thrift shop the
moment it landed in her house. Dad is quite happy to humour
her makeover fits. As long as he gets his comfort and his drop of
whiskey in the evening – and she doesn't touch his home office
or get rid of his wing chair. But three times she's had the wing
chair recovered to match the decor.

In contrast, my brownstone is a three-storey delight of
eclectic confusion. My treasures, discovered at thrift stores and
yard sales, amused Kenny, but he said he loved everything about
me, even my precious junk. Whenever I brought a further piece
into the house, I'd spend ages seeking exactly the right space for
it, moving it around until it told me it was settled. Kenny loved
each piece as much as I did, for its artistic value, its *difference* in
a world where commercialism is eradicating individuality. I
realise I'm remembering our home with a sense of pathos rather
than devastating grief and know that I've taken another step
towards healing. I never thought I'd find another love after
Kenny. In fact, I told myself I would be happy to live alone for
the rest of my life, which probably isn't true. But Kenny really
wouldn't want me to be lonely, and I know he'd approve of
Finn.

Christmas is creeping towards us, and the hotel has retreated
into silence. I am the only guest, and have a decision to make. I

suspect Grace is hoping to spend the holidays with her family, but the thought of going back to Boston bothers me. It's not just the issue of Scott, but a deeper feeling that if I leave Roone Bay, I won't find the courage to come back. I'm lying on the bed reading one of the history texts the librarian gave me when the phone rings. Dubiously, I pick it up, hoping it's not my parents, that Scott hasn't been daft enough to tell them of my decision before they leave Europe.

It's Grace. 'Erin, Noel's asked me if you'd like a chat over dinner tonight?'

'I'd be delighted,' I say but suspect he wants to discuss the ideas I'd mentioned to Grace, regarding bringing the locals into the hotel. I wish I hadn't said anything at all. I should have kept my thoughts to myself.

'Five thirty, if that's all right,' she says. 'In the dining room downstairs. You know he likes to eat early.'

'No problem.'

When I come downstairs, Noel is already sitting at the table, waiting for me. He stands with old-fashioned courtesy as I walk in.

'I'm afraid it's just roast beef on the menu today,' he says. 'I got one of the ladies from the town to come up and cover until the new chef arrives. I gave Jane a holiday before she says it's all too much for her and walks out. I hope you don't mind. It would have been just me on my own in the Big House this evening, anyway. The women in my life are all at some show or other up in Cork city. The family can eat here, too, for a few days. That should bring some life into this empty barn of a room. Unless Caitlin wants to take over in the kitchen up in the Big House. She does, sometimes, much to Jane's annoyance; says she's not used to being waited on hand and foot.'

I echo his grin, imagining Jane's rigid disapproval at someone – even if it is the owner – from invading her kitchen.

Noel's right, though – it's strange to be sitting in the large room, with its pristine new furniture and the scenic windows framed by luxurious swags of William Morris fabric, and no guests but us.

Noel is an easy man to be with. He picks up the bottle of wine that's been waiting on the table and pours. While we wait for the meal, he puts me at my ease with a story of his early years in America as errand boy for a bank and an incident that led to his becoming a stablehand, which in turn led to his involvement in the world of horse racing. It's hard to imagine the experiences he packed into his life before landing back in his home town. He then gently quizzes me about Kenny, and I find myself telling him about how we met, about falling in love, about marrying him despite the disapproval of my family and about the accident that robbed me of our planned future.

Just in time to stop me getting maudlin, a stout lady with a beaming smile puts two ready-served dinners in front of us.

Noel refills our glasses and raises his. 'May the saddest day of your future be no worse than the happiest day of your past,' he toasts.

I have to think about that for a moment, then smile and say, 'Back at you!' and we clink glasses. As we tuck into the hearty, overcooked meal in companionable silence, I feel that we have crossed some kind of bridge.

Finally, the smiling lady comes and removes the plates, and we both decline the offer of ice cream, which still seems to be the only dessert available. When she's gone, Noel says, 'Grace tells me you mentioned some ideas for the hotel?'

I'm embarrassed. 'It was just suggestions that came off the top of my head. I didn't mean to interfere.'

'Oh, goodness,' he says, his eyes crinkling into folds of humour. 'Interference is most welcome! None of us know what we're doing at all. Grace has never managed a hotel, and I only had it built because I had a pile of money doing nothing very clever in the bank. I had a vague thought that it would benefit the community, but I didn't have a clue how. So, the more suggestions the merrier. Tell me your thoughts.'

'Well, I get the feeling that the community as a whole presently feels slightly put out about the hotel. They think it will steal their livelihoods.'

Noel sighs. 'I know. That was never my intention. I just didn't know what to do about it.'

'You could easily turn it around to make them feel included. Help them see it as something to benefit the community rather than something to make more money for yourself.' I wince. 'Sorry, I didn't mean that to sound...'

He waves me to a halt, grinning. 'I won't see a return on that outlay in my lifetime, but go on.'

'I suggested to Grace the idea of cheaper meals for locals, so that they can afford to come here, rather than seeing it as a place only wealthy foreigners get to enjoy.'

He smiles encouragingly and says, 'Good, and?'

'It occurred to me that we could extend the invitation out to the wider community, all of Carbery's Hundred Isles, out of season, with special offers and events. Bring more local people into Roone Bay.'

Noel nods, his features lighting up with excitement, so I carry on, enthusiasm getting the better of me. 'At off-peak times, we could even offer rooms cheaper to encourage local people to come for weekend breaks, an evening meal with wine, and not have to worry about driving home afterwards. I mean, if the rooms are empty, it's just wasted space, after all. And that would also pave the way for some of the local youngsters to earn holiday money and get work experience into the bargain.'

Noel stares at me for a moment. 'You said *we*?'

I'm confused. 'We what?'

'You said "we could offer cheaper rooms"...'

'Oh,' I say, embarrassed. 'I didn't mean to presume...'

'No, I love it. Grace suggested you might be exactly the right person to manage the place. I'm in agreement. How about it?'

I'm stunned into silence for a moment, then ask, 'Don't you want to see a CV, or do a formal interview or something?'

'Not at all. You can let me know, whenever you like. And don't worry about the remuneration. We can discuss it later, but I assure you, you won't be disappointed.'

My finances aren't endless, especially if Dad thinks that cutting off my somewhat generous allowance will make me come home. I never minded accepting my father's money – he has enough of it, after all – but at the back of my mind, the thought of financial independence sounds rather appealing.

'Does that little smile mean you've accepted?' he asks.

I hadn't realised I was so easy to read. 'Well, I appreciate the offer, of course, but I've never managed a hotel, and you don't know whether I'd be any good. Nor do I, actually. And I really don't know whether I intend to stay in Ireland.' I think that's a lie, but it gives me an out if I truly find I don't want the commitment.

'I like to think I'm a good judge of character, and it turns out that trusting my own judgement has produced better results than believing beautifully scripted CVs. The job comes with an apartment, by the way. I'll get Grace to show it to you.' He flashes a cheeky smile, one that probably broke a few hearts over the years. 'It might help you make up your mind.'

28

NELLIE 1862

After increasing political shenanigans in America, a deepening rift between the north and south eventually erupted in civil war. As the fighting escalated, and society struggled to find its feet, the war brought a barrage of hardship and grief to everyone, including Kurt and Adelaide Becker. Their social life ground to a standstill, servants were dismissed and the family's clothes became simpler, to appease the increasing grumbles about the haves and have-nots. The Beckers' cotton factory was subsumed by the needs of the army. Private wealth didn't just trickle into the war; it flooded away, along with almost every luxury. Produce of any kind became difficult to obtain. Fabrics were simply not available, and food availability was unreliable and expensive. The meals served in the Becker household became more basic, and Nellie often found herself in the kitchen making up for staffing shortfalls, remembering with horror the hardships of the famine in Ireland.

Nellie was afraid she, too, would be dismissed, but as the war progressed, and belts were tightened, she continued to get up, dress and get on with her day in a kind of daze, hanging on for the occasional letter from Luke, letting her know he was still alive, fighting the cause. By now she'd learned that many Irish, with their history of oppression, chose to forget the cruelty that had been meted out to them as they had flooded into America, desperate and starving, and had risen to the cry for freedom.

Sarah had begged Luke not to volunteer as a soldier, but eventually, hand to her mouth in dismay, Nellie had watched Luke don the uniform and march off righteously to war. *All people should be free*, he had declared, fire in his eyes, righteous in his indignation at the slave trade. *No one should own another human. People should be able to choose their own destiny.*

He was no doubt also influenced by his own impoverished childhood, spent in the slums by the docks, and Nellie's past in Ireland, before the famine. Too poor to even imagine, she'd been victim to the English class system, her father's rich and often absent landlord benefitting from their hard labour then scarpering at the hint of crisis. Even the loss of the father he had never met, working in America as a navvy and dying in horrific conditions, ignited Luke's sense of the injustices in the world. His fervour and determination to fight injustice, be it as a lawyer, or with a gun in his hand, frightened Nellie.

In this alone he was totally unlike his gentle father. William had loathed physical confrontation, believing, as they had all believed, that their place in the world had been crafted by God, and that salvation came through acceptance and hard work. It might have been religious propaganda – Nellie knew about such things now – but she had also known a quiet pleasure in living a simple life and feared mightily for her son.

The war, which was supposed to last a few months, went on for four years. One day, as the war was on its last flurry, Nellie answered the front door to find Luke's wife, Sarah, standing there clutching an official note, tears blotching her face. It didn't take words for Nellie to understand that her precious son, Luke, was gone. She collapsed on the doorstep, so numb with grief she could not even cry.

Her parents, starved to death. William gone, buried under a pile of earth, his body never recovered. Her Annie gone, the Lord knew where, and in what circumstances. And now Luke. She was so tired of life, with its grim harvest of everyone she loved.

Sarah kneeled beside her on the step and, despite her own grief, tried to comfort Nellie, reminding her that Luke's son, her grandchild, still needed her love. Patrick, at two years old, openly wore the legacy of his Irish ancestry, like William and then Luke: a head of flaming red hair.

The official notice of Luke's death stated that he had died quickly and painlessly, which should have been a comfort but really wasn't. He had been just shy of twenty years of age. They held a memorial for him, but his body was in the South, buried anonymously in a mass grave with other soldiers.

Nellie didn't really get over Luke's demise but put it in a mental box of its own, alongside her childhood friends, her family, her parents and William, and slowly eased the door closed. But the unknown fate of Annie was a door that remained forever cracked open. She would grieve and wonder for the rest of her life, praying for the strength to bear the pain of not knowing.

Months later, Nellie learned, from one of Luke's soldier colleagues, that Luke had received a bullet wound to his leg that wouldn't heal and eventually became gangrenous. The pain had sent him into delirium. His leg had finally been amputated, too late, and with archaic brutality. He had passed out during the procedure and never regained consciousness. Imagining the pain her beautiful, talented and intelligent son must have endured drove Nellie towards depression. After everything she had endured for the sake of her family, it all but broke her. She became a ghost in the household, her strange confusion barely allowing her to do her job.

During this time, Kurt succumbed to the pressures of his decreasing fortune and died at his desk. His son, Erich, took the reins tightly and decided that Nellie would simply have to go. He could not afford, much as it pained him, to keep a servant who could not work, especially in these times of hardship.

Sarah took her mother-in-law into her home, despite the disapproval of her own parents. There she nursed her and, at every possible occasion, pushed Luke's son, Patrick, into Nellie's arms. Patrick reached out to her, his chubby little fingers stroking her cheeks curiously, and eventually, Nellie came to realise that not all of her family had gone. Luke's child was the spitting image of Luke when he had been a babe in arms, and eventually she did what she had always done.

She sealed her grief away and got on with life.

From that moment, she took control of the household, her work ethic even winning the approval of Sarah's parents. She cleaned, cooked, sewed and looked after Patrick, doing everything the servants had once done. But she no longer smiled and hummed her songs as she worked.

29

ERIN

I haven't officially responded to Noel's offer of employment and feel suspended in a limbo of my own indecision. I'm flattered, of course, but am I capable? I've never held down a job, any job, never mind being the manager of a hotel. I've had commitments – rehearsals and performances – and I did manage Kenny's exhibitions quite proficiently, if I say so myself. But I don't know about this. It seems like a huge responsibility. I know they're keen to get a decision – after all, the position needs to be filled, the sooner the better. I'm only grateful that they haven't put any pressure on me.

My parents' visit has thrown my new-found self-confidence to the wind, though, adding an element of dislocation. Can I really uproot myself from Boston? Do I really fit in with the people around me, or am I just kidding myself? I've spent the last two years trailing around after Mom and Dad like a lost puppy, so I can't really blame any of them for their mistaken understanding that I wanted to make a new life with Scott. But on the other hand, it just goes to show how little they know me. Scott and I are like oil and water, sliding past each other but never melding in mind or body. How could any of them suppose that after Kenny I'd want to marry someone without the least smidgen of artistry in his soul? His soul, like my father's, resides firmly within his bank statements and social standing. Am I being unkind? They say the truth hurts, but I can't imagine either Dad or Scott being hurt by that supposition. They'd probably take it as a compliment.

Mom has called me a few times since they returned home, ostensibly to catch up but really to try to persuade me to go home for Christmas. She's not so subtle, but she cares; she's my mom, after all. She had a ball in London, apparently, but they didn't get to Paris because Dad was keen to get back to work. I'm surprised Mom managed to lever Dad away from the office for the two weeks they were in Europe, in fact. He likes to have the final say in all decisions undertaken by his company, and if Scott thinks that will ever change, I guess he'll learn otherwise in his own time. I'll have to let Mom know I've decided not to return to Boston, in any event. She won't understand that I don't feel I have anything to go back to, not since Kenny died, and starting afresh in a totally new place will help me to move on. She'll be disappointed, sure, but it's my life.

It comes as quite a shock when Grace tells me that Scott called to book a room for the following evening. He's flying into Cork and hopes to see me mid-afternoon.

Oh, for goodness' sake. Did he not get the message the first time? So why is he coming back to Ireland? I truly don't believe it's because he's in love with me, but perhaps he sees his future in the practice as less secure without our anticipated union. Maybe it's a last-ditch attempt to bring me home.

I find I need to go out and get some fresh air, so set out down to the quay, to give myself time to think, form the arguments and find the mettle to tell Scott once and for all that I don't want to marry him.

I'm walking past the little café when I'm startled by a rapid knocking on the window. Finn is sitting there by an empty green Formica table, as if waiting for someone. He beckons me in. I didn't know he was back. I beam back at him and push the door open eagerly.

As I open the door, I'm hit by the scent of fresh coffee. There are a few other people in the room: two older women dressed in moss-green and brown garments, like hippies, and a young woman nursing a baby. A radio chat show is burbling away in the background.

Finn straightens as I walk in, his smile welcoming.

'Hi, Erin,' he says. 'This is a really useful happenstance.'

There's a strange note in his voice that instantly makes me wary. I sit down, staring at him. 'What? Has something happened?'

'Nothing happened, exactly,' he says with a faint grimace that puts me on red alert. 'Sit down. There's something I have to tell you.'

This doesn't sound good. I drop my purse beside me as I slide into a seat then pull the lunch menu out of the little wooden holder and clutch it tightly. If he's going to tell me things I don't want to hear, it's best if I'm not staring at him with something akin to panic. He leans over and replaces the menu then puts his hand over mine. His lopsided smile still makes me shiver to my shoes, and the faint pressure of his touch is reassuring.

'It's not so terrible,' he says and comes straight to the point. 'I've got a child. He's three years old. He's called Liam. Well, William, actually. His mother is bringing him to stay with me for a few days as she has an appointment she has to keep.'

I stare at him. 'You have a child?' I parrot numbly.

'I want you to meet him, because he's part of my life. You need to know that.'

I comprehend the subtext immediately: I would have to accept this child into my life, or we have no future. I feel the old sense of panic welling up, ready to overwhelm me. I want to run back to the hotel, down a few anti-depressants and let numbness seep into my brain and filter out the world, but I threw them away. Why did I do that?

The pressure of his hand on mine increases. 'You know what happened? Why I was off work?' He's looking down at the table as he speaks, a catch in his voice.

'Grace told me about the yacht that foundered. About the child inside. It must have been horrible.'

'It haunts me, the image of that baby. His hair was rippling gently in the current, and his eyes were half-closed. He looked so peaceful. But he drowned, all alone, no one even holding his hand for comfort. He must have been terrified.'

'Oh, Finn,' I say, and now it's my hands enclosing his. Tears are pricking behind my eyelids. 'It must have been awful. That's why you had post-traumatic stress.'

'Let's call it what it was, eh? It was a massive breakdown. Apparently I'm over it, but I don't know if I ever will be.' There's a long pause, then he adds, 'I never told the shrink this, but when I dived into that yacht and found the child, I thought, for a fleeting moment, that it was Liam. It couldn't have been, of course, but in my nightmares it's always him. The responsibility, you see. Of having a child. I never imagined...'

A brief flurry of rain drives past then stops just as suddenly. Clouds are scudding across a blue sky, sending dark shadows stalking over the hills. He sighs and looks out at the shining sidewalk for a moment, gathering his thoughts.

'When I knew there was a baby on the way, I felt out of control, betrayed, even. It wasn't my choice. I really don't know if it was the accident Eilis said it was, but' – he shrugs – 'it was my responsibility, and I had to get on with it. At first, everything was about the mother and the child as a single entity: the checking, weighing and us discussing how we could manage the future. Then he was born, and all the responsibility and the fear that comes with it came flooding in. I didn't choose to have a child, but there he was. I wondered about myself. Could I be a good father? Was I capable? How could I do this? It was a knock I didn't see coming.'

'But... I thought you weren't married?'

'I'm not. I never was. Times are changing. Eilis and I had a relationship. It didn't work out, and we split up before the baby was even born. Maybe I should have married her. It was what Eilis wanted, but I didn't love her. It would have been awful, for both of us. All of us. The priest wanted Liam taken for adoption, the moment he was born.' He gave a wry smile. 'Out of wedlock, you see. But Eilis's mother wouldn't hear of it. She stood up to the priest and said she'd bring him up as her own, rather than have that happen. But Liam is my son. I'm his father. I'll always be his father. I need to know you're okay with that.'

His gaze is intense, searching. I take a deep breath. I don't know if I am, actually. I'm wondering quite how to cope with this when the door chimes open.

'Dada!' a little voice yells.

'Hi, Eilis,' Finn says in greeting to the child's mother before bending to lift his son high in the air. 'And how's my bestest boy today?'

He gives his child a smacking kiss on the cheek, which somehow turns into a raspberry, making Liam scream with delight. I glance at Eilis, who is laughing. Her eyes are fixated on Finn and her son, so I stare openly for a brief moment and experience a pang of jealousy. She's beautiful. She has that dark hair and dark eyes that the Irish are famous for, coupled with a clear, almost transparent complexion. Her features are small, dainty and fairylike. I feel huge and raw-boned in comparison. How could Finn not still be in love with this woman?

Finn introduces us simply. 'Erin, Eilis.'

She holds out her hand, and as I stand and take it, she assesses me with equal intensity. She's older than she at first seemed. She's slim – fragile, almost – but her grip is firm, her expression placid and mature. He's obviously told her about me, and I wonder if she's assessing me in the light of a foster mother. I try to hide my dismay, imagining all the things Finn said about coping with a child and more.

After a flurry of activity, choosing drinks and sandwiches, Eilis leaves, and we're left with this bouncing, exuberant child. He has a mop of dark hair, a legacy from both parents, and the expression of a loved child who has no idea that life can be cruel.

I find myself drawn into conversation as Liam chatters away without pause, telling me about his playschool, his toys and about Father Christmas, who is coming to visit soon.

Of course, we're moving towards winter, and the few shops are already brightly decorated with Christmas bunting. Finn grins at me at one point, and I shake my head in amusement. My initial dismay has evaporated. I thought I couldn't handle getting to know another woman's child, but maybe it's all right, after all.

Finally, Finn stands to pay, and a waitress comes and clears up behind us. Our table is sitting in a sea of crumbs, but she doesn't seem to mind, and waves goodbye to Finn and Liam with familiarity.

Outside, Finn crooks a brow at me. 'We're going back to my place. A walk on the beach, maybe? Do you want to come?'

I shake my head. 'I need to get back to the hotel. Scott's flying over especially to see me. We have things to discuss.'

A fleeting expression of surprise, maybe a hint of sadness, crosses his face and is gone. He doesn't ask, so I assume he's learned who Scott is via Roone Bay's healthy gossip network. I don't know why I don't immediately disabuse him of the notion that Scott and I are to be married, then immediately realise I'm providing myself with an escape clause, like telling Noel I'm not sure about staying in Ireland. Finn knows I don't have plans for children, and he believes he knows why. Perhaps he thinks my meeting with Liam would provide opportunity for me to get over my hang-ups, see that having a child to love isn't such a bad thing, after all.

But Finn has thrown me a curveball. I honestly don't know if I can be with his child. Two years down the line, my grief is still raw, the ragged wound needing very little to set it weeping. Tears well as I walk back up the hill to the hotel on my own. I'd been fully prepared to have Kenny's children. I'd wanted them and looked forward to the day. But seeing Finn with his child just rubs salt in the wound.

30

ERIN

I have the window wide open in my room, despite the chill gusts of wind. I breathe in the scent of salty fishiness that is wafting up from the harbour, where the small fleet is bouncing against the quay. The choppy sea skitters between icy blue and dull ash grey as a fitful sun dodges the clouds. I'm watching from the Juliet balcony as Scott drives up the slope to the hotel, in a flash rental car he's driven from Cork. He must have come into Shannon from Boston, and taken an internal flight to Cork rather than risk the winding roads again.

When Grace calls, I tell her to send him on up. Dirty linen is best not aired in public.

He's as pristine and polished as a wax model: not a hair out of place despite the breeze, his casual gear worn as if poured onto his trim frame. I'm amused to recall the words of a friend who described him as eye-candy frosting on a man-block.

He greets me, as always, hands on my shoulders, a proprietary kiss on the cheek. I wonder if he's ever noticed that my responding air kisses aren't exactly enthusiastic.

'Are you staying long?'

'No. I have pressing work commitments. Your mom sends her love, by the way.'

'And Dad?'

He shrugs. 'Well, you know.'

I do. Dad never expresses feelings. I'm sure he must have some, somewhere, but his care for me is usually delivered as expensive gifts or dictated wisdom.

Scott looks out over the restless sea and shakes his head. 'Don't you find it depressing, seeing that every day?'

'Not at all. Scott, what are you doing here?'

'Beat about the bush, why don't you?' he says.

'Scott...'

He knows that look. 'Right. Okay. So, I understand you've put your house on the market.'

I'm taken aback. 'How on earth did you know that?'

'The realtor phoned your father to make sure it wasn't a scam of some kind.'

'Oh. Oh dear. Right. Well, it's mine to sell if I want to.'

He gives me a look of his own. 'I know that. Your parents asked me to come over to make sure you know what you're doing. In fact, I'd really like to know what you *are* doing.'

'I'm staying here,' I say. 'Noel, the owner, asked me if I'd like to manage the hotel.'

'He has?' He has to think about that for a moment. 'Why?'

'Perhaps,' I say with slight sarcasm, 'he sees that I'm capable?'

'And are you?'

'What, capable? Or taking him up on the offer?'

'Look, I'm trying to help. Be nice. We both know you're capable,' he says.

'Sorry.' For the first time, I feel I could almost like Scott. Of course, he's not stupid. 'I haven't told him, but I think I will. It's a challenge. I need something useful to do. I've been sitting around at a loose end for too long.'

'And what about your music?'

'Things have changed. I can't do that any longer. I'm still going to play, just not in an orchestra. I might teach. I don't know yet. Maybe you could have my violin couriered over?'

'Oh. Right. Of course. So, that's it? You've made up your mind – you're staying here?'

I nod. 'Absolutely.'

'I don't get it, but if it's what you want, I'll try to smooth the way with your parents.'

'You'd do that?'

'I'm not entirely lacking in understanding. Look, I thought you and I had... ah... an understanding. But if we don't, then let's move on. I didn't come here to flog a dead donkey.'

Well, he's nothing if not practical.

'So, about the house. Do you want me to deal with it?'

'I would love you to,' I say honestly. At least I know I won't be rooked over the price, and he'll make sure all my belongings are safely stored. 'And if you could let Mom and Dad down easy, that would be a weight off my mind.'

'I already have. Your mom said if I can't persuade you to come home, then I'm to tell you she loves you and she hopes you'll be happy. She just wanted me to make sure you know what you're doing. She said she wondered if you'd met someone because you "had that look" in your eye. Have you?'

I had no idea Mom was so perceptive. I say tentatively, 'I might have. But I'm not sure, but I'm going to stay here, anyway, for a while. And if it doesn't work out here, I can always come back, can't I?'

He leans back and stretches. 'They aren't going to cut you off if you don't marry me. So, what about us? Our relationship?'

'I've always thought of you as a friend, more like a brother than a prospective partner,' I say. It's a little white lie, but there's no point in being cruel.

He nods. 'Good. As I'm going to become a partner in the

firm, it would be really nice to know we can meet as friends on family gatherings without flying at each other's throats.'

At that moment, there's a tentative knock at the door, and Grace calls, 'Can I come in?'

I wonder what she thought we were doing. 'Of course.'

The door opens, and she is ushered in on the back of a blast of wind. She pushes the door closed behind her, looking more tousled that I've ever seen her. She gives herself a quick shake-down, scoots her hands through her hair and says, 'Noel wondered if you would both like to come up to the house for a snifter before dinner?'

I burst out laughing, and Scott glances at me curiously. 'I'd love that,' I say. 'Tell him thank you.'

Grace grins. 'Erin's right. Be prepared for a grilling.'

After she's gone, I say, 'Mom is going to be so miffed!'

During the 'snifter', I feel the gentle pressure of Noel's curiosity, but both Scott and I, without having discussed it, keep our business to ourselves. Noel does ask whether I'm going to return to America, or whether he can hold out any hope that I'll manage the hotel, but I tell him I'll let him know soon.

I feel kind of relieved when Scott kisses me goodbye at the door the next morning and I wave him off. I'm not relieved because he's gone so much as relieved that there will be no confusing secrets between me and my family.

He can explain to Mom and Dad that I intend to stay, though it sounds as if Mom has already guessed. And Scott and I have found an even footing with each other, which actually feels a lot nicer than the abrasive rift I was envisaging.

31

ERIN

Discovering that Finn has a child has clogged up my ability to rationalise. How can we have an ongoing relationship unless I open my heart to his child, who is so much a part of his life? And how can I make a life here and see Finn from a distance and not be with him? The dynamics have changed so drastically, the decision to run away, not have to face them, is looking increasingly like a plan.

I also have a decision to make. I promised Noel I'd let him know whether I'd take the job. I'm keen enough to give it a try, and that really has nothing to do with any relationship issues.

I used to let my subconscious make decisions for me when I played music, so I pull the violin out of the case and allow some of my orchestral pieces to flow back into my fingers. I thought I wouldn't be able to play again, but over the next few days, the bow resonates beneath my hand, and my fingers find the notes, unbidden, even after all this time. I find myself lost in the old music for hours at a time and wonder how I could have spent two years cheating myself into believing that I could live without it. I imagine Kenny looking down at me, clapping, thrilled that I've discovered the courage to pick up the instrument that had been my first love. But here, in the rustic environment of Roone Bay, as I mentioned to Dad, there's no classical orchestra within miles, and music isn't meant to be played in solitary splendour. An audience is necessary to a musician, because music is a song enriched by the souls it flows through.

I remember the music in Nancy's bar, the way the whole place had been loud with chatter, the boozy crowd drifting to silence as 'The Lone Rock' was played. The room had been charged with emotion, and although I had been too moved to see it, Finn said mine weren't the only tears.

I phone Nancy's and ask when the next music session is, with every intention of taking the fiddle. Maybe the musicians would let me join in, quietly, at the back. Next Wednesday evening, I'm told. It runs weekly, unless the musicians can't get there. I ask if it's an open session, and I'm told anyone is welcome to join in. 'But if they're really bad, they might be quietly asked to leave,' she adds with a laugh.

I take myself down to Nancy's bar on a blustery November evening, only to find that it's virtually empty. I'd forgotten to ask what time it began. 'Oh, they'll turn up some time around ten,' the barman advises.

'Oh, I thought it would have started earlier.'

He shrugs. 'It's a farming community. The men come in after the work is done. It's always been that way, even though most of them don't actually farm any longer.'

I guess it's just tradition, and people don't like change. I can't imagine sitting on my own for nearly two hours, so I ask him if I can put the fiddle behind the bar while I go for a walk down to the shore.

'No problem,' he says. 'Do you play the trad music, then?'

'I know a few tunes.'

'Weren't you here a few weeks back? With Finn Sheehan?'

'Not with him,' I say hastily. 'But I did see him here. Will he be here tonight, do you know?'

He shrugs again and carries on wiping pint beer glasses with a cloth. 'He might, he might not, depending if he's around,' he says helpfully.

I thank him, zip up my fleece and pull on the windcheater.

It's a fair walk down past Finn's house, to the bay where he discovered me that first night. There are no flickering lights in the windows, no smoke from the chimney and his car isn't parked on the road. I don't have to knock to know he's out, so I walk on, wondering if he's at Eilis's house, whether he hasn't really given up on her, as he said. They seemed very comfortable together, and she really is very lovely.

The walk takes me back to that night when Finn rescued me from the beach. It's hard to recall quite how screwed-up I was. It feels like something that happened in the dim and distant past, not just a few weeks back. Now I'm able to look out over the dark water with the sense of a new beginning – whether it's with Finn or not – rather than sink under the weight of the overwhelming grief of a lost dream.

The water is flat calm and dark, the low cloud base obliterating any possible light from the moon. It's atmospheric and serenely beautiful. The dark-on-dark shadows lend a feeling of floating in another dimension, and the silence is overpowering. No people, no engines, and even the seagulls are sleeping. Just a faintly calling wind and the soft shushing of waves lapping insistently at the shingle. The sea is like a drowsy dragon tonight, sleepily hiding her raging temper.

This is what it must have been like at night when Nellie lived here, save for the distant, regular flash of the Fastnet Rock lighthouse snatching the dark water. She must have left Ireland a few years before the lighthouse was constructed. There would have been no electric lights, no commercial factory or internal combustion engine noises hovering on the air, just this magical stillness of a lifestyle that hadn't changed for hundreds of years.

I've read that the Irish poor were thought to be contented with their lot, believing that hard work would lead to eventual salvation. I wonder if that was really true. The divide between rich and poor was so great, the rich must have seemed like ancient gods on unreachable pedestals. And yet surely the Irish had dreams? Because despite poverty, they still made time to play music, dance and sing.

How they must have felt betrayed as their livelihoods and even their lives were ripped out from underneath them during the famine. It must have seemed as if God had abandoned them. I simply can't imagine this atmospheric and serene landscape harbouring the carnage portrayed in the books I've been reading, with dead strung along the roadsides, the freely roaming dogs better fed than they had ever been while their owners were alive. I stand in absolute and silent contemplation, remembering the dead. It must have been hell on earth, but hopefully they're now at peace.

I turn and head back along the coast road, towards Nancy's bar. Finn's house is still dark, so my uncertainty about his interest is not going to be satisfied tonight.

When I get to the bar, I hear the low rumble of dialogue and realise that in the time I was away, it's gone from deserted to heaving.

I think if I hadn't left the fiddle behind the bar I might just have walked on past, telling myself it was too late, I was too tired, I didn't want to... all the while knowing I was making excuses not to walk through the door. Well, I can't rely on Finn to bolster my courage. This is something I have to do for myself.

I feel conspicuous as I open the door to a belt of cigarette smoke, stale beer and the creepy sensation of being surreptitiously watched. Every person present knows I'm a blow-in, as Grace calls it.

I fight my way through, and the man behind the bar welcomes me with a smile. 'White wine?' he asks, remembering.

'Please.' I nod and try to breathe normally. He puts it on the bar, then, before I can say no, he's lifted the fiddle case and slid it over to me. 'Go on over. I told them you'd be playing.'

I feel faint. *You what?* I want to shout. I need time to decide if I want to do this! But seeing the fiddle case in my hand, like the Red Sea creating a passage for Moses and the Israelites, the crowd parts and closes behind me as I'm ushered towards the musicians.

I'm seated during a flurry of handshakes and some mild curiosity. *Erin Ryan. I'm staying at the hotel. Yes, I've played a few tunes. I'm from Boston. No, I only met Finn recently, at Colla Quay beach. No, I don't know where he is.*

Meanwhile, as the musicians are getting out their instruments and stowing the cases out of the way, I feel compelled to do the same. I tighten the bow, rosin it automatically and clutch the violin with sweaty fingers.

'Okay, so,' the button box player says. I'm thinking that the old man is possibly the leader of this impromptu band. 'We'll start with a few steady jigs. Get warmed up.' He glances at me. 'Join in whenever you can.'

I shoot him a glance that's half-grimace, half-smile. He must think I'm a ship passing in their night, tossed in by an accidental breeze, and will blow away again in the next sailing. I suspect that they all feel a little nervous, waiting to see what kind of noise I'll produce, wondering if they'll have to quietly ask me to pack up and leave.

He can't be as nervous as me, though. In the Boston Irish Centre, I had no problem breezing in with a smile on my lips, but here in Ireland, playing Irish music with the Irish seems a bit presumptuous. He nods, beats twice with his foot and, with the cohesion of an orchestra, everyone starts.

It's amazing, mind-blowing and beautiful.

I find myself moving my fingers to the notes of the tunes and carefully lift the fiddle to my chin. I know this tune. I learned it when I was barely big enough for my fingers to reach the right notes. Despite everything I've said about Dad, he took me to the Irish sessions regularly, once he knew how much I loved them; before everyone, me included, realised that I had a genuine flair. I'm reminded, now, of the pride on his face as he told people, *This is Erin, my daughter*.

I play so quietly I doubt anyone can hear me, but I see them glance at my bow getting the right rhythm, my fingers finding the right notes. When the set of jigs comes to an abrupt end and the musicians lower their instruments to sip at their pints, there's a faint lull in the surrounding crowd. The musicians smile encouragingly at me and nod. We play a few more sets. Reels, hornpipes, jigs. Then the lead man – Tom, I finally recall – nods at me. 'Start something,' he says.

'Oh, goodness. I don't know...'

'Anything,' he insists.

This is the point of no return. I'm on trial. I begin to shake, and I'm sure all the musicians notice.

'Take your time,' Tom says kindly. 'Do something slow if you like.'

Okay, so perhaps I won't get shot at dawn. I take a deep breath and start one of my favourite airs. As I draw the bow over the strings, I realise how beautiful the fiddle truly is. That it was hand-made I knew, but the sound it produces is sweet and pure. I close my eyes and let the music soar out into the smoky bar. The song is about a man whose true love was forced to marry another for the inheritance. He's grieving for her, and his grief is entwined in the tune, even though the words are absent.

A faint vibration slips through me. I feel as if Kenny is by my side, staring at me, entranced, wondering, as he said many times, how I could produce such music out of bits of wood and wire and horsehair. I play the tune through three times then, towards the end of the last rendition, open my eyes and give a minuscule nod to the other musicians, indicating that I'm going to change.

They lift their instruments with the eagerness of a line-up of runners paused, waiting for the gun. I whack into a fast reel. Someone behind me whoops, and the musicians plough in, lifting the sound out into the atmosphere.

32

ERIN

I decide I've delved into the past too much; it's the present I need to find. Am I going to stay and manage the hotel? It's a challenge, but, strangely, it was Scott's words that make me feel as though I could do it. I hadn't expected that accolade, despite it arriving on the back of my snippy comment. I put the history books in my bag and head to the library to dispose of them.

On the way, I see Finn's Mini stopped outside the little grocery store. A smile breaks out on my face. I've taken a single step when I see him come out with Eilis. He's looking into her eyes with what I can only describe as love. I come to an abrupt halt. He opens the back and manhandles a pile of carrier bags in, then opens the passenger door for her, like a real gentleman. I know she's the mother of his child, but it somehow strikes me as a little too cosy. Their attitudes are those of people who know each other really well, like husband and wife, or lovers.

I feel something plummet inside. Is Finn playing fast and loose with me? Is he still with Eilis?

He piles into the driver's side, plumps himself into the seat and pulls her into a close one-armed embrace. He sinks his lips onto the top of her head. They stay like that for a moment, hugging, then she pulls herself away. A laugh flashes across her features, and the way she's looking at him leaves me in no doubt about her feelings.

She loves him.

As Finn drives off, I feel like a voyeur watching from the sidelines. Would Finn be that devious? String me along... I don't want to believe it. I don't... but... I shake my head. If Kenny were here, maybe he'd tell me I've been chasing rainbows, that I've been an utter fool. Am I so afraid of living the rest of my life alone that I've invented a budding relationship where none exists? Am I that gullible?

It would be so easy to cut and run, but as I've more or less told Scott to tell Mom and Dad that I'm staying, to go back now would be admitting I've made a mistake, and I simply don't want to have that conversation. The best decision now is to plough my energy into the hotel and present Finn with a cold front until I really know what's going on. I feel sorry for him, for what he experienced, but I have to protect my own fragile emotions, too.

When I answer the phone in my room a few days later, it's Finn, and my heart does a little leap. I make myself calm down. A week ago, I would have wondered why I hadn't seen him around, but now I know the reason, I'm armed to face him. It will be easier to hold him at arm's length, pretend nothing ever happened between us, than actually confront my hurt at his betrayal.

'Are you busy?' he asks. 'Sorry, I've been away. I had to work in Cork, cover for someone who was off sick. Have you got a moment? I'm downstairs.'

Liar, I think, my resolve hardening. 'Of course. I'm on my way.'

I meet him in the foyer, my emotional mask in place.

He looks grim and distant, as he had that first time I met him, when I was looking for the hotel. He indicates the foyer. 'I need to talk to you. Shall we sit down?'

Here it comes, I think. The brush-off, the explanation that he thought we might have made a go of things but he's realised that he was mistaken.

He's picking awkwardly at a thread on his shirt. There's an embarrassing silence for a moment, then he comes out with it. 'Scott came back. I saw him.'

'You did? Well, I told you we had things to sort out.'

Finn nods. 'I know. Jane told me you've decided not to manage the hotel, that you're going back to America with Scott. That you're planning to marry him. She overheard Noel talking to Grace. I just want to know whether that's true.'

I'm stunned and say somewhat acerbically, 'Perhaps Jane shouldn't listen in on other people's conversations.'

'She cares about me. I had to see Noel about another matter, and it just came out in conversation.' He shrugs. 'I'd hoped that if it was true, you might have told me yourself.'

I'm annoyed now. 'I might if you'd been around.'

'I was busy. I was working, I said. And then Eilis needed my help for a couple of days.'

'Sure she did.' My tone's probably a bit snarky, but I can't help myself. He's trying to hedge his bets.

His eyes flip up to mine. 'What? Well, she's Liam's mother, after all. I have an obligation.'

'Was there something particular you wanted?' I ask coldly.

He casts a surprised glance then changes the subject abruptly. 'I've been thinking about your Nellie.'

'And?'

'Well, it's not actually anything concrete. I want to run something by you. I was talking about it to Father Dominic the other day, and he told me that back in the day, Nellie was sometimes shortened from Eleanor.'

'Oh! I didn't know that. I thought Nellie was a real name.'

'Maybe it was that, too, but equally, your Nellie might have been Eleanor Crowley then Eleanor O'Mahoney. I asked the father about birth records, and he told me that central recording only started around 1860, so I don't know if we'd find anything there. Your Nellie was born in the 1820s, you said, and the child, Annie, was born before the famine...'

'In 1842, according to the family tree.'

'Okay, so church records were still being kept at that time. It fell apart during the famine, of course, as the priests couldn't keep up with the sheer numbers of deaths. So many people died, it would be impossible to calculate the real figure. But any older records were sent up to the archives in Dublin a few years back. Father Dominic is going up to Dublin in a week or so, and he's going to pop into the records office for you to see if he can find anything in the archives from the Tirbeg townland. If we could find Annie's birth record, it would include details of the parents, and that would give us Nellie's full name, maybe even her address, though that might simply say Roone Bay, of course.'

'I'd appreciate that.'

'Look, about Scott...'

I rise and say abruptly, 'I have work to do. I appreciate you coming to tell me that.'

He stands up slowly as I leave, confusion written on his face.

Later in the day, Grace tells me a bit more about the hotel. She shows me how the booking-in system works, explains the hotel policies and where various supplies are sourced, right down to where they keep crockery and cleaning materials. I'm well aware that she's doing her best to sell the hotel and the post of manager to me.

I can't help being intrigued by the scope of the venture. 'You still want me to give it a try?'

'Of course,' she says, surprised, and picks up where she left off. 'You wouldn't be expected to clean, exactly. But sometimes, when the staff are doing other things, the manager has to get her hands dirty, as I know all too well!'

'Don't you want to manage the hotel yourself?'

'I have so much else to do,' she explains. 'Besides being Livvy's mum, I'm sorting out Noel's memoir. He has piles and piles of stuff that has never been catalogued. You'd be doing me a real favour in taking this off my hands. If you want to, that is. Noel said you're thinking of leaving?'

'I don't think I told him any such thing.'

Grace sighs. 'Well, he's usually quite canny when it comes to reading people, and I really hope this time he's wrong. He says reading people is no different from reading horses. He says you're... skittish since Scott and your parents visited, and that you just have to know what signs to look for.'

I give a snort of laughter. 'I've never been compared to a horse before, skittish or otherwise.'

She grins. 'You know I didn't mean it like that!'

'I was joking, of course.'

'Well, he's all about the horses, so his analogies tend to go that way.'

I like Grace. She's amusing and extremely down to earth, and I suspect she didn't come from wealth, any more than Noel did. I'd like to have a good chat with her, find out what her background is. I'm thinking that if I do stay, maybe we could be friends.

'I wasn't planning on leaving,' I say finally. 'My parents were hoping I'd go home, but the idea of managing the hotel is growing on me.'

She can barely contain her grin. 'Okay. Fantastic. Shall I

carry on? Am I overloading you?' she asks. 'There's a lot to take in.'

'It's fairly straightforward, actually. I organised several art shows for Kenny, and the administration behind something that looks so serene was actually quite nerve-wracking. All those egos to stroke! And I'm not just talking about the artists!'

Grace casts me a calculating look. 'So, you like a challenge?'

That sounds like a challenge to me, but I don't respond.

She sighs. 'Look, I know you came here for a holiday, but we're kind of desperate. How about a trial for a few months? I'd just like to know whether to keep reading the CVs of dreadfully confident people with oodles of experience.'

'I'm curious to know why you think I'd be better than one of those people. Is it simply because I'm here?'

'It's because we all like you,' she answers simply. 'In this small town, a blow-in will either merge into the community or be forever a blow-in.'

'And I've merged?'

'You're merging,' she says honestly. 'It takes a while, as I learned. The people we interviewed had no intention of even trying. They would have used this job as a stepping stone, stayed for a year, if that, and moved on. And the one who actually accepted the post didn't turn up. Noel wants someone who really wants to stay in the arse-end of Ireland.'

I burst out laughing at her apologetic expression.

'Well, those were Noel's exact words,' she justifies.

'I doubt he means that. He loves this place.'

'As we all do,' Grace says. 'It has this strange effect on some people. Like we go through this magical portal and can't find a way out until it's too late. Then we don't want to leave, and we get stuck for a hundred years, like in the fairy tale. Noel blames it on the little people.'

I know what she means. I feel as though the land and the people have wrapped themselves around me, cushioned me from myself, almost. I wonder if I would feel differently if I hadn't met Finn. I have a feeling it's not going to work out between us, so there is that to consider. I'd be upset, but I'm a realist, at the end of the day. 'Well, I only came to chase my ancestors. I assumed a month would do it, then I'd head home.'

'And now?'

'I'm kind of rethinking where home is.'

She beams. 'There! I told Noel you're a keeper. It will be so nice to tell him he's wrong! If you need more time, I'll give it a couple of weeks before interviewing again,' she decides firmly. 'But I really hope you'll give it a shot.' She starts to walk away and turns back briefly. 'In the meantime, if you want to know anything, just ask. And if you have any more ideas... Well, we want to hear those, too. Oh, and how is the hunt for your Nellie going? Grandpa Noel was asking if you'd made any progress.'

I update her on progress so far, which is to say, not so much. Strangely, it was Grace calling Noel 'grandpa' in front of me that made me inch a little closer to admitting that I really do want the job. Being jobless, alone and presently homeless makes me feel kind of redundant to the world. I'd like to start digging some roots in again, feel as though I actually belong somewhere.

33

NELLIE 1883

Nellie's grandson, Patrick, was provided with the best education Sarah could afford, and as the country began to recover from the devastation of the war, Sarah's father's firm began to improve its financial stability. By his early twenties, Patrick was well on his way to becoming a lawyer and walked with confidence within the circles Nellie had once viewed from afar.

Nellie had recovered enough to be pleased for her grandson and cared for him with a slight sense of distance. He was not her son, much as he shared the superficial appearance inherited from Luke, and she was afraid to give herself over fully to this confident young man. She'd lost everyone she loved and knew she would not survive another such loss.

Before the Civil War, she'd kept in contact with Kate Kelly, but as things got tough, Kate, too had had her problems. Her rich husband had turned out to be not so rich, after all, and disappeared one day, having emptied their bank account. She carried on living in the same house, squeezed into a single room in the attic with her four children, so that she could rent out four of the rooms to lodgers. It wasn't ideal, but she was no longer the flighty young woman having fun – she had responsibilities. With her usual gusto, she flung herself into making the best of a bad job.

Since emigrating, and learning to write, Kate had kept in touch with her family. Her father and her one brother who hadn't emigrated had somehow survived the famine. Of the other brothers, one had emigrated to Australia and had a family there, and one had gone also to America, though they had never heard from him again. It was assumed he'd either died in the crossing or in the Civil War, or simply died working, as so many Irish had. She learned that her father had added a few more acres of land to the farm – Kate didn't ask how – and as the farm was starting to make a profit, and there were rooms lying empty, Kate was told she would be welcomed home with her children.

Nellie hugged Kate. They kissed and shed a few tears, sharing stories and reminiscing about the past, knowing that they would never meet again in this life. When Kate finally left, promising to write and tell her absolutely *everything*, Nellie was desolate. Eve and Danny had moved away, and it seemed that all the people she'd known and loved were gone. Patrick and Sarah tried to cheer her, saying that no matter, they were still family, but Nellie felt a weight of self-pity settle inside her that she believed nothing except death would shift. She just wanted to lie down, give up and be at peace. She dreamed of William now, and after all these years, she could finally see him again and recall his gentle soul with a hint of the love she'd once showered him with. She was increasingly homesick for Ireland; for the little house she'd grown up in, for her parents, for the rugged backbones of rock she had viewed from the hills and for the sound of the sea that relentlessly pounded them.

Nellie was so tired of grief that her eyes remained dry as she mentally reviewed her options. She knew, from Kate's letters, that if she went back to Ireland, which she still thought of as home, it was likely that the cottage her family had owned for generations, that she'd been born in and lived in with William, would be a ruin, its fields appropriated into other properties. She didn't even have that to go back to. In Ireland, she would have no income, and it was likely that all the people she'd once known there, too, would be dead and gone. She would be as lonely there as she was in America.

The night Kate left, Nellie dreamed of William, and there he was in her mind, like the last time she'd seen him, and the emigrants' song resounded through her sleep.

> Oh, Érin grá mo chroí, *you're the only land*
>   *for me.*
> *You're the fairest that my eyes did ever behold.*
> *You're the bright star of the west,*
> *You're the land Saint Patrick blessed.*
> *You're the dear little isle so far away.*

Never had she felt as homesick as when she woke up the next morning, with the hint of the dream fading into the cold Boston morning. *Why now?* Why was she able to see William so clearly now, after all these long years of trying to recall his face? Was this a portent? Did this mean she was going to die soon, and he was telling her that he was there, waiting, with his arms out, to welcome her into the great hereafter?

Nothing Patrick or Sarah did could lift her spirits. She knew they were worried about her. Sure, she was losing weight, but wasn't that normal for someone of her age? She was nearly sixty now, and there were few enough who lived much past that. So many had not even made it that far. Lost to war, or famine, sickness or childbirth... She decided that she wouldn't mind slipping away. She'd struggled long enough; perhaps it was just her time.

When the letter from Kate finally arrived some months later, it was tattered and marked as though it had its own story to tell. Nellie recognised Kate's long scrawl on the envelope. Nellie's life in Ireland was so far in her past it was hazy around the edges, like a dream not quite recalled on waking, and she opened the envelope with a certain apathy. Yet she found herself quite moved by Kate's news, and was hit once again by nostalgia and her own inherent sadness.

She struggled to decipher Kate's amusing account of the journey, which had not been half as long or as bad as the journey to America, as steam ships had mostly replaced sail, so the passage took just two weeks, landing her in Dublin. She had shared a cabin with three other girls, but it wasn't so bad, apart from the *facilities* (the word was underscored heavily). The worst part, she said, was the journey down to Cork by coach and thence to Roone Bay, and a four-hour wait for her brother to pick her up from Skibbereen and take her to the farm, as he hadn't realised she'd arrived. And didn't her brother look just like her father! And he being just eight years old when she'd left to seek her fortune.

But, Kate added (also underscored), *the best bit of news is yet to come. I told you my news first, my dear Nellie, as once I added my most exciting discovery, my biteen of news would be of little interest to you. You see, my darling Nellie, I have discovered that Annie is alive and well. She is here, in Ireland, living near Bantry with her husband, Andrew Nolan, who is a doctor, and two of her three children. You should have seen her face when I told her you were still alive!!! And I can picture yours now, my dearest friend. So, cry yourself to sleep with happiness, my lovely Nellie, because your baby is alive. I could tell you her*

*story, but it's hers to tell. Just believe me that she thought you
dead all these years, or she would have come looking. Come home
to us here, in dear old Ireland. We are all waiting for you. Your
best friend, Kate.*

Sarah came into the kitchen, where Nellie was staring numbly
at the wall. She stopped short, hand to her breast, and asked
what was wrong. Nellie was so choked she couldn't speak. She
handed the letter to Sarah, tears spilling silently down her
cheeks. She didn't know what she was crying for, whether it was
happiness that her daughter was alive or sadness for all the
years they had missed together.

Her Annie was alive, and not only that, she was married
and had children!

Sarah read the letter and put it down slowly. 'What will you
do, Nellie, love?'

Nellie had no hesitation in saying, 'I love you dearly, Sarah,
and my grandchild, Patrick, but I have to go home. You do
understand, don't you?'

The two women hugged and cried, because no words could
express their fluctuating emotions. Nellie, to find that her lost
child hadn't suffered the ills she had been imagining all these
years, and Sarah, happiness mixed with grief, because her
staunchly supportive mother-in-law would disappear back over
the water, and she would likely never see her again.

34

ERIN

It's early evening when there's a knock on my door, and Grace's voice asks, 'Erin, can I come in?'

'Of course,' I say, jumping up. I open the door and indicate the low seats by the Juliet balcony. 'Come on in and sit down. Can I get you a drink or something? I've got a bottle of wine somewhere.'

'No thanks. I need to speak to you.'

She sounds a bit awkward, so I prompt her. 'About managing the hotel?'

'Maybe indirectly. I'm sorry if you think I'm prying, but I'm a little confused. On the one hand, you seem interested in managing the hotel, and on the other, you said something about your parents organising a wedding for you and Scott.'

'My parents wanted me to marry Scott. I never said I was going to. He came here to propose, and I told him absolutely not.'

'Oh. Was he disappointed?'

'Not as much as he should have been.'

'I see,' she says, hearing the wry note in my voice. 'So why does Finn think you're going to marry him?'

I flush violently. 'I might have given him that impression.'

'Self-defence?'

I nod glumly. 'I thought maybe we had a connection, but I was wrong. He's still in love with Liam's mother, Eilis.'

'What makes you think that?'

I glance at her, surprised by the question. 'I saw them together. You can't fake that kind of intimacy. He told me he wasn't with her, but...' I grimace. 'I saw the look on her face, too. She loves him to bits.'

'Oh,' she says. 'I see. Well, it's true, she does, but she knows it's not reciprocated. She came to terms with that a while back.' A spark of amusement lights her eyes as she leans forward and pats my knee. 'So, Finn thinks you're with Scott, and you're not. And you think he's with Eilis, and he's not.'

'But I saw them!'

'No wonder you thought that.' She sighs. 'Right. Maybe he should have made it clear. Eilis has been diagnosed with a particularly virulent form of bone cancer. Finn takes her to the hospital for her chemo and looks after Liam while she's there. The chemo isn't going to save her life, but it might give her another few years to be with her son. Eilis's mother is prepared to take on Liam because Finn has to work, but Finn wants to be there for him, too. He doesn't love Eilis. He's just doing what any kind man would do and helping her cope with something that really isn't fair. So young and pretty, having to face, well, you know, instead of planning some kind of future. Not easy.'

'Oh Lord,' I say guiltily. 'Poor girl. I had no idea.'

'I didn't want to interfere, but Eilis called to ask me what was going on with you. She said Finn's really miserable because he thought you liked him, and now he doesn't know what to think.'

She smiles gently as she rises and walks to the door. 'I guess you need to let Finn know it's all a misunderstanding, don't you?'

'I don't have a contact number for him.'

'He doesn't have a phone, but his father does. Or you can call his work. I'll get the numbers for you.' She puts her head back around the door. 'Oh, and about managing the hotel? Have you made a decision?'

I'm so embarrassed by my own stupidity, I feel like getting the first bus out of here, but, clearly, I will have to talk to Finn. 'Yes,' I say. 'I'll give it a trial, like you said. But I can't make any promises.'

'No promises expected.' She nods and leaves.

What a lovely person she is, I think. They all are, in fact. Everyone I've ever met here. They are all absolutely wonderful. But there's no time like the present. I make the call to Finn's work and pass on a message, asking Finn to please come and speak to me at Roone Bay Hotel.

A day later, Grace calls me from the foyer to tell me Finn is here. I go down the stairs slowly, knowing I'm going to find myself embarrassed and tongue-tied. He's wearing his normal uniform of jeans, checked shirt and Doc Martens, and he looks stunningly desirable with the outside chill on his cheeks, his hair mussed by the wind, a worried expression written over his features. I don't doubt he can see the heat reaching my cheeks. This teenage-crush thing is kind of embarrassing.

'I got your message. Is everything all right?' he asks, concerned.

'I'm not marrying Scott,' I blurt out. 'I let you think that. I'm sorry.'

There's a pause while he takes this information in, but his expression remains puzzled. 'Then why? Is it because of Liam? Is that too much of a problem for you?'

I shake my head violently. 'No. Not at all. I thought it might be, but I got past that.'

'Good. I'm glad. But I still don't understand. Unless you just want me to leave you alone. The last thing I want is to be chasing someone who isn't interested. Grace said you're going to be managing the hotel. We can agree to be friends and draw a line under this?'

I shake my head miserably. 'It's not that, either.' I take a deep breath. 'I saw you with Eilis. It seemed as if...'

'Ah,' he says, the rigid furrow between his brows fading slightly.

'It looked as if you were still with her. I didn't understand.'

'But why didn't you ask me?'

'I was embarrassed. And hurt.'

'Of course you were. Damn it, girl! You must have thought I was playing fast and loose. I should have told you about Eilis. It just didn't seem necessary. I'm an idiot.'

He closes the gap between us and pulls me into a close hug. A shiver of anticipation runs through me, from a cold spot in the top of my head, to my toes. I put my arms around him, hesitantly at first, then clutch as tightly as I can. We stand like that for a long moment. All my fears evaporate, the vacuum almost instantly replaced by a rush of relief and happiness and hope for the future.

'It's a difficult situation,' he says, his lips against my hair. 'You see, it was me who left her. She didn't want me to go, but after the initial fling, I realised that we really didn't have anything in common. I didn't love her. I didn't want to be with her for the rest of my life. I didn't even fancy her, if the truth be told, not that I could tell her that. I think I told you that I did wonder if she'd got pregnant to try to make me stay. Then, of course, she got diagnosed and needed my support more than ever... I should have explained all this to you.' He pushed me back, bent his head and stared at me closely. 'I feel that I have all those things with you. A connection. Something so indefinable that I couldn't even find the words. I fancy you like crazy, but I knew you had issues to work through.'

He fancies me like crazy? When Eilis is so beautiful?

'So, are we still heading in the same direction? Do you think we stand a chance?'

I nod, tongue-tied in a way I'd never felt with Kenny. But then, I'd never had any doubts about Kenny. I never had to feel guilty for doubting him. Even if my doubts about Finn are of my own making, it's still awkward.

'Do you want a coffee?' I ask in a rush, pulling free and indicating the empty seating area.

'I wouldn't say no to tea, but I don't want to...'

'I'll go and get it. It won't take a moment.'

It does take a moment because I'm all fingers and thumbs. I fill the kettle but can't find any teabags. Then I find a tin of loose tea and remember being told that the Irish think loose tea has a better flavour. I swear under my breath. I really don't know how much to put in the teapot, so shovel in several generous spoons and finally take the loaded tray back to the table by the window where Finn has seated himself.

'Here we go,' I say brightly.

'It's a lovely view,' Finn comments, probably trying to make me feel less gauche. 'I hated the idea of Noel building a hotel here, but I kind of got used to it. It's actually not the eyesore I was afraid it would be. More like a sort of gothic fairy tale than a hotel.'

I pick up the heavy china teapot, and the handle promptly slips through my hand so that I'm forced to plonk it back onto the tray. It sends a gush of tea from the spout towards Finn, who jumps back hastily.

'Sorry,' I say, but then we're both laughing, and for some reason that makes everything better.

'No bother. Here, let me.' As he pours, he says, 'So, you

aren't going back to America, and you aren't going to marry Scott. You have no idea how happy that makes me.'

'I never was,' I admit guiltily. 'Though he did come here with a big fat diamond ring and proposed.'

'He did?'

'I told him it was never going to happen. Even if you didn't want me. And I just couldn't get my head past that. Because Eilis is so beautiful. I was jealous and upset, and thought I'd imagined what was between us and didn't want to embarrass myself by acting like a jilted lover.'

'Well, thank goodness for Grace and her endless common sense. But what led Scott to believe you would welcome his proposal? I feel a bit sorry for the guy, actually.'

'Well, don't. He's so full of himself, it didn't occur to him that I wasn't smitten. He'll find someone soon enough. The problem was, when Kenny died, I went back to live with my parents. Scott was often there, working with my father. I was spaced out on anti-depressants a lot of the time and just went along with everything my parents suggested, which often included the four of us going out as a party. They all read more into it than I did. It turns out that he asked my father for permission to ask for my hand, and they all agreed that it would be a wonderful solution to my unhappiness.'

His brows rise. 'Isn't that a bit last century?'

'Yes, well. He's Dad's protégé, and they both have a high opinion of themselves. Apparently, they all decided I'd had enough time to grieve and should get on with my life, and Scott thought that was where he came in. He was a bit taken aback when I said no. He's a lawyer, too. Dad's going to let him buy in, become a partner, and I suppose I was perceived as the bonus deal. At least he had the sense to ask me when we weren't in a public place. And he didn't go down on one knee, which would have been even more embarrassing. I certainly wouldn't have said yes to save his face. I think they've all been browsing wedding catalogues on my behalf.'

'Oh dear. Your parents are going to be a bit put out.'

'I think Mom realised, and Dad will have to get over himself. I told Scott not to mention it until after they got back home. They think Scott's a good catch, but he really isn't my kind of person. They never much liked Kenny. They thought he was a freeloader, after my money. But he wasn't.' My tone betrays a hint of the anger I'd felt when I realised that was what they thought.

'Did you ever think he was?'

'Not for a second. I'll grieve for Kenny until the day I die. He was a talented artist. It's just not fair. And don't say "life isn't", because that would really annoy me.' As I snap out the last sentence, my face collapses and tears prickle to the surface. I mutter, 'Sorry, I wasn't thinking of Eilis.'

He comes over and kneels in front of me, wipes my eyes with his thumbs then hugs me. 'Don't ever apologise for mourning someone you loved. These things can't be hurried. I want to get to know you, Erin, but in your own time. When you're ready.'

'I'd really like that.'

'No more secrets, eh?'

'No more misunderstandings.'

'Not until the next time, anyway.'

We both laugh at his wry comment, then he adds, 'So, you've decided to stay. And will you take the job Grace offered you?'

'I've told her I will, but I can't make any guarantees.'

'You'll be great. I know. Okay, so. We're all good, then?'

I nod.

'Good. It's a weight off my mind. When I came around before, it wasn't just to tell you that maybe Nellie was maybe called Eleanor. I wanted to talk to you, but you were so distant, I thought I'd got it all wrong.'

'Sorry.'

'No more apologies. Moving on, okay?'

'Okay. Talking of Nellie,' I say, 'I was chewing over the whole handwriting problem after you discovered it. It came to me in a flash. Why would someone else do that if she was still alive?'

'You did say maybe she lost her sight.'

'It's possible. But there's another possibility...'

Finn leans forward, captivated.

'Because she was leaving Boston,' I say triumphantly.

'But why would she leave Boston, where her grandson and his family were living?'

'Maybe she was homesick and came back to Ireland to spend her final years. If she did, it's possible that she actually did place that stone for her parents. I know that's a huge lot of what-ifs. But if she did, maybe she's buried locally.'

I see the spark of understanding dawn in Finn's eyes.

'So, we were looking for records of her parents, when we should actually be looking for Nellie or Eleanor O'Mahoney,' he muses. 'Or even Annie. What if Nellie had word that Annie had somehow found her way back to Ireland? That would surely be a good reason for her to come back.'

'That's unlikely,' I say. 'But we know the exact date of Nellie's death, from the bible. It might be worth putting a request for information in the various church publications, maybe get the wider community interested in finding her grave.'

I'm tickled by a little thrill of excitement, even after Finn says, 'It's all conjecture, though. She might not have come back at all.'

We both pick up our cups and take a sip. The tea is really strong and bitter, and looks like tar. We exchange a look of amusement.

'Shall we go to the café?' Finn suggests.

We share a grin. 'I'll nip up to my room and grab my wind-cheater.'

'Okay, so.'

It's actually quite cold outside, and there's a brisk breeze flying in from the sea. We're walking side by side down the slope from the hotel when he reaches for my hand. We don't look at each other, but warmth trickles through me.

'So—' he begins.

'I wondered—' I say at the same time.

He laughs. 'You first.'

'Oh, it was nothing.'

Over a decent cup of tea and a hot buttered scone, Finn lets me know that he's going to be away in Cork city again for a few days. 'I'm jumping through psychiatric hoops,' he says. 'Even though I've been signed back to work, I'm being made to work in the office for a bit. They're afraid to let me go out to play on the boats.'

'Maybe they're right?'

'Maybe. But I wanted to let you know why I'll be away, so you don't jump to any wrong conclusions.'

'I won't – I promise,' I say guiltily.

'And when I come back, I don't want you to feel rushed into anything, so we'll take it easy.'

I feel chastened by my stupid reaction. 'I should have spoken to you before allowing my hurt to write the wrong story.'

'I totally understand,' he says. 'Eilis really is beautiful, and that's probably what attracted me in the first place, but that wasn't enough, in the end. We just had nothing in common.'

'Thank goodness I'm not beautiful,' I joke.

'I didn't say that. Your beauty is more subtle – it's in the way your lips move when you speak, the way your eyes go distant when you're thinking. I fell in love with the idea of loving Eilis rather than her as a person. I feel bad about that. But Erin, I'm learning to love you from the inside out, which hopefully is how Kenny felt about you. Now, I have to go. Are you okay about everything?'

'Absolutely. We'll take it easy.'

He hugs me, and we kiss outside, softly and quickly like an old married couple parting, and I feel very mature because we're doing the right thing by not rushing into a relationship on the back of our respective mental issues. And at the same time, I feel cheated that the kiss didn't deepen and turn into something more.

35

ERIN

I write the outline of Nellie's story and add my notes about what might have happened. I drive the canary-yellow car out to the neighbouring townlands, sourcing the vicars and priests who produce their own community pamphlets, to spread my search out into the wider community. I find myself welcomed everywhere I go, brought into church vestries for cups of strong tea, shown around graveyards and provided with so much fascinating local lore it would fill a book. It occurs to me that I should be taking notes, that perhaps such a book is just what's needed in the foyer of the hotel, something for visitors to take away and read at their leisure. Not the big stuff, about the famine, but the little stuff: people's stories and anecdotes and photographs. I must mention that to Grace. Given that she's writing Noel's memoir, when that's done, she might be scratching around for another writing project. The elders of the community have a wealth of tales, amusing, sometimes sad and always human, which encompass a world that's fast disappearing.

But then, I suppose every generation thinks that.

As I'm driving around, I finally realise another truth: I'm

not afraid of driving any longer. I should buy a car. The rental on this one is astronomical, and it spends most of its time sitting in the parking lot. I check out a few cars that I happen to see in passing and am amused by the outright dishonesty of Irish car salesmen. They are shameless hawkers who even seem proud of their blarney.

I'll get Finn to help me buy a car when he comes back.

I'm hoping he'll be back Wednesday, in time for the music session at Nancy's bar. I really want to play again. I need to play again; it's who I am. Kenny's art and my music were the glue that joined us, and our bond is slowly coming adrift through my association with Finn, and the other wonderful people who now surround me. Kenny is stepping further back into the mist with every bridge I cross, but I know he'd be pleased to learn that my love of music has been rekindled.

The various priests and vicars I chat to take my notes and promise to include them in their magazines, which can be anything from weekly, to bi-monthly, to just at Christmas. I might have a long wait or never hear anything from anyone. My search for Nellie is also an unfinished story, and I wonder whether it will remain unfinished. I am getting the strangest feeling that I'm close to her, even though she remains annoyingly just out of reach.

Finn isn't back by Wednesday, though he did say he'd try to make it. This time I walk into the bar with my fiddle case in my hand, and I'm instantly welcomed into the session. I feel as though I've come home. As I play, lost in the atmosphere, the old tunes and the new compressing time, I have the strangest feeling that history isn't something that happened in the past. It's here, around me, not just in the music but in the people, in their comradeship, their community spirit. They have a long history of oppression but somehow have discovered the ability to not allow it to burden their souls, but move into the future, bringing the old values with them.

I close my eyes and let the music wrap around me, and just briefly I imagine Kenny is beside me. But when I look up, it's Finn, grinning madly as he joins in, note for note, his leg fluttering in time to the beat, as mine is. I've never been able to put my finger on just what it is that I love about Irish music; I guess it's in my genes, like the hint of red in my hair.

We play for a few hours, and I'm exhausted when the box player puts his instrument down, yawning widely. I've barely spoken to Finn since he came in, but we say our goodbyes, and he follows me through the depleted clientele to the door. We walk out into the dark night. He takes my elbow and steers me towards the hotel.

'You weren't surprised about my playing,' I accuse.

'Tom told me. He said you were stunning.'

'He exaggerated.'

'No.' He shakes his head, smiling. 'He didn't.'

'It's late,' I say. 'You don't need to walk me back up the hill.'

'I want to,' he says. 'Where on earth did you learn to play like that?'

'The Boston Irish Centre, and' – I glance slyly at him – 'the Boston Symphony Orchestra.'

'I knew you were going to be good,' he admits. 'I just didn't know how good. So, tell me.'

What was it Livvy had said? *It's not bragging if it's the truth, is it?* 'It's what I did,' I say. 'It was my job. Playing, I mean.'

'What, full-time musician?' His brows are raised.

'Yes. Sometimes as lead violin, sometimes solo.'

'Oh my,' he says softly.

We walk side by side, savouring the silence of the night, the soft sigh of the sea, the dark sky a dome of stars, the moon a sickle of white. I feel at peace. Maybe even happy as we turn away from the sea towards the bright lights of the hotel.

At the door, Finn turns me to face him. 'Sorry I was late,' he says. 'I wanted to get here early, make sure you didn't wimp out. You didn't. I'm proud of you.' He leans in to kiss me goodnight. It's a peck on the lips. My smile must speak for me. I can hardly contain it, so he leans in closer and kisses me properly. 'Goodnight, sweet Erin,' he says.

I want to say 'goodnight, lovely Finn, but something else comes out. 'Will you come in?'

There's a long pause while we both think of the implications, maybe give ourselves time to reconsider. Then he nods. 'If you're all right with that?'

For some reason, I am.

I wake up slowly, pulling myself out of a deep sleep. I didn't revisit the accident in my dreams, something I haven't experienced in a long time. Finn is already awake, lying beside me, his dark eyes dreamy with the satisfaction derived from good music, good company and satisfying sex. And it had been good. I was a little worried that Kenny would be inside my head, watching me make love to Finn, but he'd been noticeably absent. I hadn't felt as though I was being disloyal. I simply knew it was time to let Kenny go, and he'd taken it in good part, drifting away, leaving me in peace. I lie back, hands behind my head and smile.

Finn heaves himself up onto one elbow. His ragged hair is mussed, his face stubbled. He leans down and kisses me. 'Thank you,' he says. *What for?* I'm thinking, when he carries on. 'I know you're still grieving. I'd have left any time, you know. I wouldn't have wanted this if you hadn't wanted it, too.'

I pull his face down to mine and we kiss properly. Our bodies move to the age-old tune, and this time we make love in the half-light of a dull morning. His eyes close as we slip into time, the slow air, the happy jig, the frantic reel and the moment when the music stops, when we just breathe and let it slide dreamily away…

Later, he gestures to the sheet covering me with a lift of his brow. *May I?* I smile wordless acquiescence. I suppose it's time. He's slipping the sheet back with the intense curiosity of opening an unexpected present. I expect to see the moment of change on his face. The shock, the indrawn breath as he takes in the scarring on my belly. The puckered skin, the stich marks, the trauma. But there's no shock.

'I saw this,' he says quietly, 'when I undressed you, that first night – when you were freezing, in those wet clothes. I've been wanting to know but didn't like to ask.'

'Does it bother you?'

He pulls me into his arms. 'It bothers me that you experienced such trauma. But…' He pauses, seeking the right words. 'You don't have to tell me. I assume that's from the accident Kenny died in? It looks bad enough.'

'Yes. I nearly died, too. The paramedic at the scene saved my life. He saw I was bleeding out. A few minutes later and it would have been too late. But the thing is…'

'What's da t'ing?'

I smile at his Cork accent, loving it, and pull myself up, hugging my arms around my knees. I stare through the glass at the dawn clouds sweeping in over the Atlantic.

He sits up and pulls the sheet over us both, a sensitivity I'm grateful for as I admit: 'I can't ever have children. When I awoke, in the hospital, I could see it written on my parents' faces that Kenny was gone, even before the doctor came and told me. I was so spaced out with drugs I just felt as if my life was irrevocably over. I was stunned, empty, bereft. The accident didn't just take Kenny; it took everything. I needed you to know. If you want a family…'

'So that was why you gave me that strange look when I said I had a child already? It must have hurt. I'm so sorry.'

'I was a little jealous, to be honest. And I wondered, if we ever...' I flush slightly, take a breath and continue. 'I was afraid you wouldn't want me if I said I couldn't have children.'

He hugs me. 'Daft girl. Have you never heard of adoption? There are countless children who need a good home. We'll get as many as you like. Ten? Twenty?'

Despite myself, I burst out laughing at his amused but intent expression, and say seriously, 'I wondered, if we became a couple, how I would cope with someone else's child. Yours, anyone's. Could I love it? I don't know...'

'Do you have a problem with Livvy? Or the children at the school?'

'No, but—'

'Well, there it is. Trust me, I know you'll be a good mother, and if we have to adopt a few, well, I'm not precious about my own sperm bank!' Then his face becomes serious. 'But, Erin, I need you to understand that Liam will always be in my life. Even if he's living with his grandmother after Eilis dies, I will always be his father. And that kind of means he'll be in your life, too.'

I understand that I'm being given a kind of warning. If push comes to shove, Finn will choose Liam over me – of course he will. But he doesn't want to have to make that choice. He wants to know that I will be there for him, that I can handle it.

'I don't have a problem with Liam being in my life.' I smile, maybe a little sadly. 'Maybe Eilis will be a little happier knowing that.'

He hugs me. 'You're very understanding. It's hard being a parent, you know. Always worrying, trying not to be overprotective. Being a parent means living with the joys and hardships, and tragedies, too. Think about your Nellie, losing her William then literally losing Annie on the docks when she got to Boston, never knowing what happened to her, and then her son dying when he was still no more than a child himself. She didn't give up on life. Hey, what have I said? I didn't mean to hurt you. Oh dear. This is too soon, isn't it?'

In dismay, he scrapes a hand through his tousled hair, seeing the silent tears dripping down my face.

'No,' I whisper. 'Not too soon. Just hurdles. One at a time, as my therapist would say. And I don't have casual sex,' I add, sniffing.

He glances at me, askance. 'I didn't think you would.'

'So, if this is possibly the start of something...'

'What do you mean, possibly?'

I take a deep breath. We're still on the same music score, so there's no point in holding back. No more secrets. 'There's something else I haven't told you. It wasn't just Kenny who died in the accident. I was pregnant. Five months. Long enough to feel her move inside me. They told me I'd been carrying a daughter. I would have called her Esther. She died in utero, and when they operated, they had to remove my womb, too. I found all that out when I woke up.'

'Damn it, girrul,' he whispers. He hugs me close, and the strength in his arms is more than just physical. He's absorbing my hurt, sharing it. 'What a nightmare. It must have been so difficult to come to terms with all that. I kind of gathered it had been bad, but no wonder you were having problems regarding children.'

Later, we get up and shower – me first, he insists. Finn sings loudly, a happy, silly ditty about bringing in a goat for milking, while thoroughly enjoying the hot water. His current accommodation might be basic, but he's no stranger to modern life, and from what I gather, most homes in Ireland still have baths not showers. He comes out, a towel wrapped around his middle, his hair an explosive riot. I laugh at the sight, and he pulls me close and buries his nose in my hair. It feels good.

'Ah, showers,' he says with satisfaction. 'The man who invented them should get a medal.'

'Perhaps it was a woman?'

'Not a chance,' he says between kisses pecked on my body, from my lips down my breasts to the crisscross of scars. 'Everyone knows women don't have brains. It's in the genes.'

When we're dressed, I suggest we go and grab breakfast.

'What, here?'

'Grace won't mind. I'll pay extra.'

'You don't want me to sneak out quietly?'

I shake my head. 'Not unless sneaking is your preferred method of exit?'

He shakes his head.

The hotel is empty, but I feel as nervous as a bride walking down through the foyer after her wedding night, expecting to be greeted with subdued but suggestive comments from guests with massive hangovers. There's no one in the dining room, and we help ourselves to orange juice, cereals, toast and marmalade – the works. There's no doubt that a good evening demands a substantial breakfast.

'All that's missing is the full Irish breakfast,' Finn says sadly, a dreamy look on his face. 'Sausages, black pudding, bacon, eggs... Haven't they sourced a chef yet?'

'They have, but Robert has to give notice. He'll be here soon. I don't doubt he's as nice as they say he is. Grace says Noel is a good judge of character, but she's pretty good herself.'

We're grasping mugs of coffee when Grace marches in, saying, 'Erin, I've been thinking— Oh, Finn! You're up and about early.'

Finn grins, and Grace colours wildly. 'Oh,' she says, understanding hitting her. 'I'll just go and—'

'No, we're fine,' I say. 'Grab a coffee and join us.'

By the time she sits, she's recovered her composure. She

glances from Finn to me with the hint of a smile. 'Does this mean what I think it means?'

'Maybe,' I say.

'Yes,' Finn says.

'Good. Great.'

'So, what did you want me for?'

'I was just going to ask if you could cover the desk on Monday, give me a break.'

I glance at Finn. 'We weren't planning anything, were we?'

'No. I have to clock in at work later. Sort out my shifts with the supervisor.'

'You're going back to work?' Grace asks, the question loaded.

He nods. 'I've been pronounced fit and healthy.'

'And are you?'

'I'm getting there. I have to get back on the horse, so to speak.'

She lays her hand on his. 'Be kind to yourself, eh?'

He gives a kind of grimace. 'I'm on drug-smuggling detail at the moment. It's kindness to kids I'll be thinking about.'

'Good. Go and get the bad guys. And be careful.' She stands. 'So?'

I realise I haven't answered her question. 'Of course I will. Are you going somewhere nice?'

'Sean and I thought we'd just have a day together, in the city. It's been a while. My mother will be collecting Livvy from school and bring her to the Big House, so Sean and I might catch a show or something.'

'That will be lovely. Have fun. And don't worry.'

'Thank you. And' – she glances from me to Finn again – 'I'm pleased. You both deserve a second chance.'

'Thank you,' we say in unison, making her laugh.

After she's gone, Finn stands. 'I need to get on, too.'

'Me, too, apparently.'

'So, it looks as if you have a job?'

'It does, rather.' I hesitate then say, 'About the future. They've offered me a suite here.'

'That's fine. I can't ask you to join me in my house, and I can't bring Whiskey to live in the hotel. But we have a whole future to plan, so one step at a time, eh?'

Grace has told Noel that I've accepted the job, and he gleefully has my belongings brought down into the manager's apartment, which, incidentally, hasn't got such a good view of the bay.

In the evening, Noel, Caitlin and Grace arrive with a bottle of champagne, and we toast to the future. After which I give a large burp, hand over my mouth in embarrassment. As we all laugh, I explain that's why I could never have bubbly drinks before performing, because a bit of wind expelled in a quiet piece of music could bring the house down.

I love that I can laugh with these people.

I phone Mom and tell her about my decision. She sniffles down the phone at me and says she'd had a horrible premonition that I was going to do that, but Scott had already hinted that I'd met someone, and is it true? I say I don't know, but maybe. I hear Dad, over the other side of the room, tell Mom to stop worrying, I'd come to my senses. I tell her that's why I put the brownstone on the market, so that I can buy a house in Ireland. There's a shocked silence as they both realise that I'm serious.

I'm shaking my head and grimacing as I put the phone down. One day they'll understand that I've already come to my senses, absolutely and permanently. But they'll get used to the idea. At least, I hope they will.

36

ERIN

It's nearly a year after my arrival in Roone Bay. Finn and I share music in a way I never thought possible. We divide our time between work, my apartment, and his tiny cottage to play music and walk on the beach. Tucked away in his home by the ever-moving Atlantic on his days off, we learn new tunes together then rattle them out later in the music sessions. He still prefers to spend his evenings after work alone in his tiny cottage with its total lack of amenities. I know he spends time sitting by the water, staring out to sea, with Whiskey, his faithful companion, leaning against him. But his trauma is his to work through, and I know from experience that these things can't be hurried.

Through my association with the school, where I've been seconded into helping with a Christmas musical production, I've had to spend a lot of time around the children. I once thought I couldn't handle that because it would aggravate my own loss, but now I accept that this isn't the case at all. I enjoy Liam's company as much as I enjoy being with the children at school. Liam often stays with Finn at the little cottage on odd weekends, or during the days Eilis is not well enough to cope.

He's part of Finn's life, and so his child has become part of my life, too.

My past is now an open secret in Roone Bay.

I haven't lost hope for my quest to find Nellie's story, but it's no longer driving me. Knowing that I have finally come home, I do give quiet thanks to Nellie, for the bible that brought me to Roone Bay, and maybe for my deep and abiding love of Irish music that's surely a legacy handed down through my ancestry. And as I network my way further and further through the west of Ireland, seeking news of Nellie through the various church connections, I have come into contact with many other individual tragedies.

My brownstone sold almost immediately, and the funds have now been transferred to Ireland. Scott has his uses. He knew exactly how to get things organised, and now Dad has offered him the chance to buy into the partnership, I guess we all have discovered our slot in this life. I suspect that Scott will one day traipse to dinner with Mom and Dad with some pretty and adoring showpiece on his arm. She'll probably even give him babies that Mom will take under her wing in the absence of mine.

It's strange how the months have flown by since my arrival in Roone Bay. There was a time I thought I could never be happy again, when I didn't think it was even worth trying. It took me months to get over the physical trauma of the accident, but a lot longer to face the joint tragedy of losing my husband and child. That double loss was a void, deep as space itself, into which I poured myself, leaving no room for happiness. And here we are, Finn and I, looking for a house to share. Although Finn still loves his little snug by the sea, we'd like a home we can share. We haven't found the right one yet, because Finn needs to be within sight and sound of the sea, and to deprive him of that would be a sure way to end the relationship before it's really been consolidated.

. . .

I work weekdays, and Grace does the weekends, but the new girl, Maeve, has taken the pressure from both of us. Another of Noel's instant decisions, she's a godsend. Good on the phone, an excellent administrator, she also has endless patience dealing with awkward clients, of whom we get our fair share. I spend my days in the hotel planning, making lists, accepting phone bookings and generally getting to know every little thing about the hotel.

The new chef, Robert O'Neil, is young and inexperienced. We're to call him Robbo, a nickname he's had from birth. He isn't averse to hard work and has a wicked sense of humour. Noel liked him at first glance, as did I. Unpretentious and down to earth, he doesn't want to win medals or work in some high-flying establishment, so I have a feeling he's going to be a fixture here for a few years. In the volatile hotel trade, that's a bonus and, as Grace said, Noel's success came on the back of his own ability to judge horses and he measures humans with the same yardstick; less by their achievements to date than their characters and potential, given the opportunity to prove themselves.

I guess that's how he measured me.

My biggest task at the moment, for which I can only blame myself, is the sumptuous Christmas buffet and party I'm organising for just about everyone in Roone Bay, something Noel has been badgering me to do ever since I broached the subject to Grace a year ago. I wondered if local antipathy might have over-ridden curiosity, but as the acceptances flood in, I realise we're going to be hard-pressed to fit everyone in. Noel and Grace are quite excited about it, but I wonder if I've jumped a little too quickly into the deep end of the pool.

Nellie remains a shadowy figure in the back of my mind. In a strange way, she saved me. We both lost a child, in different circumstances, sure, and maybe she eventually found hers, maybe she didn't, but her loss reached out to me when I was at my lowest ebb. Seeking her roots in Ireland means that I actually found mine and gave myself another chance at life.

My therapist once told me I had given up music to flay myself with the guilt of still being alive. She was right, of course, and with a new beginning, I've rediscovered music. I can never go back to the person I once was. I've changed. Those days are gone. Maybe I never quite gave up on hope. If I had, I might just have said yes to Scott's proposal and drifted through the rest of my life with regret for the past. Finn has provided me with a new love; different from the old but, in some respects, equally as beautiful. The therapist also assured me that my life would one day change, that I wouldn't see it coming, but would just turn around one day and find it had arrived.

I hadn't believed her at the time, but I do now.

37

ERIN

Finn is away down the coast, assisting in an operation to stop cocaine being brought into southern Ireland. Apparently, the ragged coast on the south of Ireland, with its many little hidden beaches and tiny quays, provides a perfect drop for drugs being shipped in from the continent. I'm pondering this when Grace hands me a telephone number scribbled on a piece of scrap paper. 'It came via one of Olivia's friend's parents at school,' she tells me. 'Her name's Estelle Green. She says she can shed some light on your Nellie's missing child, Annie?'

'Really? Did she say what?' I ask, surprised. I haven't actually given up on finding out about her, but between Finn and work, it somehow ended up on a back burner.

'I didn't speak to her as I had someone in reception, but it's a local number, Bantry.'

'Well,' I say, 'nothing to lose by giving her a call, eh?'

'Absolutely.'

I phone Estelle, and after explaining who I am and why I'm calling, she sounds really interested, keen to meet up.

'It's not every day you do a bit of detective work going back several generations and actually make sense of it,' she says on the phone. 'But it's strange to discover that Nellie was alive, after all, because as far as I've known all my life, she died on the ship going over to America.'

I'm confused. 'Why on earth did you think that?'

'It's just the story I was told. You see, one of my ancestors was a woman called Dervla Doyle. She was the one who rescued Annie O'Mahoney in Boston and eventually brought her back to Ireland with her after her own husband died. Annie herself told Dervla that her mother had died on the journey over to America. That's the story that came down from the grandparents.'

I'm stunned. 'So she did come back to Ireland! But really, why would Annie tell people her mother had died? I can safely say she didn't, because she was my great-something grandmother.'

'That's really weird. I think we've both got stories to exchange. How about we do it in person? Are you mobile? Can you come over to Bantry or shall I come over to Roone Bay?'

'Which is easiest for you?'

'Well, I have a baby and a toddler, as well as Mikey, who knows Grace's Livvy from the gymnastics club.'

'No bother, I'll come to you. I'm managing the Roone Bay Hotel, so I'll have to get Grace to cover for me.'

'Ah, yes. Grace told me about the terrible accident you were involved in, by the way, about losing your husband and child. So sad. I can't imagine coping with that. I'm so sorry for your loss.'

'Thank you. So, tell me when and where, and I'll talk to Grace about cover.

Estelle has a little semi-detached, modern house on a new estate at the north end of Bantry. She opens the door, welcoming me in with a smile before I can knock. 'Erin, I'm so pleased to meet you. Come on in.'

I follow her through to a neat kitchen, where she unceremoniously puts teabags into mugs, tops them up with boiling water, and dumps packets of biscuits and a bottle of milk onto the table. 'I hope you don't mind being basic? With two pre-schoolers to cope with, one tends to cut all the corners possible.'

There was a time a woman might have had ten or more children, if she survived the trauma to her overworked body, which many didn't. Not all changes are bad, after all, I think.

After quizzing me a little on my own background, she gets going. 'It was my grandmother who told me the story of how her mother's great-grandmother rescued the little girl, Annie, in Boston. I think I've got the *greats* right, but it doesn't matter. Anyway, they thought she might have been about five years old, but they weren't sure. Dervla and her husband – I think it was John – had a farm out of the city by a hundred miles or so. That was a long way back in the day, what with the roads being just packed earth. They used to drive their horse and wagon into Boston for supplies every few months, which used to take a few days, depending on the weather and the state of the roads. That particular day, apparently, they had also picked up a boy from the harbour, the son of one of her Irish friends, which is why they were at the docks. Serendipity, eh? The youth had been put on the ship by his parents who couldn't afford the fare for themselves, too.'

I lean forward, eager to hear the missing chapter of Nellie's tale.

'That's a sad story in itself,' she remarks, 'because Dervla later learned that his parents had died in Ireland during the famine, not long after he'd been shipped out on his own. They'd undoubtedly saved his life. I think Dervla sent him the news that his parents were gone, but that was a good while later, after she'd gone back to Ireland, and he was a grown man by then with a family of his own. But he did write to thank her for putting his mind to rest. There's nothing so bad, he said – I have his letter somewhere – as just not knowing.'

'Did his parents know he'd arrived safely before they died?'

'I suspect not. As far as I know, he never got word from anyone back at home until Dervla told him that news. But don't forget that a quarter of the population, even more down this part of the country, were dead or dying, and the priests who tried to keep the faith were struggling to cope. If a letter from him did end up with them, it might just have been put aside, forgotten, in the horror those brave men were dealing with.'

I nod, recalling reading that the population had been ravaged by disease as well as starvation, and that the priests were lucky if they didn't die from cholera or dysentery or typhoid, simply from handling the dead.

Estelle pushes the mug towards me. 'Sort it out – I don't know how strong you like it. And help yourself to the biscuits. When the kids come in, they'll demolish the rest in two seconds flat.'

I like her informality, but feel strangely guilty at enjoying tea and biscuits while discussing people who had lived through more poverty and tragedy than I can ever imagine.

'Dervla and John weren't from Roone Bay,' she carries on, 'but from a small town between there and Bantry. They had emigrated a few years before the famine and bought a farm, so they must have been doing okay, from the sound of it. Anyway, it took them a couple of days to find the boy, Dominic, as the ship had come in a week early. The docks and the immigration situation in Boston were a nightmare, and so many had died on the ship, you see. Dominic was just twelve years old, and she was afraid she'd find he was one of the missing. She must have been vastly relieved when she discovered his name on the immigration list, so they were able to track him down and bring him home.

'They were leaving the docks, on their way home, when they saw a commotion in front of them. This is the story, anyway. John pulled the horses to a standstill as the crowd was blocking the road. Hearing screams, Dervla stood up on the foot-plate to try to see what was going on. There she saw a small girl backed into a corner, surrounded by people, like a terrified animal surrounded by feral dogs. Dervla's maternal instincts were triggered. She told Dominic to mind the horses and not let anyone steal anything, and instructed her husband to help her. She must have been one strong lady! She forced her way through the crowd and finally realised why no one was doing anything. It turned out they couldn't understand the child, because she was screaming in Irish. They all thought she was mad, rabid, you know?'

I'm horrified. 'A child – what was she, five, six years old – in distress like that, and they just stood and watched? No one thought to give her a cuddle, calm her down?'

Estelle shrugged. 'It was the times, though, wasn't it? Irish were flooding into the country, they were starving, diseased, wearing rags, and I suspect the Bostonians were afraid of catching something.'

'Still,' I mutter. 'Where was their Christian charity?'

Estelle gave a humourless laugh. 'There was no such thing as charity, not then, nor social welfare. It was everyone for themselves. And if the child had been eventually picked up and taken to the orphanage – and trust me, plenty of Irish children ended up there – it's likely she would have died. They were seen as an infestation, like rats, not children who needed love and affection. They were treated brutally. Besides that, the Irish were mainly Catholic, somewhat less than Christian in the eyes of the majority of the citizens, who were Protestant.'

'How do you know so much?' I ask curiously.

'I think it was Annie's story that prompted me to read up on it. Nothing like a little personal touch to instigate curiosity, is there? Most of this came down through the family largely by word of mouth, though. My grandmother had a way with telling a story.'

I smile. 'It seems you've inherited her gift.'

She grins. 'I used to fib a lot as a child! And, sure, I don't know how much I'm telling is truth or fiction.'

'Never mind! Go on.'

'Right. Where was I? Oh yes. Dervla Doyle heard the girl's terrified voice calling for her mother in Irish, and in her own words, in the letter she later wrote, she said, *The Lord told me to save the child.* So she did. She shushed the child and held her until she calmed down, and asked her what her name was, and where her mother was. Annie told Dervla that her mother and her brother and her father were all lost. Eventually she learned that Annie was from Roone Bay, and her parents were William and Nellie, and she realised they were her one-time neighbours. She'd never met her, but, sure, didn't they all know who was who back in the day? So, she took Annie in and brought her up as her own.'

'I get that *lost* is a euphemism for dead, but maybe she really meant lost, as in couldn't find them?'

'Oh my, you could be right, there! Anyway, Dervla and her husband assumed she meant dead. They had a farm to run and were on their way home. They sent word to the immigration office that the child, Annie O'Mahoney, had been found, and where they were taking her, just in case someone was looking for her, but they didn't expect to hear anything, and they never did.'

'It doesn't sound as though Nellie was ever given that information,' I say. 'According to the stories I heard, she spent weeks – years – looking for her, in the orphanages, around the docks and immigration offices.'

'Well, I guess the authorities were inundated with immigrants because of the famine. Anyway, the Doyles took Annie back with them and brought her up, but they made sure she always knew who her real parents had been.'

'But if these people, Dervla and John, had a farm in America, how did they end up back in Ireland?'

'About ten years after she found Annie, Dervla's husband died. His father had survived the famine, and the farm was by then viable once more. He had more land and just the one surviving son who had never married, so there were no heirs. He sent her a letter saying if she came home, John's children would inherit the farm, so she sold up in America, brought her children and Annie back to Ireland.'

She looks at her watch. 'Erin, it's been lovely telling you all this, you're a fantastic listener, but I have to go to pick up Mikey from the school, and get Sally and Ben from my neighbour, who's been minding them for an hour.'

'But there's more?' I say eagerly as she stands up. 'You can't leave me hanging!'

She laughs. 'If you can wait a few days, I'll go over to Mum's and pick up the old papers. There are a few letters, bits and pieces, you know. I can't recall who's who after that, but we can go through it together.'

I'm reluctant to leave with the story half told, but she's looking at her watch worriedly. 'Shall I call you?'

'I'll let you know when I've got the stuff.' She sees me hesitate, holds out her hand, grins and says, 'Pinkie promise!'

We do the link-shake, and I leave, filled with exuberance.

Annie was alive and came back to Ireland, just as I guessed! That lends credence to the possibility that Nellie eventually got news of her lost child and came back to Ireland herself, but goodness knows how she ever found out. Oh, I'm so excited for her – it's as if she's still alive and I'm gunning for her to actually meet up with her lost child.

I will be devastated if I never find out.

38

NELLIE 1884

Patrick argued against Nellie's decision to go back to Ireland. After all, Boston was her home now, and Annie would be a stranger to her, as would Annie's husband and children. And as Nellie had spent twice the years in America than she had spent in her native Ireland, it would be like a foreign land to her. Nellie wondered if Patrick was thinking more of Sarah's possible loneliness than her own happiness. When she refused to change her mind, she experienced the full brunt of his patriarchal implacability, which must surely have come from Sarah's family. It certainly hadn't come from the emotionally fragile Luke or her gentle William.

It was Sarah who paid for Nellie's passage back to Ireland, and who provided her with a small nest egg to tide her over until she found Kate or Annie. She said Nellie should come back if things didn't work out – she was and always would be family – but Patrick made it clear that if she went, his door would be shut behind her; he didn't like his will being crossed, and he didn't tolerate disloyalty. Nellie refrained from saying she had been nothing but loyal all her life and bid goodbye to

Sarah in the knowledge that they would never meet again in this life.

Nellie passed her precious bible to Sarah and asked her to keep writing the family tree. Even though Patrick had never met his father, he should at least remember his name. Kate's letter had included the name of Annie's husband and their address in Bantry. Armed with that information, she booked her passage. She sent a letter to Kate informing her of the shipping details and, with her few belongings in a small cardboard suitcase, stepped on board the steamship bound for Ireland.

Nellie knew she was sick because she had pains inside that she had not bothered anyone with, but the fire in her breast was rekindled. She wasn't afraid of dying, if that was her destiny, but to set eyes on her little girl again before she died became a compulsion that would keep her alive.

During the two weeks she spent on board, the strength of spirit that had driven her to survive the famine, the loss of her sweet William, the loss of her first child, then her second, and those dreadful first years in America now drove her to eat, even though eating made her want to vomit. For two weeks, she ate, prayed and slept, and when she was not doing those things, she sat ramrod straight on the bunk, her hands clasped in her lap, simply waiting to arrive on the other side of the Atlantic, to her home. She knew Ireland would have changed as much as America had since the war, but she couldn't envisage anything other than the Ireland she had left nearly forty years ago, with the tiny cottage she had lived in with her parents and William, and behind it, the hill on which she had stood with Annie, watching William's boat sail away. She was glad she had not known, back then, that she would never see William again. It was the thought of being with him again that had kept her going for the following two dreadful years as people were dropping around them, and herself secretly hoarding the turnips that had kept them alive. How it had pained her to do that. But how upset William would have been if she had not found the courage to keep his little treasured daughter alive and bring her to America to be with him once more.

Nellie was nearly sixty years old now and had been preparing herself for death. Her little Annie would be nearly forty. Though she could not imagine the little girl she had lost as anything other than a stick-thin little figure, with milk-pale skin, and William's wide blue eyes and red hair.

When they finally disembarked, it was a civilised affair, not like the horrific scramble she had experienced in Boston. The first-class passengers left first, dignified by their clothes and their huge travelling trunks, and everyone else followed behind carrying their baggage in neat cases. The passengers were tired and a little grubby, but there were no bundles tied up in rags, no bare feet, no desperately thin children whose hollow eyes and caved-in stomachs spoke of a death sentence waiting to happen.

At the immigration desk, Nellie held her head high and answered the questions without faltering. Yes, she was an Irish national, born in Roone Bay. Yes, she had means. No, she wouldn't be vagrant. She would see if her old house was still there, and if not, she would live with her daughter. That wasn't a lie so much as a lack of care. If she got to Bantry and found her daughter alive but unable to take her in, she would be happy to walk down to the shore and sit and wait for God to collect her soul. She was so tired of living.

She walked out of the immigration centre at Cork, placing her feet on her native soil with a strange sense of unexpectedly finding her way home after being lost for forty years. She wondered if little Annie had felt the same way when Dervla Doyle had brought her here, or whether she had become so American, like Patrick, that the thought of going to a little back-ward country like Ireland had seemed like a retrograde move.

Nellie, though, had crossed the Atlantic twice now, and this was her destiny. She would not do it again.

She found the railway station and discovered the line to Bantry was closed for repairs. She closed her eyes briefly with dismay then rallied. She was advised to go to Skibbereen and find onward transport from there. So that's what she did. She might find a carriage or a farmer going to Bantry. But if she had to walk, so be it. So much had happened, she wasn't going to allow the prospect of a ten-mile walk to stop her.

What a strange thing, she thought. Once, before her great adventure, even going on a coach was so beyond reach she might well have dreamed of flying, but now she was going to ride in a carriage pulled by a steam locomotive.

How the world had changed!

In Skibbereen, she found a room for the night, and in the morning quietly set about cleaning herself up after the journey. Working in a wealthy household for so long had provided her with standards that had not even been thought of during her childhood. She changed into the one set of decent clothes she'd brought with her: a white blouse with a high neck, onto which she buckled a little silver filigree brooch Margarethe Becker had given her one Christmas, and a long grey skirt that fitted tightly to her middle, flaring slightly over her hips, ending wide at the ankles, good for striding. She laced up her leather boots then brushed her grey hair, twisting it up into a knot on the back of her head before pinning on the hat she had made herself and decorated with ribbons. There was a small mirror in the room, and she stared at herself. Behind the severe cut of her mouth and the lines carved by hardship, she sought a trace of the happy, barefoot bride who had once promised to honour and obey the beautiful William until the day she died. No one could have foreseen what would happen in the intervening years.

For the first time, a tendril of misgiving slid through her. What if Kate had been wrong? What if the woman was not her Annie? Surprisingly, that had not occurred to her until this moment. She had so wanted to believe Kate that it had not occurred to her to doubt it. She found herself shaking.

Would she even recognise Annie?

She doubted Annie would recognise her.

And what if it was Annie but the girl had fostered hatred towards her mother all these years for losing her in Boston? She sat back down on the bed and folded over with a sharp flash of pain. But even as these things flooded through her mind, she knew she had no option. She had come this far. She would take the final steps, because truly there was no other way. Even if her daughter hated her, she needed to see her, know it was her... Well, then she would die happy.

She stood by the Bantry road and held her hand up to three carts that went on by, the donkeys' heads nodding in rhythm to their clopping hooves. The fourth pulled to a stop and asked if she needed a lift to Bantry.

'I can pay,' she said proudly.

'Sure, now,' the man said, heaving her bag into the cart, atop sacks of flour piled high, and holding out his hand. 'Why would I be taking money from a lady like yourself? Sure, it's no bother. I'm going there anyway. So, who might you be visiting in Bantry?'

'My daughter, Annie,' she said decisively. 'She's married to Andrew Nolan, the doctor. 'The house is on Orchard Hill,' she added nervously.

'Oh, sure, that will be Doctor Andrew. A good man, he is.'

'You know him?' Nellie was fearful of seeming ignorant. Perhaps if Annie was, indeed, married to a doctor, he would be too important to want to know his wife's forgotten mother, who had been a poor girl during the famine, then a servant to rich Germans in Boston.

The man shook his head. 'I've heard of him, but I've never

had to pay for his services. But people say good things. So, where have you come from?'

He was curious about Nellie's accent, and she felt obliged to provide some details of her life with the Beckers. She didn't tell him of the hardships she had endured before she reached that point or her various tragedies. He had probably heard enough tales of hardship in his day. She regaled him with some amusing anecdotes from her days as a lady's maid, making him smile, and another that made his eyes widen with surprise.

'Sure, and that didn't happen! What a strange place America is, to be sure.'

It took nearly the whole journey before Nellie realised that they had been speaking in English. When she had lived here before, everyone she knew spoke the Irish, and she asked him now, in Irish, whether this was the language of the people.

'Sure, and I understand you,' he answered, giving her a sad look. 'But it's only the old ones who are speaking the Irish now. Aren't we all after speaking the English? The children learn in English, and it's for the best, really. The good jobs are over the water, and no one would employ someone who can only speak Irish.'

She nodded but thought it sad that in the years she had been gone, the language of her parents had been superseded by the language she had spoken in America. Little Annie had only known the Irish, but no doubt she, too, had been obliged to adjust.

'Here we are, my friend,' the driver said, pulling into Bantry market square.

She climbed down painfully, and he handed her bag down as she looked around, wide-eyed. While she had lived in Roone Bay, Nellie had only ever visited Bantry twice, but even she could see the changes that had been wrought. The bigger shops and houses, the cleanliness of the street.

He pointed up the road with his switch and indicated to the

right. 'Orchard Hill isn't so far up there. May God be with you and bless you, ma'am.'

'And may the road rise to meet you,' she responded.

With a tip of the hand to his flat cap and a brief twitch of his switch, he jogged his donkey on. Nellie turned and walked up the road. The sun was shining, and her feet made little clouds of dust in the earth, but she found herself smiling. God willing, she had come to her destination and would accept whatever He handed to her.

Orchard Hill rose steeply to the right, and there she found a real town house with two storeys and glass windows with a sign hanging outside: Surgery. Falling back to her early years, she crossed herself, walked to the door and rapped on the brass knocker.

Footsteps inside tripped to the door, which was opened. A woman smiled at her kindly. She was neatly built, her fading red hair faintly flecked with silver, but her eyes were William's eyes, blue like the pale forget-me-nots that grew in the hedges.

'Do you have an appointment, ma'am?' she asked. 'The doctor has someone with him at the moment.'

Nellie froze, and the woman on the doorstep faltered, staring with shock and dawning recognition mixed with disbelief. '*Mathair?*' she whispered. Her hand went to her mouth, and her breath drew in with a long, shuddering sigh. 'Mam? But...'

Nellie's eyes filled with tears, and she couldn't speak for a moment, then finally took a deep breath and said, 'Annie, sweetling. Are you going to invite me in?'

It was a strange time, during which Nellie and Annie quizzed each other about their lives, and Annie gradually got used to the fact that this wasn't some bizarre joke. Doctor Andrew Nolan was at first taken aback by the presumed-dead mother-in-law turning up on his doorstep from America. He took it in good part, though, when he realised that his wife really did recognise the stranger; that it wasn't some horrible swindle. Nellie was invited to stay while they all decided what to do.

It turned out that the letter Nellie had written ahead to Kate had never been delivered, which is why Annie had been so shocked when her mother, whom she had firmly believed to be dead, turned up on her doorstep.

'Apparently, I told Dervla you were dead, when she found me,' she explained to Nellie. 'I don't remember, though.'

They were sitting quietly together in a furnished parlour, which looked out over an apple orchard. Annie couldn't stop herself from reaching for her mother's hand at any opportunity, as if fearing she would disappear the moment she was out of sight.

Nellie was more pragmatic. Having experienced so much in her lifetime, she felt slightly distanced from the reality of this strange meeting. The weight in her heart had disappeared when she recognised Annie. She knew she was not well but would now face death with equanimity, even with a sense of relief. Her life was all but done, and finally she could stop struggling and be at peace.

She dragged her mind back to the present.

'But something in the back of my mind always thought that wasn't right,' Annie was saying. 'Because I didn't recall you dying on the ship, even though I was lost and alone when we disembarked. I had a vague memory of you walking off the ship with me and little Luke, but Dervla wouldn't have lied, not at all. She will be so pleased to meet you.'

'She's still alive?'

'Oh, yes. She's been a mother to me, and the children call her "grandmama".' She grimaced and stroked Nellie's hand. 'Sorry, that was insensitive.'

'Not at all,' Nellie said with true practicality. 'I would like to thank her. But, Annie, I wanted to know if it really was you. I just wanted to see you before I died. I didn't give a thought to what I'd do when I got here or how it would affect you.' She gave a dry little chuckle. 'I haven't a clue what I'm going to do now. Well, aside from one thing.' Annie's brows rose in query. 'I'd like to see the house where I was born, where we lived as a family, with my mother and father, and William and you, before everything went bad.'

'And Luke, too?'

'Luke was born after William left. Your father never knew he had a son. He would have been so proud.'

'I don't remember what my father looked like.'

'He was beautiful and strong and kind. He had the sweetest smile. His grandson, Patrick, has the look of him, just a little.'

'He used to sing,' Annie said thoughtfully. 'And I remember sitting on his shoulders, and he yelled at me for holding on to his hair too tightly. It was red, wasn't it?'

'It was. Like fire. And so was Luke's, and Patrick's is red, too, though not as bright.'

'I only remember Luke as a baby, and they all look the same; except mine, of course!'

Nellie laughed out loud and wondered at herself. It was a long time since she had truly laughed, then the laughter died.

'Poor Luke died as a soldier in the Civil War. It was a horrible death. And William has been gone such a long time now. But maybe you can meet Luke's son, Patrick, one day. It's getting easier to travel, what with the steam ships. It only took two weeks from Boston to Cork.'

'Maybe,' Annie said doubtfully. 'I don't have any desire to go back to America. My life is here now.'

'So it is, and I'm so very happy for you, Annie. And you have children... It's amazing, so it is!'

'We have three daughters, one married and pregnant. I'm going to be a grandmother.'

Nellie shook her head. That was truly bizarre.

'You'll meet them soon. Andrew has told them about you, and they're giving us a chance to catch up before descending upon us. They are keen, and curious, of course, to meet the grandmother they never knew they had.'

A few days later, Andrew closed the surgery and had his pony and trap brought around to the front door. The wooden seats faced inward, and Nellie climbed up in amusement, able to see the scenery and watch her Annie at the same time. She saw herself reflected in some of Annie's mannerisms, but also saw fleeting glimpses of William in her wide smile and optimism.

The trip to Roone Bay took a little over an hour, and once there, Nellie's eyes welled, looking at all the houses, many now in ruins, remembering all the families she had known, all now gone. She wasn't inclined to seek out anyone she had known from the past; if any had even survived it would be too traumatic. The only thing they would have in common would be counting the lost souls, and that was pointless.

She directed them through the town, past Roone Manor, once a bastion of wealth, now derelict. And so it should be, she thought. Let the birds and wild creatures take it back to nature, for all the good that ever came from it. They carried on up the hillside that faced towards the bay. And there it was, the tiny cottage, its empty windows open to the birds, the roof gone. 'Have we time?' she asked Andrew, pointing. 'I'd like to walk up the hill to the rock.'

He nodded. 'Annie, you go with your mother. I'll wait here.'

They stopped at the cottage, and Nellie felt no sense of nostalgia. It was just another thing ticked off her list of regrets. She and Annie toiled up the steep slope, past the remains of the well, until they reached the overhanging rock. Nellie turned to the sea and put her arm around her daughter. 'This is where

William proposed to me. And this is where we came to watch his ship sailing away for America. You were with me. I was so young. It never occurred to me that we'd never meet again in this life.'

'Are you all right, Mam?'

'I'm fine.' And she was. She thought it would upset her, being here, but instead she felt that things had come full circle. She had come home, and soon she would be joining William and Luke, and one day Annie would be with them, too.

'I'm ready to go now,' she said calmly.

39

ERIN

When Finn arrives home after five days' absence, we hug silently, breathing in each other's presence like perfume, before I push away and say, 'I think I found us a house.'

'You have?'

He sounds tired and plonks himself down on the couch. He rests his head back, yawns widely and eyes me lopsidedly with a lazy smile. I never tire of seeing him and am continually amazed that this beautiful, sexy, practical, wonderful man has walked into my life. I sit beside him, and he puts his arm around me, pulls me close and kisses me with honeymoon urgency, his touch exciting me in a way I thought was gone forever. That it will eventually morph into something gentler, I know, but I'm enjoying the newness, the overwhelming and surprising joy of another love, something I had never expected to experience again.

But at this moment I need him to listen. 'The estate agent doesn't think it will hang around long. It's going to be your home, too. If you don't love it, I'll be very disappointed.'

'That good?'

I nod. 'I haven't viewed it yet, just looked at the picture and read the spec. The estate agent gave me the key. It's vacant. We can go and look whenever we like.'

'Has it got a garden?'

For Liam, of course, and Whiskey. Finn's house has a small yard, and a teenager walks Whiskey before and after school when Finn's away, but it's not ideal, and it worries him that the big German Shepherd spends so much time in a tiny space, alone.

'It has a rather big garden.'

'Okay, sold, so. Now can we go to bed?'

'Finn, I'm serious. This is important!'

'So is... Oh, okay. Can I see the brochure?'

'No. It's a surprise. I want to see it with you. It came on the market last week. The man who owned it lived there alone since his wife passed. He died a couple of months back, and his daughter, who is selling it, moved to Australia many years ago. She's coming over to Ireland next week to clear it. The place is in need of some serious TLC, according to the estate agent.'

'That probably means it's damp, mouldy and is inhabited by mice.'

'Well, we can light a fire and evict them.'

He laughs. 'I love you, you know, Erin.'

'I love you, too.' I'm still amazed that he wants me, with all my hang-ups, but as he says, my history is what it is. We can only move forward, and at the moment that means setting up a home. 'It dates from the early 1900s, and...'

'It's by the sea?'

'Half a mile, downhill all the way. It has a view over the water.'

'Already sold,' he says, his hand gliding up underneath my T-shirt.

I slap it down. 'We could go now?'

'We could go to bed?'

'Let's look at the house first thing in the morning then, before someone else snaps it up.'

'I'm picking up Liam in the morning,' he says.

'Good. If Liam hates it, that's something we need to take into consideration.'

In the morning, I collect the key and we drive down to Finn's cottage to pick up Whiskey, who's standing with her nose pressed to the front door as we arrive. She's accepted me into her life, but she'll always be Finn's dog. Her expression of devotion must surely be echoed on my own face.

'Come on, girl,' Finn tells her. 'In the car. We're going on an adventure.'

She leaps in eagerly, taking up the whole of the back seat. We drive to Bantry where Liam leaps in and shoves the reluctant Whiskey to one side. Whiskey immediately sticks her head on Liam's lap with the same adoration that she gives to Finn. I wonder if Whiskey can sense the biological connection.

Finn follows my directions, three miles west, towards the Mizen peninsular, along a winding lane and finally through a pair of huge cast-iron gates, one of which is hanging by a single broken hinge, and up a curving drive. And there it is, exactly as portrayed in the brochure, in all its gloomy gothic glory.

Finn pulls the handbrake on and turns to me, stunned. 'That's it?' he asks. 'Ashley Point Lookout? I've seen it from the sea and wondered... You can't afford this!'

'Well, I can actually,' I say apologetically. 'Shall we go and look?'

He shakes his head, running a broad hand through his shaggy mane of hair in amazement. 'It's even got a turret!'

I smile, knowing he'd sold himself on the house long before I even knew it existed. Liam climbs down and grabs Finn's hand, and Whiskey bounds off into the undergrowth. She has no doubts about the place at all. I don't think the garden has been tended for thirty years. The rampant gorse is like the thicket around Sleeping Beauty's castle. I hope Whiskey finds her way out when it's time to leave.

'Is this your house?' Liam asks me.

'It might be,' I say. 'Do you want to explore?'

'Sure,' he says.

I unlock the front door, and it opens to a waft of musty air. Finn's right about the damp. We walk around, our awe combined with suppressed guilt. It feels as if we're trespassing. The owner's possessions are still scattered around. Furniture, books, wellingtons in the tall lobby, coats hanging on the hooks, even a pair of glasses on a small table.

The ceilings are high. The kitchen is from the 1930s, if not earlier. The lounge and dining room have the faded grandeur of a stately home, and the turret, accessed by a circular concrete stairway, was obviously the old man's snug, with a 360-degree view that spans from the curved horizon of the sea to the backbone of the peninsular. Of course, that's like a magnet to Liam, who clambers up instantly and disappears around the corner. We follow and discover him kneeling on an upright armchair in front of a huge brass telescope.

'I can see the sea!' Liam exclaims, peering through the eyepiece.

I can't help grinning. I can see the sea without the telescope, but there is an ambience to the room that sends us back in time. I almost expect to see a sailing ship cross the horizon.

'It's like being in a lighthouse,' I say, turning a full circle in astonishment.

'It's sad,' Finn says, echoing my own feelings. The room, with a single fringed rug on the wooden floor, is scattered with shipping memorabilia. I get the feeling that the man who'd inhabited this room had been lonely, living on memories.

'It is,' I agree. 'Apparently this place was built by the

previous owner's grandfather, who was the captain of a sailing ship. It's been in the family since. But the estate agent said that the daughter who inherited it called it a "ghastly monolith" and just wants it gone.'

We carry on exploring. The house is a solid square block, with an entrance hall, kitchen, lounge, dining room and another small room, downstairs. Upstairs, we find four spacious but mouldy bedrooms, and a small set of stairs off the landing that lead to a large attic. There are cumbersome old radiators in the downstairs rooms, and a massive old boiler in the kitchen that looks decidedly dangerous. The bathroom is built onto the side of the house like an afterthought.

There's plenty of scope for renovation, and I suspect the upkeep would be huge. A smear of discoloured wallpaper down one corner of a bedroom indicates that the roof has been leaking for quite a while.

'It's not sensible,' I comment.

'No,' Finn agrees.

'So, shall we buy it?' I ask.

Finn's face is that of a child stunned by an unexpected Christmas present. 'Are you sure you can...'

'I'm sure.'

'Then bloody hell, yes!' he swears exuberantly.

I can't stop grinning. It's time Finn and Whiskey and I became a family of three instead of bouncing between jobs and apartments and dog duties.

'What do you think?' Finn asks Liam. 'Would you want to come and stay here sometimes with us? Like an adventure?'

'Can I have a swing in the garden?'

'Of course,' I say.

'And can Mum come and stay here for a holiday, too? And my granny?'

Finn glances at me, brows raised.

'Of course,' I say. 'But we will have to do a bit of work first.'

Liam considers this, seriously, then nods. 'I think that will be nice,' he says.

When we're back in my apartment, still coming down from the euphoria of our impending and indisputably impractical purchase, I show Finn the photocopies of the old letters that Estelle's mother had hoarded and talk him through what I now know about Annie.

'The letters are interesting, of course, but they don't add anything to what Estelle already told me,' I tell him. 'But the thing is, we now know that Annie married a doctor, Andrew Nolan, in the 1860s and apparently they had three daughters.'

'Shame she didn't have sons. They would have been easier to trace.'

'True, but she didn't. The daughters aren't mentioned by name in the letters, unfortunately. But if we can find records of the births, we could trace other relatives, who might be able to add a little more to the story.'

Finn, who is sprawled on the couch, looks up from the photocopies and puts them aside. I'm standing between his knees. I place my hands on his shoulders and lean down to kiss him on the nose. 'It's so exciting, just as Estelle said, like a detective story!'

'Do you think we could forget Annie and Nellie just for a moment, and think about us? You realise we have just a couple more days before I lose you to Christmas? All these things you have planned for everyone else – do they include me, just maybe, somewhere along the line?'

'Soon we'll have a house of our own.'

'A great, cold, wonderful barn of a monolith,' he says. 'It's hard to believe. I've seen that place from a distance so many times, from the sea, and thought it was like something out of a fairy tale. I never in a million years imagined living in it. Erin, you're a wonder, so you are.'

He stands up and lifts me. I wrap my arms and legs around him like a child. He kisses me and asks, 'Are we going to get married any time soon?'

I laugh and say, 'Yes, yes, yes!'

'Because I can't risk someone else getting that house.'

He carries me to the bedroom. I open my mouth to speak, but he puts a finger over my lips. 'No more about Nellie. I have other things to think about right at this moment.'

I had invited the school children, on their last day of term, to come up for a tree-decorating party at the hotel, for which I laid on sandwiches, sausage rolls, cakes, and jelly and ice cream. It was a riotous success. The huge, gaudy Christmas tree in one corner of the hotel dining room is draped in a somewhat haphazard fashion with fairy lights, tinsel, plastic reindeer, and paper angels they'd made in school and plastered with glue and glitter.

And now, in the evening, I feel justifiably pleased with myself. The room is packed. It seems that everyone from Roone Bay has turned up for our Christmas party, some for the free supper, some undoubtedly from curiosity, but that's all right. In fact, it was the whole point. There will no longer be a 'them and us' feeling about the hotel. Instead of referring to it as 'the eyesore', I'm hoping the inhabitants of Roone Bay will now refer to it as 'our hotel'.

I have a glass of wine in one hand, Finn's hand in the other. I can't stop beaming and guess I'm a little merry, with the wine and the relief that it's finally come together after several weeks of frantic activity. Although I'm taking a back seat, I'm well aware that this wouldn't have happened without me.

It's not bragging if it's the truth.

Grace is, just like her name, a beautiful and gracious hostess, drifting through the crowds in a chic dress, welcoming, chatting. She seems to know everyone. Noel and Caitlin are seated at the head of a large buffet table, like royalty, enjoying themselves enormously. I see Noel hide a yawn behind his hand, and suspect he and Caitlin will soon slip out quietly, as will some of the parents with children. The DJ is setting up to one side, and the music will soon be thumping out. *No diddly music tonight,* I said to Noel. *Let's give the young people a night to remember.*

I turn and catch Eilis sitting on a seat to my right. As our eyes meet, she gives a little smile, and I move to talk to her. Liam comes running over with a toy train to show me. I kneel and let him run the train around me. I laugh involuntarily at his *choo-choo* noises, then go and sit beside Eilis. 'I hope you're having a good time. Liam is, anyway.'

She nods. 'It was kind of you to invite us.'

I smile. 'No bother.'

'I've been wanting to talk to you. I don't want it to be awkward between us. Finn loves you, and that's okay with me.'

'Um,' I say, at a loss for words.

'Well, Finn said I can come with Liam out to the house some time. I just wanted to make sure it's all right with you.'

'Of course it is. You're Liam's mum. You can come any time.'

'Well, that's not really what I wanted to talk to you about.'

She looks a bit nervous, so I hide my own disquiet behind a smile. 'Come on – spit it out!'

'I suppose you know...' She waves a hand down her body. I wonder if she has difficulty saying the word 'cancer'.

I grimace and nod. 'Yes, of course. I'm sorry.'

'Yes, bad luck, sure. My mother is all set to take on Liam, of course, but...' She looks as if she's going to stop, but takes a deep breath and presses on. 'I think it would be better for Liam to be with younger people, with his father, when I go. And you.'

'I don't know if...' I must look horrified as I find myself unable to finish the sentence, because she lays a hand on my knee.

'I know about your accident, your loss. But maybe this is God's way of solving the problem. Yours and mine.'

I'm shocked. I've never before come into close contact with a young person facing certain death, and with a young child, too. I don't know what to say.

She smiles gently. 'Think about it. There's no hurry. The doctors tell me I might have a couple more years.'

'Of course,' I say faintly, words failing me.

Grace taps me on the shoulder. 'Sorry to interrupt, but the DJ needs another extension lead. We haven't got one lying around, have we?'

'Sure. Excuse me,' I say to Eilis, and as I walk away, I feel myself growing faint. 'Oh shit,' I say under my breath and take a deep breath. She wants me to take her child? Finn and I have talked about Liam staying with us, in an abstract way, like weekends or something, but he hasn't suggested that he come live with us permanently. I wonder if they've spoken about it.

I don't know how I make it through the rest of the evening.

'Did you know that's what she was going to suggest?' I ask Finn, later, once the last partygoers have straggled home and the DJ has packed up his kit.

He compresses his lips then sighs. 'She's never asked, not directly. It does make sense, but I just didn't know how to broach the subject with you, in light of what happened. I didn't want to upset you.'

'But she doesn't know me!'

'She knows me and knows I wouldn't be with someone who wasn't absolutely wonderful. I guess when you're facing death, as she is, with a child's future to think about, the logical solution is one that just needed to be said. I think she's right. You'd be a good mother.'

I feel my eyes welling. 'I just don't know if I can. What if I can't do it? What if I'm not a good mother? What then?'

'You can never replace the child you lost,' Finn says, hugging me with sympathetic understanding. 'When Dervla Doyle, all those years ago, found Annie on the docks and took her in, she never tried to take away the knowledge of who her mother was. But she still became a mother to the child, when the child needed it.'

'How can you be so reasonable?' I grumble after a pause. 'What am I supposed to say? She as good as asked me.'

'You know Liam well enough now, and he's happy to be with us both. Get to know Eilis a little. Get it all out in the open.'

'I don't know if I can do that.' I find myself pacing.

'No one's going to force you, one way or the other.'

My voice nearly breaks. 'Did you tell her I can't have children?'

'Sweetheart, everyone knows!' Finn holds me closer. 'She understands your grief. And perhaps she thinks you understand hers. She's already grieving for Liam because she's going to leave soon. She knows he won't understand why his mother's gone away and is trying to find ways of coping.'

I wince, feeling pressured. 'She can't know what I feel.'

'You already know she does.'

I mull over Eilis's words – and Finn's. When Finn and I are together, with Liam, it's as if I'm his substitute mother already, telling him how to behave, teaching him as if he were my own. I just hadn't wanted to see it. But if I can be his substitute mother on weekends, why not always?

'Ashley Point Lookout is big enough,' I muse to Finn a few days later. 'If Eilis and Liam moved in with us, it would be an easier transition for both of them, when the time comes.'

Finn smiles gently and says, 'You're a wonderful person, Erin. I always hoped I'd meet the right woman one day, and I have. I love you so much it scares me.'

'It scares me, too,' I admit and add, 'I'm not actually worried about being a substitute mother to Liam. It took me a while to realise that I'm worried about loving him and losing him. I've been through that once. I don't want to go through it again.'

'I know. But do you wish you had never had those few years with Kenny? Do you wish you had never experienced the joy of impending motherhood?'

'Not for a moment.'

I realise that life is knocking on the door, and I'm going to open that door and let it back in.

40

NELLIE 1884

Over the following week, Nellie told Annie about Danny, and Eve, and Luke, and Sarah, and her grandchild, Patrick. In return, Annie told her mother, in bits and pieces, about her life in America. How she had found herself alone on the dock in Boston and was rescued by Dervla Doyle. Annie said, 'I was so confused. I was sure I remembered getting off the ship with you and baby Luke, but Dervla said I told her that you and Luke had died on the trip, so in the end I wondered if I was wrong.'

'And you came back to Ireland.' Nellie sighed. 'If only I had known, I would have come home all the sooner.'

'Well, it wasn't my home,' Annie said bluntly. 'Mama – I mean Mrs Doyle' – she cast Nellie an apologetic glance – 'was so excited. But all I had ever known was America. I wasn't at all happy about coming to Ireland, not for a while. I was only six when we left Ireland, and the little I do recall is all mixed up.'

'You do recall some things, though? Your grandparents? Our cottage? Your father?'

Annie shook her head. 'I remember being on Dada's shoulders, looking out over the sea, but precious little else. I can't recall his face, or my grandparents, and I have no recollection of the cottage. I asked around to find out where it was – went to see it, of course, when we got back. Mostly, I remember being on the boat with you and Luke. It was horrible.'

'It was,' Nellie agreed. 'How strange that the things we most want to remember get lost, and the horrid things stay in the memory forever.'

They were sitting close together on the settle. Annie hugged her mother, and they both cried a little. 'Well,' Annie responded, wiping her eyes, 'now that we have found each other, we'll make a point of finding happy things to put it back into balance. I grieved for you both. You for your terrible life, and I thought how sad it was that baby Luke died so young. I wish I'd known him.'

'I wish that, too.' Nellie sighed. 'I came to realise that Luke was very much like his father. He grew up to have strong morals and ideas. He believed that everyone deserved the right to be happy. Unfortunately, it didn't work out that way for him. But you, you're happy now?'

'I missed America for a long time. And I did think about staying. There was a young man who wanted to marry me. Timothy, the son of the farmer who rented some of the Doyles' fields.'

'Did you love him?'

'He was nice enough, but...' Annie giggled. 'He was eight years older than me and was beginning to look suspiciously like his father, who was a strange shape and quite bald! To be honest, leaving the only home I'd ever known, to go to a small island in Europe, halfway across the world, wasn't as frightening as the thought of marrying Timothy and living in the same house with his mother. I would have had to milk cows! Just think! I didn't particularly want to be a farmer's wife. His mother thought me vain, but it's not wrong to want pretty clothes, is it?'

'I guess not,' Nellie said, who had never had pretty clothes.

'Well, it was Dervla who made my mind up for me. She said, "If it's Timothy or the unknown, if I were you, I'd take the unknown any day!" So, there I was,' Annie continued, 'in Ireland, travelling in an ancient cart pulled by a shook old nag, freezing in the cold rain, wondering what I was doing in this horrid little country, when it was too late to change my mind. But when we got there, the old farmhouse had a fire brightly lit, and John Doyle's father welcomed us all in, with tears in his eyes, because he still had family alive. And I grew to love him, and Ireland, after all. And then I met Andrew.'

God moves in mysterious ways, Nellie thought. If John Doyle hadn't had a son who emigrated and married Dervla, and if they hadn't been going to Boston on that very day, Annie wouldn't have been rescued or come back to Ireland. Kate wouldn't have found her, and to the day she died, Nellie might never have known of her daughter's fate, never mind actually meet her again. She would go to mass and give thanks.

'But you love your husband? It wasn't just, ah, convenience or because he was a doctor?'

'No, Mam. I love him very much.'

Nellie was pleased. She was glad she had experienced love herself, even if it had been just for a few precious years. And she was glad her daughter had married for love, not just to provide her with a home. 'So, how did that come about?'

'Well, I was never meant to be a farmer, but Grandpa Doyle kept a few chickens in the barn. I enjoyed looking after them, and worked out how to bring the eggs in and incubate them by the fire. Soon we had so many chicks, Grandpa Doyle was scratching his head saying what are we supposed to do with all the eggs? I'll get out and sell them, I told him, and that's what I did. I began to drive the old cart around the countryside delivering eggs to whoever would buy them: the homes of priests, the convent in Skibbereen, small shops, and any individual who heard the mare clopping along the boreen and called out to me for a half dozen. Sometimes I got soaked,' she said, laughing, 'but it was better than milking cows!'

'And the good doctor?'

'Well, that's the point of the story. I was driving along a tiny boreen with my eggs and discovered Andrew, stranded, with a broken axle on his sulky carriage. He told me he was a doctor, much in need of rescue. He had urgent business at the Stringers' farm where it seemed one of the sons had fallen from a roof and needed a broken arm binding, and it would be a mercy, so it would, if I would bring him there. He said, later, I was the angel who had come to rescue him, and it was love at first sight!'

Nellie saw her young self in Annie's smile.

'I married Andrew Nolan eight months later, and he brought me home to this cottage. Now, Mam... Oh, it still feels strange to call you that when I've called Dervla "Mam" all these years!'

She laughed, and Nellie found herself welling with tears of gratitude because her daughter was truly happy. Then one of Annie's daughters came in and said shyly, 'Mam, I'm to tell you Papa has brought the sulky around.'

'So,' Annie said, leaping up, 'now we're going for a ride. I'm to take you to Dervla. She dearly wants to meet you.'

41

ERIN

It takes two months for the purchase of Ashley Point Lookout to go through, and we've also ended up keeping a lot of the furnishings, which is quite bizarre. I asked the estate agent if the daughter who had inherited it wanted the furniture. It's not inconceivable that she might ship it to Australia, given the sentimental as well as antique value. He arranged for her to meet us at the house to discuss it.

I don't like her on sight.

If asked, I probably couldn't pinpoint exactly why, but it's one of those instant first impressions that I usually discover are essentially truthful.

She collects her mother's jewellery and says everything else can go, that it is all junk, anyway. We settle on a figure for some of the pieces, and I say I'll send the rest for charity, if that is all right.

She nods, says 'okay' and leaves without looking back.

I later learn that she hadn't visited her father since she moved away, some twenty years previously. I'd never met the old man, knew nothing about him, and he might have been a horrible father for all I know, but at least I'll dispose of his personal belongings with a little dignity.

I'm in the hotel a while later when Grace hands me a letter. 'From Australia,' she says, indicating the stamp and the airmail sticker.

For a moment, I wonder if it's from the woman we'd bought Ashley Point Lookout from and have a couple of moments of panic in case she decided she did want the furniture, after we'd given most of it to charity! But inside there's a handwritten note with a signature I don't recognise and a flimsy copy of something old in flowing copperplate script.

I read the handwritten note and sit down with a thump. 'Oh, goodness!'

'Bad news?' Grace asks anxiously.

'No, quite the opposite,' I say with a little laugh. 'It's the end of my story. Listen.

'*Dear Erin, I understand you're seeking details about an ancestor called Nellie O'Mahoney. My mother was from Bantry originally and emigrated to Australia some thirty years ago. Once a year, her brother sends her the Christmas magazine, so that she can keep abreast of the news. Mostly to see who is still alive, I expect! But anyway, I read your plea for information and found it fascinating. You see, Annie Nolan was my great-times-two-grandmother, and her mother was Nellie O'Mahoney, who emigrated to Boston from Roone Bay.*

'*I always found the story fascinating, how Nellie lost her little girl Annie in Boston and eventually was reunited with her in Bantry nearly forty years later. Apparently, a friend of Nellie's who had emigrated ended up going back to Ireland, where she discovered Annie. She sent Nellie a letter with the news, and Nellie came back to Ireland to be reunited with her daughter. I have a vague recollection that Gran told me Nellie ended up living with a lady called Dervla Doyle – I'm not sure, but she might have been the woman who rescued Annie in Boston and brought her back to Ireland. I don't know who wrote up Annie's childhood account, but it came down to me from Gran, and I enclose a photocopy. There is some hint of a breakdown in communication with Nellie's grandson in Boston, who maybe felt that Nellie had 'abandoned' his Boston family to go chasing after the lost daughter.'*

I look up at Grace. 'That might explain why Grandpa Gabriel never knew what happened to Nellie or Annie? If Patrick felt betrayed, he might have just cut her out of his life?'

I carry on reading. *'What an adventure! And with a happy ending, too! From your article, I think Nellie's son was your ancestor and her daughter mine! That means that Nellie O'Mahoney is ancestor to both of us! That makes you and I kind-of cousins, so many times removed I can't even think of calculating it. But wouldn't it be fun to meet? I was planning a visit to Bantry in the summer, just to see where my mum came from, so I was wondering if you would be interested in meeting up with me? Do let me know, I am quite excited about the prospect. Yours, Melaney Wilson.'*

I look up and see the tears in my eyes reflected in Grace's.

'She found her Annie, after all,' I say. 'Isn't that just perfect?'

EPILOGUE

ERIN

Eilis's wake is beautiful. It seems as if the whole populace of Bantry and Roone Bay have come out to wish her well on her final journey. I am awed by the stream of people who trail past, cross themselves and say their goodbyes. It's not something I have ever experienced. In Boston, I recall my grandfather being shuffled from our lives amidst a heavy shroud of reserved grieving, but the party atmosphere here is like a wedding, with Eilis presiding as the happy bride. This wake epitomises the Irish for me. The laughter, the copious quantities of drink, the stories, the acceptance that death is simply a part of life. I have discovered that the underlying cohesion of continuity and community in Ireland is so much more than faith.

The funeral brings Kenny and my lost child to the fore, and some of my grief is for myself. The scars will remain, of course, physically and mentally, but the open wound has healed over, and I can think of them with gentle sorrow rather than crazed grief. I have Finn's child to bring up, and I love him as if he were my own. How can it be otherwise?

Finn and I don't require Liam go and kiss Eilis goodbye, though, as some of the old ones had tried to insist was necessary.

We have been saying our goodbyes for a year now, as Eilis gradually faded, until all that was left of her beauty was the love that shone from her moss-green eyes whenever she saw her son. I will speak of her often to Liam. I think he should remember his mother as the vibrant and beautiful girl who had borne Finn's child for love, not as the faded shadow who died of cancer.

There were times I felt like an interloper in Eilis's life, even though she was living in my house. It was certainly a weird relationship, with Finn and myself married, and his previous girlfriend and their son in the same house with us. But despite my apprehension, we formed a bond that transcended convention, Liam being the glue that held us all together.

Now she's gone I know I will miss her, as surely as Finn will, but we're entering a new phase of our lives. Eilis will leave a space in our hearts and souls that only time will heal, if only for the brave and uncomplaining manner in which she accepted her fate and entrusted her son to us.

As the evening descends, the stream of cars gradually diminishes, and the lights of the last car fade. Finn and I stand in the little lookout, by the brass telescope, holding Liam's hands between us. The sun is sinking behind the sea, a trail of flickering gold leading out of the bay and over the horizon, flooding the clouds briefly with such beauty it might be Eilis's soul on its last journey.

Tomorrow will bring a new dawn for all of us.

Liam is young – he will survive, and we have all done the best we can to prepare him. He has lived with us at Ashley Point Lookout for two years, and we haven't tried to hide from him that his mother was ill and would soon be leaving. It's strange how accepting he was of something so big. But his grief is cushioned by his surroundings, a good home, a father, myself and a whole community of people who care for him.

'How different this is from what poor Nellie and Annie experienced,' I say softly to Finn.

Strangely, I have been so consumed with the present that the past kind of got forgotten. It reminds me that I intend to write up Nellie's story, as well as I'm able, and fold the typed sheet into her bible in case someone in the future inherits it. Even as I want Liam to remember his mother, I want Nellie and William and Luke and Annie to be more than just anonymous names and dates scratched on parchment.

'Who is Nellie?' Liam asks, looking up at me curiously.

'A woman who lost her little girl, a long, long time ago,' I explain softly.

'But did she find her?'

'She did, in the end.'

'Like the lady in the swan story?'

I'm not entirely sure which story he means, we have read so many, but I nod.

'And she lived happily ever after, like Mam will, in Heaven,' Liam states.

'Absolutely,' Finn says. We share a tear-filled glance. 'So, it's been a long day. Shall we go and sit by the fire and read another story?'

'I'd like that. I'm very tired,' Liam says, yawning. 'Will we play some tunes tomorrow? Mam would like that.'

'I think we will,' Finn agrees.

A LETTER FROM DAISY

Dear reader,

Thank you so much for reading *The Irish Child*. I would love it if you kept up to date with all my novels and any other significant news from Bookouture, so do make sure to sign up at the following link. Your email address will never be shared, and you can unsubscribe at any time.

www.bookouture.com/daisyoshea

Novels can be prompted by a spark of thought, little observations or experiences that make you wonder what might have happened if...

I had an early miscarriage between my two living children, as so many women do, and I've often wondered what that lost child might have been like. Might that child have turned out to be like me: a dreamer, a musician, an author? I wondered, too, how I would feel if the baby had been a little older before I lost it, old enough to shift inside me, make its presence known, old enough to have reshaped my own body to accommodate its growth. Old enough, perhaps, that I knew its gender. I tried to put myself in Erin's shoes, facing the double loss of husband and baby, coping with depression, knowing that she could never bear another child.

Happily-ever-after often means crossing seemingly insurmountable hurdles, solving one's own life problems and actually choosing to be happy. I hope you empathised with the way Erin's gradual uncovering of Nellie's story helped her find the strength to overcome her own personal tragedy.

One of my most gratifying experiences as an author is to know that readers enjoyed the novel and closed the last pages with a sigh of satisfaction, even maybe a little tear. If you did, then I'd be delighted if you would leave a review to let other readers know how much you enjoyed the story. Be sure, though, to dwell on the characterisation, the writing style and your own emotional responses, and don't give away any critical plot points.

I've lived in West Cork since early retirement, and it's been the most fulfilling time of my life. The wild countryside, the rocky seashores, the call of the sea, the scarred history, the underlying myths and legends, and most of all, the inclusive warmth of the dauntless Irish people. There's a wisp of fey here, in rural Ireland, that subtly underpins all our lives and which quietly infuses my stories.

I do hope you're looking forward to my next book as much as I'm enjoying writing it.

All the best, Daisy

www.daisyoshea.com

facebook.com/DaisyOSheaAuthor
x.com/westcorkwriter

HUSH LITTLE BABY

Hush little baby, don't say a word
Papa's gonna buy you a mockingbird

And if that mockingbird don't sing
Papa's gonna buy you a diamond ring

And if that diamond ring is brass
Papa's gonna buy you a looking glass

And if that looking glass gets broke
Papa's gonna buy you a billy goat

And if that billy goat don't pull
Papa's gonna buy you a cart and bull

And if that cart and bull turn over
Papa's gonna buy you a dog called Rover

And if that dog called Rover don't bark
Papa's gonna buy you a horse and cart

And if that horse and cart turn around
You'll still be the sweetest little baby in town.

— *TRADITIONAL AMERICAN*
LULLABY

TWINKLE, TWINKLE, LITTLE STAR

Twinkle, twinkle, little star
How I wonder what you are
Up above the sky so high
Like a diamond in the sky
Though I know not what you are
Twinkle, twinkle little star

— NURSERY RHYME ADAPTATION OF
JANE TAYLOR'S POEM 'THE STAR'
(PUBLISHED IN 1806)

AUTHOR'S NOTES

DISCLAIMER

Roone Bay isn't a real town, and any individual homes
and businesses mentioned are fabrications. There are
many families in the area with the surnames I've chosen
to use, but any similarity to real persons, alive or dead, is
entirely coincidental. All views in the work are those of
the characters, not the author.

OVERVIEW OF IRELAND

Ireland is divided into the four provinces: Connacht,
Leinster, Munster and Ulster. Cork is located in
Munster, the bottom-left section of Ireland, where its
rocky fingers reach out towards America. Within the
four provinces, there are thirty-two counties containing
around 64,000 townlands: historic areas that once
might have been clan boundaries and which can be
anything between 100 and 500 acres. Roone Bay is set
on the southern coast of Ireland, in the mythical townland of Tirbeg, somewhere between Bantry and
Skibbereen.

a chara: *a* (as in apple) *kaara* (my love/close friend)
Caitlin: *Kat-leen*
Cú Chulainn: *ku hu* (as in look) *lenn* (mythological Irish hero)
Eilis: *eye-leesh*
Gabh mo leithscéal: *gov muh leshkale* (excuse me?)
mo chroí: *mo kree* (my friend/my dear)
O'Mahoney: *oh-mah-nee*
Shook: as in *shook old horse*, simply means tired, run down, used up
Tírbeg: *Teer-beg*

a stór mo chroí: *a* (*as in apple*) *store moh kree* (treasure of my heart)
Érin, grá mo chroí: *Erin gra* (*rhymes with far*) *moh kree* (Ireland, love of my heart)
Mavourneen: *ma* (*as in mat*) *voor neen* (my love)

ACKNOWLEDGMENTS

My thanks go first to my husband, Robin, who's believed in me in every way from the moment we met. A staunch supporter of my passion for writing, he's the first critic of my work, my best friend and also my 'til-death-us-do-part love. Thanks to my lovely mother, Alma Yea, one-time librarian and teacher, for encouraging me to read fiction when I was a child. Thanks to Susannah Hamilton for 'discovering' me, also thanks to the external editors & proofreaders and the whole team at Bookouture, who manage the process so efficiently. Last, but certainly not least, thanks to all the readers who enjoy my fiction. Without you, my work would be pointless, so don't be afraid to reach out and provide me with much-needed reassurance.

PUBLISHING TEAM

Turning a manuscript into a book requires the efforts of many people. The publishing team at Bookouture would like to acknowledge everyone who contributed to this publication.

Commercial
Lauren Morrissette
Hannah Richmond
Imogen Allport

Data and analysis
Mark Alder
Mohamed Bussuri

Cover design
Dissect Designs

Editorial
Susannah Hamilton
Nadia Michael

Copyeditor
Angela Snowden

Proofreader
Laura Kincaid

Marketing
Alex Crow
Melanie Price
Occy Carr
Cíara Rosney
Martyna Młynarska

Operations and distribution
Marina Valles
Stephanie Straub

Production
Hannah Snetsinger
Mandy Kullar
Jen Shannon

Publicity
Kim Nash
Noelle Holten
Jess Readett
Sarah Hardy

Rights and contracts
Peta Nightingale
Richard King
Saidah Graham

Printed in Great Britain
by Amazon

48014945R00179